A Streak of Sandalwood

Anand Nair

Published by YouWriteOn.com, 2011
Copyright © Anand Nair
First Edition

The author has asserted her moral right under the Copyright, Designs and Patents Act, 1988, to be identified as the author of this work

All Rights reserved. No part of this publication may be reproduced, copied, stored in a retrieval system, or transmitted, in any form or by any means, without the prior written consent of the copyright holder, nor be otherwise circulated in any form of binding or cover other than that in which it is published and without a similar condition being imposed on the subsequent purchaser.

A CIP catalogue record for this title is available from the British Library.

This book is a work of fiction. People, places, events and circumstances are the product of the author's imagination. Any resemblance to actual persons, dead or living, is purely coincidental.

Every effort has been made to trace or contact the estates of the copyright holders of two Malayalam songs and one Hindi song, two lines of each of which, have been used in this manuscript. Their authorship is gratefully acknowledged.

For

Kitta, Raghu, Ranju and Manju

and our precious

Asha

1

Thankam surfaced from a troubled sleep to the sound of Seetha, her maid, clattering steel pans downstairs. She looked to her right at the empty space in the bed and felt anew the crushing weight of hopelessness, which was her constant companion since Unni's death. She pushed all thoughts away from her head, except those related to getting dressed and out of the house, as soon as possible.

By the time she had brushed her teeth and bathed, Seetha was at the door with her morning offering of hot coffee and unasked questions. Thankam looked at her saris remembering bleakly that widows, especially new ones, were not supposed to wear bright and happy colours. Her hands quickly rejected the must-wear whites of mourning and returned again to the yellow *Kotah* in her wardrobe, soft and light as cobweb. Yellow was her get–happy colour. And God knew she needed something to get happy about.

Seetha, at the sink, washing yesterday's pots and pans, would know something was afoot, but would wait to be told. Thankam drank her coffee in a hurry, as though she was late for an appointment. 'Seetha, I won't need breakfast,' she called out, collecting her house keys and handbag as she ran out of the front door. No one was there to stop her, but she knew that if she thought about it she would not manage to get out of the house and into the real world, yet again. Her husband had been dead for six months now, and during that time she had been unable to summon up the will to go out, to do her own shopping, to meet people and be part of that outside world. Today she was determined to start living again.

Thankam walked quickly down the short path from her front door to the gate. As she reached the road, the auto-rickshaw man who always parked at the corner was getting into his seat. Thankam rushed up and climbed in. 'Panampilly Nagar,' she gasped, unsure where that 'Panampilly Nagar,' came from.

The vehicle put-putted its way into Sahodaran Ayyappan Road, away from the centre of Kochi, and clattered over potholes, almost toppling over as it turned the corner. Once over the bottleneck of South Bridge it gathered speed and Thankam looked at a world she had almost forgotten. Hoardings advertising every conceivable product and service lifted their ugly box-heads over the buildings on either side of the road, making the crowded highway look cluttered, untidy, but strangely alive.

'Where to?' asked the driver.

'The Panorama Flats,' she said, thinking of the one person she knew in that area. Her good friend Raji would ask no questions and understood a great deal about widowhood, having lost her own husband as a young woman of thirty-six. Perhaps, somewhere in the bottom of her mind, Thankam always knew that was where she needed to go.

Raji's face lit up with obvious delight when she saw Thankam.

'Thankam, how lovely. Been thinking about you. Did you hear my thoughts?'

Her smile of welcome was like sunlight creeping into the dark corners of a room. Raji seated Thankam down at the kitchen table as though an unannounced visit at eight in the morning was normal. Then she busied herself making two mugs of coffee and chatting about her children whilst turning the *doshas* on the griddle pan.

'Coffee smells good,' Thankam said, smiling.

'Let's have breakfast when the children have gone. Hate eating alone, though I'm getting used to it.'

Soon the doshas were on the table and the children were clamouring for breakfast, ironed uniforms, missing socks… Thankam was glad to be in the middle of a noisy family meal; it was almost as good as being invisible. Recently, she had been quite contrary: hating the hordes of commiserating old women who constantly surrounded her, as though they had a special lien on grief, at the same time, not wanting to be left alone. She had redefined "alone". Alone was when all the people around you were the ones you did not want and your mind listened for the footsteps and voices of only the few loved ones you desperately needed near you.

The young ones, sated, scattered like crows at a handclap, collecting school satchels and umbrellas from the hallway on their way out. The dosha and coconut chutney were good and tasted a little different from Seetha's. Thankfully, at least taste was coming back to her. She was now past the stage when food stuck in the gullet in a hard, merciless knot, like traffic at Kochi's rail-crossings.

The world, and time in it, had blurred in the aftermath of Unni's death; all the senses had concentrated in a fierce, destructive grief holding her in a python's coil. Seeing, eating, bathing and all the other things that meshed the day together had disintegrated. Now, Thankam knew that the world was slowly returning to focus. Perhaps, if she tried hard and long enough, the kaleidoscope of herself and her world would fall again into familiar patterns.

Raji cleared the used plates and steel mugs into the sink.

'I should have come to your house – looked after you the way you cared for me and my children when *my* husband died. But with two school-going children -'

'I know that. That's why I came.'

Thankam's voice held no reproach. 'I just wanted to get out of the house today as I have been nowhere since … Well, Manju, my daughter, takes me home in her car sometimes, but that's not the same thing, is it? I have tried to get out on my own, but I seem to have lost the will. And then it became habit to stay at home.

'Every one tells me I should sell the car,' added Thankam. Why do I need a car now that Unni is not around? they ask. I wish they'd just leave me alone for a while, until I am ready to make my own decisions.'

'Tell them to mind their own blessed business,' Raji burst out. She dipped the washing-up sponge into the *Sabena* powder next to the sink and scrubbed hard at the starch on the frying pan as she talked, almost as though she was scrubbing away all those unpleasant memories.

'Bad enough losing your husband, and then the whole world wants to tell you how to live. Busybodies!

'I suppose they mean well, but my mother wants me to live with her in Thalassery, leave Kochi altogether.' Thankam grimaced.

'I am not ready for that; I doubt I ever will be. To be Mother's little girl again.'

Raji abandoned the breakfast dishes, walked over to the kitchen table and sat herself opposite Thankam. 'Don't tell anyone anything,' she insisted. 'First they want to know how much money you have, then what you do with it. If you let them, they will want to know how you spent the day, where you went, and if you met anyone going there. Bad enough having to rearrange your life without having that lot staking off little bits of it.

'Actually, it took me a year to feel like a human being after Madhavan's death. But being inside the house all the time – that's dire. Why don't we go to that widows' place near the hospital next week?' Raji suggested.

She tucked her sari ends into her skirt as though getting ready for a serious bout of housework. 'They meet every week; I think they helped me to see things in perspective.'

'Counselling, speakers and such like, was it?' Thankam's voice was tentative. She looked vulnerable as she leaned forward and put her elbows on the table, resting her chin in her hands, ready to listen.

'Mmm... That too, but not quite.' Raji had a faraway look as though she was seeing pictures in her mind from long ago. 'I think meeting other women who had lost their husbands and talking to them helped.

'And thing is,' she added, grinning mischievously, 'my in-laws cannot blame me for gallivanting so soon after my husband's death. What can be more sanctified than a Widows' Association? My mother-in-law would like me to stay indoors all the time, maybe put a streak of sacred ash or sandalwood on my forehead for good measure.'

'Family!' Thankam said ruefully.

'Can I just walk into this widows' place just like that?' she asked.

'I'll take you. You'll make friends there; they know what it's like to be alone in Kochi.'

'I have to think,' Thankam said. The thinking to be done was like a gargantuan task waiting to be started. Thankam's mind, so strong and certain in the past, appeared to have fragmented like a scattered jigsaw.

'I must go home,' she muttered.

Raji walked out to the gate with her and down to the auto-stand at the corner, near the Cross Roads restaurant. 'Take this madam home to Carrier Station Road,' she said. 'Where the plantain crisp shop is.' Everyone knew the little shop, *Kozhikode Chips*, which produced the best plantain crisps in town.

The driver nudged the nose of the auto with one hand and swivelled it around, turning the steering wheel with the other. Thankam was grateful to be on the far side from Raji. The black dogs had caught up with her again, making her retreat into her dark hole to hide.

Thankam was not really used to going about in an auto. She held on grimly to the bar in front of her as the vehicle gathered speed past the Manorama junction, turning sharply to the left without stopping, to enter the dense Kochi traffic towards South Bridge.

She was conscious of the many new things she had to attempt. Life had been quite straightforward and simple when Unni was in charge and all she had to do was look after him. Now she had begun to realize that a woman trying to live alone in Kochi had to have a feel for that urban mess. For so long she had been content to be one of many married, middle-class women who learned to drive when the family first acquired a car, and then never actually bothered to practise the new skill. She had been happy to leave the car entirely to Unni.

He had often tried to coax her to take the wheel. Unni was one of those rare men who believed women could do most anything men did, and do it well.

Thankam smiled as she remembered Unni saying, 'Now if you did the driving, I could sit quietly in the passenger seat and smoke my cigarette, look at the scenery… Now that bit of scenery in the green sari is worth a second glance, don't you think?'

'Watch the road for now. I'll drive next time so that you can watch the scenery.'

Next time she would have an excuse, 'I am not wearing the right slippers; these will fall off my feet while I am driving.'

Eventually, Unni got the message.

Unni is driving, one arm draped over the window of the Maruthi, *cigarette hanging lazily almost like an extension of his fingers, the other hand resting lightly on the wheel.*

'I am uneasy when you do that.'

Thankam is staring right ahead, but she can hear the amusement in his voice as he answers, 'Do what?'

'You know perfectly well what I am talking about.'

He is still mocking. 'Well... There is the arm hanging over the door and the cigarette in my hand ... You are wondering which will kill me first.'

'You will kill both of us with that one-arm driving.' Unni throws away the cigarette and places both hands on the steering wheel.

'Ten - past – two o'clock position on the steering wheel, ma'am, and textbook driving for you.'

The look he turns on her is a melting mixture of affection, trust and a little boy's desire to please.

Thankam is a little shamefaced. 'I just don't want you to get hurt.'

Unni's left hand comes out briefly to caress her neck.

Thankam smiles. 'This could get even more dangerous.' She laughs, feeling herself tickle and respond to his touch, as always, like a well-loved veena *to the maestro.*

As soon as they reach home, Thankam hurries off into the kitchen to put her special mix of milk, water and AVT tealeaves into the pan. When the tea is strained, she carries it out to the veranda where Unni has collapsed from the major effort of driving to the grocers and back.

'Mmm, nothing like a hot cup of tea to make you feel rejuvenated. I could move mountains now,' he says as he leans back in his armchair, sighing luxuriously.

'Moving the gates will do for a start.' Thankam replies. 'I can see our daughter's juggernaut coming this way in a hurry. Do you reckon she will stop long enough for us to open the gate for her?'

'Something is wrong with Manju,' Unni remarks. 'Recently, she's irritable and tense. Have you noticed how she no longer rushes back to her house when she comes this way?'

'That husband of hers, Gopi.' Thankam remarks. 'Away in Dubai most of the time and a sullen presence when he is around.'

Unni looks thoughtful as he gets up, carrying his mug of half-drunk tea to the gate. He uses his toes to nudge the bolts at the bottom and pushes the gates wide open as Manju turns sharply into the short drive, brakes screeching in protest.

The little ones, Asha and Latha, tumble out and their clamour for attention fills the veranda with happy cacophony. Unni is trying unsuccessfully to hold the mug of tea out of the way of little arms and legs and tea slops on to his arm. Manju watches them, a distracted smile on her face, as though she is not quite part of the scene.

By the time Thankam has made another mug of tea for Manju and fussed around in the kitchen, warming up chappathis *left over from breakfast, for the children, it is getting dark. Manju spreads jam on the chappathis and listens to the children's chatter to their grandparents.*

'Sometimes I wonder whether I am so lucky to have my parents in the same town, near me,' Manju suddenly says, apropos of nothing. Thankam looks up sharply and Manju hastens to explain.

'What I'd love to do is spend a month here and forget I am a married woman, be a carefree child once more. But it seems a lot to ask to sleep over when my husband's home is only ten minutes' drive away.'

Manju pauses as though to gather her thoughts.

'Gopi is becoming a stranger after he started working in Dubai; I don't recognize his expensive shaving lotion or the designer shirts he has acquired.'

Thankam does not want her daughter to dwell on her discontent, so she does not ask more questions. Instead she watches Manju as she sits around in the fading daylight until her emotional battery is recharged and she is ready to go back to her home.

2

Seetha seemed a little concerned at the unusual activity going on in the house: phone calls, sorting out of clothes, fiddling with the car... She hovered, clearly trying to find out what all the hyper-activity was about, without appearing to ask a question.

'If you are taking the car out, I think I'll give the garage a good wash down. It's some time since anyone's gone in there. Might be a few snakes nesting for all you know.'

'Snakes in the middle of Carrier Station Road. That will be the day! The pollution will drive out anything but crazy human beings.'

Seetha laughed at seeing her Amma's caustic humour coming back; it had been missing since Unni died.

Thankam ate her *poori* and potato *masala* quickly; going out to Raji's house appeared to have released some inhibition in her.

Thankam had called the Perfect Driving School since coming home from visiting Raji, and arranged for some brush-up driving lessons. If she was to have a life of her own she needed to get about without depending on anyone. She knew it was a small thing, but it would make her feel she was moving on, gaining control.

When the driver Sudhakaran turned up at nine in the morning, his surprise showed; maybe he had expected a young woman from the voice.

As Thankam went inside to collect her bag, the driver from next door looked over the low wall and greeted Sudhakaran as if confirming the brotherhood of all drivers, who spent most of the day waiting in forecourts of houses for their instructions.

'Who's learning?' he asked indicating Thankam's house with a toss of his head.

'That lady, I think,' Sudhakaran answered.

'Bit old to learn driving,' he mumbled, darting a quick glance at Thankam's front door. 'I've never had a woman client as old as this woman; she must be at least forty. Men of course, when they buy their first car. For instance; last week I took on a new client in his mid-fifties. This man got his first company car just that week. But, women this old? Strange!

'Doesn't she have a son or someone to drive her around? Or a driver? Huge house; she must have enough money to afford a driver. So many looking for jobs these days.'

He shook his head at the way the world was going. Thankam came out just then, so the driver next door ducked behind the hibiscus bush, where he could have a clear view of the proceedings.

'You can take the car out,' Thankam said to the instructor. 'Let's find somewhere quiet to practise.' Thankam made it clear right from the start who would be in charge.

Sudhakaran took the Maruthi out, letting it roll out on neutral, down the slight slope of the garage floor. As Thankam got into the passenger seat, a faint whiff of sandalwood soap wafted in the car.

'No empty spaces around here,' he said. 'We will go down to the exhibition grounds near SRM road.'

They spent an hour on starting practice and parking in various tight places, between the cassia trees and the cardboard and iron-sheet *bastis* of the Tamil migrant workers, who camped in that area. The car twisted and glided over the blue and white plastic bags, scattered by the wind from the rubbish heaps on the edge of the road. Half-naked children from the lean-tos stood around staring at the car and its occupants. Sudhakaran shooed them away impatiently, but Thankam smiled at them when they came near the car. If she touched them with the vehicle, the parents would scream 'accident!' and extract a sizeable sum from her in compensation. Both of them knew this.

'We will go out on the roads tomorrow,' she said at the end of the hour. 'I need to get over my fear of Kochi traffic.'

'It might be easier to get a driver; I know a really good one who is looking for a job,' Sudhakaran offered. She gave him a look, which was intended to make him feel the size of a matchstick.

When the driver came the next morning, Thankam climbed into the driving seat without comment and took the car out.

'It's too early to venture on to MG road,' she said, after she had negotiated the tight corners in the cul-de-sac where she lived. She turned left just before the junction and reached the South Bridge; most of the traffic was coming into town. They had a smooth ride to the Vyttila junction in the opposite direction.

She got on to the national highway and went as far as the Kalloor turn-off; and there she got into heavy morning traffic. An L-board was displayed in the rear but no one was paying any attention or giving any quarter. She leaned forward in her seat, tense with the effort of taking in all the disorder around her. Finally she stalled in front of Kurien's Supermarket and cursed to herself.

'Easy,' Sudhakaran said. 'You are doing fine. Get into the left lane and don't give them room to pass on your left. You are feeling crowded because they are coming on both sides.'

Thankam could see the wisdom of what he said; she thawed a little. She sat still for a moment, gathering her courage, looking out, listening to the morning pandemonium around her.

A stray, young elephant walked sedately, trailing the chains, which were looped round his neck and secured on one front and one back leg. He clutched his lunch of palm fronds in his mouth, and a big bunch of golden yellow coconut blooms was tucked behind his left tusk, ready to eat when he fancied a special nibble. The handler walked beside him, with a confidence born of familiarity, holding his steel-edged thong, which he used for a steering device. No one took much notice.

Thankam passed within inches of him.

'I'll need a fair amount of confidence to come out in this kind of traffic,' she admitted, eyeing the buses hurtling past her.

'This is a bad time, when everyone is going to work and the buses are competing with each other for custom.'

She was grateful to Sudhakaran for trying to restore her courage.

Thankam watched the waiting passengers duck back as the vehicles careered towards them, shedding the tailboard brigade of night shift workers, and splashing dirty puddle-water on synthetic silk saris, frayed trouser turn-ups and starched-crisp dhotis.

When she got back home she breathed a huge sigh of relief; then she arranged more lessons, every alternate day, for two weeks.

'Anil mone phoned,' Seetha called out, as she walked in. 'He says he will be here for dinner this evening.'

Anil had got into the habit of phoning his mother daily and coming to Kochi more frequently since his father died. Thankam often thought Anil had become more caring, as though he had sloughed off some hard, outer skin of selfishness.

Anil arrived in the evening while Thankam was having her evening tea on the terrace upstairs. He had been driving all day and was hot and sweaty.

Thankam touched him lightly on his arm, as though confirming his presence. He had dark circles of sleep deprivation under his eyes and a shadow on his chin, which had gone well past five-o'clock. She noticed the ever-present biro, which had leaked in his shirt pocket and his jet-black hair, too long at the nape to be tidy. He always looked as though he had got out of his house in a hurry. But he could get away with all this because he was a naturally handsome boy, the kind women wanted to mother.

'You look done in,' Thankam said. 'Tea?'

Anil ignored his mother's concern.

'How are you, then?' he asked. 'Getting about? You weren't in when I called.' This, with a slight edge of grievance. 'Seetha said you'd gone out with the driver. Have you got one now?'

Seetha came in with a hot mug of tea and a plateful of plantain crisps.

'We'll talk about all that in a minute. Here, drink your tea.'

Manju arrived soon after with her two sunbeams in tow. It was rapidly developing into a full family reunion. The children had a great time climbing all over Anil, who always seemed to have infinite patience for his nieces. Mercifully, they had got past the stage when they demanded to know when grandfather was coming back. Someone had taken the easy way out by telling them Unni had gone to his village near Thalassery.

'What's all this driver talk?' Manju asked as she walked in. 'You should be careful about getting a driver; some of them are right rogues and will pinch money from your handbag if you leave it on the car seat for a moment.

'*Illa, Moley*,' Thankam explained, a bit sheepishly 'I am getting driving lessons so I can do my own running around.'

'Why didn't you call me if you needed a lift?' Manju asked guiltily. 'Would have,' Thankam interrupted. 'I am not getting a driver. I am learning to drive. Another week of lessons and I will be zipping around Kochi; you'll be proud of me. And watch out, *Moley*. I shall turn up on your doorstep at all sorts of hours; you're not going to like it.' She appeared quite happy at the prospect.

'I could do with someone turning up. It is getting pretty boring with both the girls in school now.'

Manju stopped a moment and leaned forward as though she was asking permission.

'There is a job going at the local British Council library here, thought I might apply for it.'

'What does Gopi say?' Thankam came straight to the point. 'And your mother-in-law is not well. Isn't it a bad time to start working after all these years?'

Manju sounded a little uncertain. 'I know,' she said. 'But I can't sit at home forever, while Gopi is in Dubai living it up, and the children are in school all morning. Perhaps something part time. I can get a woman to stay with *Amma*, I am sure, for the mornings.'

'It's all expense; you will find you have no change left from your wages.'

'Money seems to be all I have,' Manju said verging on the bitter. Thankam looked sharply at her, but nothing more was forthcoming.

'Are you sure you are up to all this driving around in Kochi? MG road is pure, undiluted hell on a morning,' Manju warned.

'Must manage my comings and goings,' Thankam said firmly.

'Can't sit at home alone all day, waiting for some kind soul to come and keep me company, can I? In between having good thoughts, looking after my grandchildren and visiting temples - eh?'

Thankam called out to Seetha to clear the plates away as she started stacking them on the centre table. Asha, the younger of the two little ones, climbed up on her lap as soon as she sat down; as though sensing the tension in the room, wanting to be reassured. Thankam hugged her and she put her thumb into her mouth, sucking herself to sleep.

Thankam rubbed her nose with her knuckles, thinking aloud. 'Lots of things to do,' she said.

'I haven't paid the corporation tax for the year or the car insurance.'

'Why don't you let me do all that?' Anil sounded as though his role as male head of the house was being questioned.

'But that is exactly what I don't want you to do. I have to do all these things myself.' Thankam smiled at Anil, to lessen the effect of what she was saying.

'When your dad was alive, I didn't even have a bank account. But first things first. Get mobile.

'How long are you staying, Anil?'

'Just until day after tomorrow. I could do all your paperwork while I am here – taxes and all that?'

'You are going to pay her taxes, insure her car, deal with the lawyers and the will, all in one day,' Manju broke in, laughing.

'And while you are about it, you can collect the test results for my mother-in-law from the hospital, and take the girls for a haircut.'

Anil frowned at the women who were obviously teasing him, then gave up and retired to bed.

Anil went back to Bangalore early next morning.

'So, when are you coming my way?' he asked, as he put his overnight case on the front seat of his car. This was an oft-repeated query.

'I'll let you know. I have a few things to attend to. For instance, no one has gone into your father's school for a long time.' Thankam was referring to the tutorial college, which Unni had managed, profitably, for the last fifteen years. 'After all the effort your father put into that school; I would hate to think the business died because of neglect.'

'You're not seriously thinking of taking over father's work, are you?'

Thankam knew Anil could be blamed by all and sundry if it looked as though she needed to work for a living. It was his traditional role to provide for his widowed mother.

'At the moment, I don't know what I am thinking,' Thankam answered. 'I'll know when I have been to the school and seen a few things there.'

As soon as Anil left, Thankam took the car out. She was still a bit shaky with her driving, but it was a short distance to the school in Kadavanthara and once inside, she wouldn't have to fight the steering wheel to park the car, because the school had its own parking lot.

The rains had stopped. Street-children came out to play in the puddles, in which telegraph poles and scraggy, urban trees were reflected. Pie dogs and threadbare kittens appeared, to pee and scavenge for food in the rubbish heaps on either side of the road.

The multicoloured fruit and vegetable stalls on Sahodharan Ayyappan Road were already up, though trade was weak at nine-thirty in the morning. The new crop of potholes after the last rainy season was lying in wait for the unwary driver, and Thankam, in her nervousness, often went into the holes, making the front of the Maruthi bounce up and drop heavily. The engine died a few times and had to be restarted when her foot came off the pedal.

As she drove in to the school compound, she noticed that it was already full; obviously the staff had arrived and the school was in session. At the reception, Savithri was on the phone and Thankam caught the tail end of the dialogue.

'No, it finishes on Monday. Kumari went. Lots of cotton saris and the prices are good. I'll meet you during lunch break if you want to …'

She saw Thankam waiting in the doorway and came to a sudden, guilty stop. Thankam let it go for the moment; she had not come to find fault with anyone; indeed she was not certain why she had come.

She took a deep breath and walked towards her husband's old office, afraid to confront that empty chair. While he was alive she had come in here so many times, and Unni would push his papers aside, however busy he was, order tea, and talk to her, tickled pink to see her in the middle of the day.

Thankam, in her mind's eye, saw an orphaned, empty room; a notepad with familiar handwriting on the desk; gathering dust; an electric typewriter that had been a birthday present …She summoned up all her courage to face that bleakness, so she was taken aback when she walked in to see Jacob, Unni's assistant, seated behind his desk, having a conversation with one of the pretty young teachers on the staff. Jacob looked at home as though he had been there forever. The two of them didn't seem like they were discussing last month's test results either. Thankam remembered Unni's constant advice to his staff: 'Don't play in your own backyard.'

And his comment about George Jacob: 'Excellent professional. But he can't keep his hands off the young teachers. He'll get himself into trouble one of these days. As it is, we've had one or two muttered complaints. Harassment of women at work is not something he can get away with in this day and age.'

When Jacob saw Thankam at the door, he jumped up, knocking down a sheaf of question papers from his desk in his agitation. 'I was just telling Vasanthi here that we have to do more work with past question papers in Maths. And to keep some solved papers ready for all the staff to use.'

'Yes, of course,' Thankam said lightly, hoping her disapproval did not show. And it was unreasonable of her not to expect the signs of Unni's presence here to be wiped out, in a busy institution like this.

'I hope you don't mind my dropping in when you are obviously busy. It is not fair to leave the whole burden of this office on your shoulders, but I will be around from next Monday. And I must thank you for your kindness to me when Unni died. Also for looking after the establishment all this time on your own.'

Now, from where did that decision to involve herself crawl out, she wondered. She had not decided anything before she walked into the office, now she had committed herself.

'There is really no need,' Jacob did not sound enthusiastic. Vasanthi was edging to the door as unobtrusively as possible. 'Do you really want to take all this on?' He waved expansively to include the office, the school, perhaps even the road outside.

Thankam was firm. 'I need something to do and Unni would want me to make sure everything is going well here.' Her tone did not invite discussion.

Why was every single person relegating her to an ineffectual widow's life, while suggesting it was in her best interests?

Thankam got up and walked to the door, 'Could you get this office cleaned up for me by Monday?'

She didn't wait for an answer.

Thankam went in to the school next Monday morning, quite early, before the staff arrived. A sweeper, sari hitched up, was lazily dragging a broom across the corridor outside the classrooms. Thankam called her in.

'Sweep and swab this office right away. I'll wait outside while you do that.'

The woman muttered something, but was clearly tsurprised to refuse. Thankam collected all the ashtrays, spilling over with last week's butts and ash, and gave them to her to empty and wash.

When Jacob drove in a few minutes later, he found Thankam ensconced in what he had recently thought of as his office. His morning newspaper, the *Manorama,* was sitting on the mat outside the office. He picked it up, said a brief greeting to Thankam, and strode off briskly to the 'senior' section where his own office always had been.

Thankam spent the morning at the school, looking through the enrolment lists and last year's results. She asked Jacob to arrange a meeting of the staff to thank them for their work, and for the results, which were excellent. This was the kind of thing Unni did and it was somewhere for her to start, to get the feel of the business.

She spoke to some of the students she met in the corridors. These were the backbone of the institution, students who were here for the whole year, doing repeats. The school had no laboratories and offered only arts subjects, and Bookkeeping and Commerce, during the day classes. In the evenings, Mathematics, Physics and Chemistry were included, but no Practicals were possible. Those who came in the evening shift would be here only for a few months until the exams came round. She noticed students were more comfortable talking in Malayalam; their English was hesitant and inadequate. In the back of her mind Thankam flagged the general problem of spoken English in the school.

All ten members of the morning staff came to the meeting in the main office.

'The results last year were above average – thanks to Mr Jacob and all of you; you have been doing a wonderful job. Now it is time I did *my* bit. You will find me in the Principal's office all morning in future and please feel free to talk to me on any issue that troubles you.

'I would be especially grateful for any ideas on how to improve the spoken English of the students. They won't find it easy to get jobs if they can't manage an interview in English.'

Thankam drove home after the lunch hour, thinking about the school. Seetha was waiting for her at the front door when the little red *Maruthi* protested up the slope into the garage.

'I nearly rang Manju. It is unlike you to come back this late from your morning trips; it is nearly two.'

'I went to the school. You mustn't worry about me if I am a little late. I'll have to go to the school now and then; it puts the food on our table, remember.'

'Are you starting work, then?' Seetha seemed to want a straight answer. 'Will you come back daily at this time? Because I won't get lunch ready by twelve-thirty as I normally do, if that is the case.'

'I should look after our business, Seetha, shouldn't I?' Thankam was thinking out loud.

'It is good for you; it will give you something to do, but Anil won't like you working.'

'If Anil had his way, he'd put me in a big plastic bag, with just my head outside, and keep me safe – and useless – forever. But we mustn't get annoyed with Anil. He feels it is his job to look after me now.

'Mind you, I doubt he can look after himself. After all the time he spends running around to Madras and here and Hyderabad, for his work.'

3

On days when Seetha couldn't come to work, Thankam would walk from room to room, looking out through the windows, a little lost, waiting for her. That day, Seetha arrived late in the morning and offered no excuses.

'So you couldn't be bothered to phone, could you?' Thankam lashed out. Usually Seetha would go down to the nearest teashop to phone if she was going to be delayed.

Seetha kept her head down and continued to walk through to the kitchen. This refusal to meet her eye angered Thankam even more, so she followed her into the kitchen.

'The kitchen is in a state -' As Thankam ranted Seetha looked up, and Thankam saw the huge black and blue welts on her cheek and temple.

'Oh my God, Seetha, what happened to your face? Here, let me take a look.' All Thankam's ire was gone in a second. She fetched *Iodex* from her bathroom cabinet and put it on the bruises.

'There, that will make it better. What -?'

Seetha winced and the kindness in Thankam's voice brought the tears that she had, with much practice, learned to keep back.

'That *chaithan*, Amma,' Seetha said, sobbing, 'last night he came home on all fours again and he knocked me into the door. Preethi also got hurt when she tried to get between her father and me.'

Thankam put her arms round Seetha; this made Seetha sob even more.

'"You and your daughter dress up every morning and go in search of men." That's what that beast said. "Look at your clothes; don't tell me you wear all this to go to work," he shouted. Then he pulled out all my saris from my *almirah* and threw them on the floor. Swept the fish curry off the table.

'You give me all my clothes Amma; he never buys my daughter or me anything. Not even food. Some months he doesn't pay the rent and I've had to pawn the little gold I had. My daughter's earrings, which she bought, working at a neighbour's house, are also gone.

'We like to dress neatly when we come out; gives us some self-respect. What has he got against that?'

Thankam didn't know how to comfort Seetha. So she said, 'Here, come and sit down. I'm going to make a cup of tea for you and then we are going to do lunch together. I'll give that man a piece of my mind one of these days. You and Preethi will have to live here with me if this goes on.'

Seetha perked up and it looked as though she was ready to forget her griefs. 'No time for tea. It's getting on for twelve. I have to clean the rice and grind the coconut for the fish curry…'

Thankam smiled to herself: Seetha's griefs always vanished as quickly as they came; she had no time to dwell on them. 'Let's have some beans *thoran* with the fish curry,' she said as she walked out of the kitchen.

Next morning, Thankam called Jacob. Unni had always consulted him about most things.

'Jacob, something I need your advice on. I am thinking of renting the self-contained annexe to my house. A young couple perhaps or even a single person, so I don't feel I'm alone on the premises at night.'

'A live-in maid, I'd say, is the best solution,' Jacob suggested.

'They're so hard to find these days. And I don't think I can take the responsibility. With a young maid in the house, I would be forced to stay at home guarding her virtue so she's never left alone.

'In any case, the place is getting untidy and old with being empty for so long; no one's used it since my son, Anil, went off to Bangalore.'

Jacob phoned the next day.

'Guy I often see at the Rotary - name is Mohan - is looking for a place in town. Would you be interested?'

'What does he do for a living? And do you know him well?'

'Can't say I do. But then, does anyone know anyone else well in this town? I think he is a businessman – but what in I have no idea.'

'What do you think?' Thankam knew she could trust Jacob's street wisdom. Jacob was a Kochi person, whereas Unni and Thankam had come from the sticks in North Malabar.

'No harm in trying him out. He wants a place for himself and his sister, who is a student at Maharaja's College. Can't go too far wrong with a young sister in tow, can he?'

'All right then. Send him along if you can contact him.'

They turned up bright and early next morning, when Thankam was in her bath.

'Two people to see you,' Seetha shouted through the bathroom door. 'Say they have come about the annexe.'

Another example of Jacob's efficiency, she concluded, as she quickly dried herself, wrapped a sari round herself and hurried downstairs.

They were looking at her cannas when she found them, a tall, middle-aged man, and a girl, who looked too much like him not to be a sister. She was relieved this wasn't a case of a man trying to set up a mistress in a flat; Kochi's urban anonymity encouraged men to set up their "little house" here.

'Do come and sit down,' Thankam called out.

'Lovely garden,' he said, as he turned round. Thankam saw a man, no longer young but certainly not old, thin, almost willowy, so much so he appeared to stoop a little. He pushed a recalcitrant forelock back with his left hand, revealing hair so straight it had a will of its own. Light brown eyes regarded Thankam quietly before he spoke. The girl hung back behind her brother, obviously shy about this encounter.

'We heard from Jacob at the college that you have a flat to rent.'

Both man and sister appeared tense and diffident. Thankam wondered what exactly Jacob had told this man about her. However, she instinctively liked the look of them; there was something touching about this brother-and-sister pair looking for a place to live, something young and wholesome that reminded her of her own brother, Appu, and herself when they were young.

'I don't know whether Jacob told you. I lost my husband recently and don't like living in this large house on my own. So I thought, maybe, I could rent the annexe out.

'I'll show you the rooms and you can decide whether this is what you want. I'm looking for tenants who'll be friendly – feel like family. But I suppose that's a lot to ask.

'I've never had tenants,' she added in explanation.

As Thankam talked, she led the way upstairs through the outside entrance. A stone stairway painted white spiralled up to a small covered landing.

'This would be your entrance; the flat is self-contained. There is a door from the main house but it is locked from my side and you'd have a bolt on your side.'

The heavy, teak door opened on to a large, light-filled sitting room and a bedroom at the back. Geetha, the young sister, had a look at the kitchen and bathroom. She came back and whispered in her brother's ear. He laid a hand on her shoulder as he tilted his head to listen to her.

Thankam showed them the door leading from the sitting room to her side of the house. When they returned downstairs they discussed rent and Mohan paid an advance of one month's rent. They clearly could not believe their luck in finding such good accommodation, so near the centre of town.

'My sister really likes it and the rent is reasonable for this part of Kochi. We'll try to be good tenants and not disturb you at all. With you next door I shan't worry about Geetha'

A huge sigh of relief escaped from him as he left with a grateful smile for Thankam. Clearly they had been desperate to find somewhere for the young girl to live, where the brother could also visit.

The image of the brother and sister stayed with Thankam as she continued sitting on the veranda; they were a striking pair to look at. The girl was slim like her brother and her thick, lustrous, black hair was plaited loosely; the end swayed from side to side at her waist, behind her, as she walked. They had the casual grace of the very beautiful, who knew they did not need any artifice to adorn them.

When they had gone, Thankam's thoughts went back to the time she had grown up in Thalassery with her brother, Appu. Life had been simple then. Now Appu was far away trying to make a living in Dubai and she was in cold-blooded Kochi. She also had a sense of anticlimax; it had all been so sudden. So she phoned Manju to tell her the news.

4

Thankam was slipping into deep sleep when she was jolted awake with the sound of a window banging on the back veranda. The wind, she decided, and turned over to go back to sleep, but sleep would not come easily.

The tense hush was suddenly broken by a thud as someone jumped off a ledge, landing heavily on the lawn, and ran swiftly across. Thankam tumbled out of bed and rushed to the window in time to see a shadowy figure escaping over the back wall.

Grabbing her housecoat off the hook on the door, Thankam struggled into it, her fingers clumsy at finding the buttons, and tying the belt a major feat. She then dropped heavily on to the bed, as though the whole effort had exhausted her, and stared at her trembling hands. Her body shrank into itself trying to become invisible.

Eventually she got herself together and walked downstairs, all thought of sleep having fled. She wanted to tell someone, anyone, about the intruder, but it was too late to call friends for comfort, so she made a cup of tea instead and walked back into the living room with it. As she put the tea down on the side table, she looked around her as though predators could pounce on her from any dark corner in the room. Was the front gate padlocked? she wondered. It was frightening to part the curtains open, so she made a chink in it with her fingers and looked out.

The solitary porch light shed its tired beams on the car and the gate seemed secure. As she stared anxiously at the mottled shadows outside, she could hear a motorcycle revving down in her lane, then the clang of a front gate opening and shutting. The lights came on in the house opposite; Vijayan, the college student, coming home after an evening out, she decided.

Down the lane a man cleared his throat deliberately loudly, hawked and spat, probably the security guard confirming his presence at sight of Vijayan. The thought that neighbours were awake was reassuring. She could hear the put-put of auto-rickshaws on Station Road, where the last train from Malabar must have disgorged its passengers. The odd horn blared its impatience somewhere far, and upstairs, in her tenant's flat, a toilet flushed. Normally it would have irritated her at this time of the night, but now it was a welcome sign of other friendly presences; Kochi was still awake and pulsing, though it was beginning to hunker down for the night.

When she switched on the television, all the Malayalam channels were showing old films in black and white. Thankam surfed around a while and returned to a music channel; it suited the fragmented nature of her mind right then. I've become one of these insomniacs browsing the TV channels in the early hours of the morning, she thought; how the mighty have fallen.

Thankam got up late the next morning with the night's intruder still uppermost in her mind. When Seetha brought the coffee she found her mistress lost in thought, looking bedraggled and tired. The coffee spilt on Thankam's unsteady wrist as she took the mug and she wiped it impatiently with the edge of her kaftan. She did not meet Seetha's eyes or greet her: engaging with anyone or anything looked like too much trouble.

'Dark shadows under your eyes, Amma. You look really wasted,' Seetha said.

'Some one tried to break in last night. Didn't get much sleep.'

'Now they know you are on your own here, thieves can't wait.'

'Yes. We widows are a race apart. Every human vulture targets us. We have to batten down hatches and live in fear.'

As Thankam sat sipping coffee, her tenants came down the stairway and went through towards the gate. Mohan let Geetha through and turned to close the gate behind him. He must have seen some thing in Thankam's face, which made him whisper to his sister and hurry back.

'What's the matter?' he asked. 'You look…'

Thankam realized he never saw this private face of hers; she normally came downstairs after dressing for the day, hiding her bouts of despair in a starched, crisp cotton sari and a business-like attitude. No wonder Seetha had been so concerned.

'Had a bad night,' she answered, dismissing the question quickly.

He hesitated, smiling tentatively. 'We are upstairs, not far. You can call one of us if something disturbs you.'

'Thanks, I wish I had,' Thankam said; she felt grateful for the offer but his kindness made her feel even more bereft for some strange reason. 'I thought someone tried to get into our house through a window last night,' she added.

'That must have been awful,' he exclaimed. 'A shout would have brought one of us down. I'll have a look at the windows downstairs when I return, if you wish,' he added.

'I have to go now; I'll see you later.'

Thankam thought of that fleeting smile, and how his face lighted up with it. She wished she could have opened her heart to him, but would it be humiliating? She watched him as he walked away from her: he moved with a dancer's grace. Perhaps he had learned *Bharathanatyam* in his youth. Looking at him it seemed to her he should have been wearing the flowing *kurta* rather than the prosaic work-uniform of trousers, shirt and tie.

After he left she wanted to call him back and tell him all that happened, hear the sympathy in his voice, but the moment had gone. Would she feel protected if she confided in him? Suddenly she was jealous of Geetha, with Mohan to look after her. No nightmares to banish, no predators to escape.

Thankam shook herself awake from her reverie. Must do something about all this, she decided. The Widows Association that Raji mentioned perhaps.

Thankam waited for Mohan to turn up in the evening to check her windows, but there was no sign of him. She felt a little abandoned; he doesn't sleep here every day, she reminded herself. Maybe he had to go out of town.

Mohan turned up early the next day. She was on her usual perch on the veranda ledge and didn't greet him, partly because she had felt let down the previous day, and partly because she was still in her morning kaftan. She was not really ready to face her own face in the mirror, let alone Mohan. But he spied her as he walked over purposefully towards the dining room window.

'Sorry. Couldn't make it yesterday,' he said perfunctorily.

She heard him testing the metal burglar-bars on the windows. He clattered around for a while on the outside of the house before returning to her.

'The downstairs bedroom window seems to have been disturbed recently,' he remarked. Someone did try to loosen the grid but did not succeed. You know, your windows are pretty impregnable.'

'That's a relief.' Thankam answered, but her voice was dull, distant, almost uninterested.

Mohan must have noticed her lack-lustre demeanour. Even the way she sat, slumped into herself showed how dejected she was. He hesitated as though reluctant to leave.

'Look, I'll tighten up that window for you. Might need another bolt, which I will get from town.' Mohan was standing on the other side of the parapet where she was perched.

The brown and white lungi he was wearing failed to reach his ankles. He had picked the left hem up in his hand as men tended to do if they were bustling about. He was also barefooted; obviously he had meant to get back upstairs very quickly.

'If you are going to stand around barefooted, you might as well come up and sit yourself on the veranda,' Thankam said without enthusiasm. She then remembered he was doing something for her and she should be grateful.

'Thank you for your help,' she added dutifully.

Mohan came up the steps, pulled a wicker chair out and brought it near her. He seemed to be considering what to say next.

'Coffee,' Thankam announced brightly. Mohan put a hand out as though to stop her from calling for coffee, then withdrew it to push back his hair, which threatened to fall into his eyes.

'I think you need to get out of this house more often and forget this burglar – and everything else.' He sounded thoughtful. 'For a little while at least,' he added. 'I am going to Vyttilla this evening; why don't you come along for a ride?'

She smiled; despair curled at the edges of that smile.

'Evening then,' Mohan said decisively, as he got up and went back upstairs.

When Mohan turned up at dusk, he found Thankam squatting in front of a bed of multi-coloured dahlias with an old kitchen knife doing duty for both secateurs and fork. She was busy chopping the dead leaves and sprucing up the area around the new tubers by loosening the mud with the knife. She had tied up her waist length hair in an untidy knot on her head and pulled the sari pallav tight and tucked it willy-nilly into the waist. A wet smudge of mud was drying on her forehead where she had been wiping off the sweat from her face with the back of her hand. Clearly, she had not bargained for him keeping his word.

'Just the right time for a ride,' he said, looking down on her. She looked up at him and couldn't find an excuse for not being ready.

'I didn't….' she began.

'You didn't think I would come or you didn't want to come? It's a lovely time of the day for a ride,' he cajoled. 'C'mon, keep me company.' He made it sound as though *she* was doing *him* a favour.

'These dahlias -,' she started tentatively.

'And I'll tell you what,' he interrupted before she could finish. 'I'll help you clean up that dahlia bed if you go out with me today.'

'All right. Give me ten minutes.' Thankam walked quickly to the house and went upstairs. Mohan sat down on the veranda ledge, whistling an old Malayalam tune.

She was as good as her word and came down very quickly, washed and changed; the transformation was amazing. Mohan stared at her as though he had never seen her before, and then turned away deliberately. She had tied her hair in a neat coil at the nape of her neck and the spring-up curls near her face framed it softly. She was wearing a crisp blue voile sari and a *choli* to match. As Mohan jumped off the ledge, she slipped into her *chappals*, which always rested at the bottom of her veranda steps.

'Haven't been out for a ride in months,' Thankam remarked. 'Unni used to love this time of day when dusk is creeping up. We often drove to the island and sat around watching the crowds on a Sunday evening.'

He gave her a strange look; she understood that look only when they got to the road where he usually parked his car and realised he meant to take the motorcycle out, not the car.

'I've never –'

'Good heavens. Really? I thought everybody graduated from a motor bike to a car.'

'Not in my time,' Thankam pointed out. 'It wouldn't do anyway.'

Mohan was quick to understand her half-stated concerns.

'You are right. We should take the car instead.'

He went over to his car parked at the kerb and opened the door for her.

'I'm really sorry, I didn't think.' He sounded contrite.

He eased the car out and drove towards Vyttilla. He was whistling again, the same tune that he had been whistling earlier. Thankam relaxed back into the seat and let her mind wander.

Graciamma next door, the obese, diabetic, old woman, permanently parked at that window in her wheelchair, would have much to talk about, she thought, if she saw Thankam on a strange man's motorbike. The news would have reached her very conservative Nair community in no time at all and she would have been labelled a slut. It was amazing how gossip had no caste distinctions; it spread like flood waters in South Kochi, going with the flow, gathering more and more filth as it crept along. All sympathy for her would vanish overnight. Much as she wished otherwise, Thankam knew the opinions of her community were important to her.

Did he really think she could get on his pillion and hold on to him and no one would notice? Still, it might have been fun. Perhaps, if he volunteered to take her out late in the evening one day, she would be tempted.

Her thoughts turned to Mohan sitting beside her. He was quite innocent really - and impulsive. Very generous with his time too. She looked at his hands resting lightly on the wheel; they were a dancer's hands, graceful and well maintained. Unni used to have nicotine stains, she remembered, and his fingers always smelled slightly of the Scissors cigarette, his favourite brand. How she loved that smell of his!

What would Unni have made of her going out for a ride with Mohan? Thankam wondered briefly; then she pushed the thought away.

'Don't you smoke at all?' Thankam asked Mohan instead.

'No,' he said and turned to her, grinning mischievously. 'I thought you were not going to say a word till you got home.'

'This is nice; I am enjoying this drive. I am not talking because I am savouring this. But didn't you have to see someone in Vyttilla?'

'I am arranging an evening's entertainment for a family here. But it occurs to me it wouldn't be a good idea to do it with you. There's no hurry anyway.'

'Is that what you do?'

'Well. Yes and no. I own a music shop in Kottayam; that's run by my cousins, but I am there a lot. I also manage a small estate agent's office in Kochi. But my family were always singers and dancers. Geetha and I learned Carnatic music and *Bharathanatyam* early in life. So this, arranging concerts, is a sideline. More fun than work. But it pays well when there is work to be had. In the marriage season mainly.'

He drove on to the National Highway out of town towards Alwaye for half an hour and turned round and returned home. When Thankam got out of the car she tried to thank him, but he would not let her.

'That was a good idea. You were right; I needed to get out,' she insisted.

'It is strange,' Mohan said. 'I feel as though I have done this many times with you before. We must do this again soon.' He had a faraway look in his eyes.

As Thankam went up the stairs she felt disembodied; the substance of her self seemed to have changed in some fundamental way. She went to the *Puja* room and lighted the wicks slowly, mechanically. *Sandhya,* that neither-this-nor-that time when devotional lamps are lighted in Hindu homes had come and gone.

As the oil-drenched wicks caught and the pungent smell of hot oil and burnt matchsticks spread through the room, she stood with joined hands before the deities near the lamp, trying to pray. But Mohan's voice and the image of his friendly face kept intruding, so she gave up and left quickly, thinking she would now have some thing to expiate with the gods in that room.

Raji turned up on Wednesday afternoon for the visit to the Widows' Association. The pink and brown granite floor in Thankam's sitting room looked cool and inviting. The whole room shone with the brass images on display; they were everywhere.

'What do you do with your time?' Raji asked suddenly, apropos of nothing, as she bent down in front of a glass cabinet to peer at a miniscule statue made of ivory. 'You need something really engrossing at this time, to get you through the days and make you so tired you fall into deep sleep when your head touches the pillow. I had small children when Madhavan died, I didn't have time to think, neck-deep as I was in homework, science-projects and revision for tests.'

'I have to be a little careful with that. Nobody here wants me to step into the job which was Unni's, but that is what I want to do. I am sort of starting slowly.'

'Nobody as in -?'

'Well, Manju is not too bad, she thinks I mustn't do too much and get stressed, and I'm inclined to agree, if only because I haven't done anything for so long. But Anil worries. He also thinks people will say he is not taking care of me if I go back to work. They may think I need the money.'

'We all need money, whatever Anil thinks. What work is it anyway?' Raji settled down on one of the dining chairs to drink the tea Seetha had brought.

'I've sort of begun working at the school in the mornings. I don't think that Jacob, Unni's assistant, likes my sniffing around. He's very efficient, but –

'But?'

'Long story there – Jacob and the women, to begin with. Must tell you some time.' Thankam giggled.

'Right. Time to go then.'

'Let's take my car. I need some driving practice.

'And get out of this blasted house!' she murmured under her breath.

'It's near here actually. On top of a mattress shop on Press Club Road.'

Thankam took the Maruthi out, a little less eager, faced with the prospect of finding parking on Press Club Road.

'I am still quite bad with gear changes,' she warned. However, she was lucky; the lane was empty, so she didn't have to do any of that slow nudging past that the professional drivers in Kochi were so good at. As she approached Carrier Station Road, she could see the annual gift of wet slush the Corporation cleaners had piled up on the left of the road. It was a squelchy two feet wide in places and decaying coconut fronds and twigs stuck out from the heaps. She knew no way of avoiding them, so she drove infinitely slowly along the edge of the slush, the Maruthi tilting dangerously to the right.

'They won't clear this for months.' Thankam was speaking from experience, as both women held their sari ends to their nostrils against the stench of decaying vegetation.

'You know something? I am going to need an automatic if I do a lot of driving in Kochi; my back is never going to stand all this waiting around. I am finding it hard to decide on my own, what car to buy.' She eased the car finally on to MG Road and joined the traffic going north.

'You haven't got any choice; otherwise friends and family will try to inflict decisions on you,' Raji argued

'You are right, my mother rang up; she heard I was learning to drive. She's not at all happy; wants me to go home and live there for a while, do the bereaved widow act. And I haven't told her I've started working part-time either. I can't live with her for two weeks without us getting on each other's nerves.

'She'll freak out if she hears about my intruder on Sunday night,' Thankam confided, as she drove into Park Avenue.

'Sundays are bad days anyway; Unni and I had all sorts of special rituals we enjoyed, especially after the children left home.'

'I can imagine,' said Raji naughtily.

Thankam laughed. 'Actually, it was getting up late, eating too much and a drive out to old Kochi to look around Jew Town, if you *must* know.'

Thankam parked next to the embroidery shop with a huge sigh of relief and leaned back in her seat to recount the events of Sunday.

'Oh, dear.' Raji said when Thankam had finished; she sounded as though she had heard all this before.

'He tried to get in through a window, I think. I saw him running away across the back garden. What if he got in?' Remembering it made Thankam shudder. They got out and secured the car.

'They must get a list of widows and single women from somewhere,' Raji said, as she gingerly negotiated the cracked paving stones on the side of the road. 'They always seem to go for houses where there are no men.'

The two women ducked under the kaftans hanging in shop fronts and past the Modern Mattress shop to get to the stairway leading to the meeting hall.

'How else do they get to the widows so easily? Anyway, you'll probably find a few others at the Widows' Association who have had similar experiences.'

The stairs were mean and dingy, littered with cotton fluff, orange peels and bits of paper and plastic; they smelt of stale urine and the women held their breaths going up. By the time Thankam and Raji reached the meeting place, some women had arrived and were arranging the folding chairs stored at the back of the room, in rows facing a chair and table. The hall was large; the few women there hardly filled a corner of it.

The curtains at the small windows, opening out on to Press Club road, appeared soiled with the dust and pollution of central Kochi. A naked bulb hung dejectedly from the ceiling and in the corners, puddles had formed where the rain had leaked into the room. The cement on the floor was cracked in places, making the unwary stumble.

However, this first impression was soon wiped out, as the crowd of women grew bigger and the noise level from their chatter louder; clearly they were happy to be there and looking forward to the day's events. As more arrived the room took on a life of its own; shards of sunlight appeared in corners as if by magic and the room no longer seemed merely unprepossessing.

'All widows,' Raji whispered, as Thankam glanced round the room.

'That young girl as well?' Thankam gestured in the direction of a pretty woman who appeared to be no more than twenty. She was dressed smartly in a pale blue *Salwar-Kameez* outfit, which complemented her fair complexion and curly black hair, with red henna highlights in it.

'That's Nisha; it's a very sad story. She is a *Nair* girl, but she fell in love with and married Vinu, who was from the *Izhava* caste. He died within the year. Her people disowned her; so she still lives with her mother-in-law, who believes this girl brought bad luck into the family.'

'That's terrible,' Thankam interjected.

'The old woman won't stop reminding her of this, so now she suffers from bouts of depression. Never says anything and walks out after a little while when the rest are still talking. What she needs is her family, but they won't talk to her.

'By the way, they'll ask you to say something about yourself when the session begins,' Raji murmured. 'You can just give your name and address if you don't want to say more.'

Soon the crowd began getting bigger and little groups of friends collected in the corners of the room. They appeared to be all sizes and ages and as they talked, they stole glances at the new face in the gathering.

'I come here from time to time, but some of these faces are new to me,' Raji whispered as she introduced Thankam to the women she knew. Within minutes the crowd of over thirty women greeting each other and catching up on the week's happenings had converted the room to a happy, bustling place.

'Went to visit my daughter... my in laws dropped in, I moved, got a job with the … had a bad cold and cough …'

Thankam, a quiet talker herself, wondered whether anyone could hear anyone else in this din.

'They take turns chairing the meeting,' Raji pointed out, speaking into Thankam's ears to get heard. 'If any action is decided, one of them will take responsibility for following up on it and reporting back.'

'Who started this group?'

'That was Grace; she's not here today. Her husband died in a traffic accident on National Highway, forty-seven, within a year of her getting married. You know, how it is with Christians: her family had parted with a huge dowry, all her share of her inheritance, they said. When Ouseppachan died, her in-laws would not give the dowry back to her and her family had nothing more to give her. She wanted to go back to college, to obtain some qualifications and get a job, so she took her in-laws to court with the help of her family, and won most of her dowry back.

'She then started this group to help women in the same situation as her. It grew from there, and now, widows meet here for all sorts of reasons: to exchange experiences, to know their rights, to make friends …'

'And where is Grace now?'

'She works in Ooty; comes here occasionally when she is in town. Very courageous girl that. Her husband's family won't talk to her at all, of course, and they slander her a fair bit when they get the chance.'

Soon one of the women came to the front of the hall and called them to prayer. She started with a song praising

Shivan, in which all the Hindus joined. The Christians and Muslims listened respectfully with folded palms. Thankam was the only newcomer, but all the women gave their names to the group for her benefit, as the meeting started. So Thankam did the same.

'I'm Thankam; I live near Carrier Station Road. I lost my husband some months ago.' Looking around at the motley bunch, she wondered what she expected to gain from this meeting. Did they have anything in common except their widowhood?

As usual, one woman had to relate how she was managing her bereavement; this was the way they always kick-started the gathering. This week it was Nancy, whose husband had succumbed to a sudden cardiac arrest. The chairwoman, Parvathy, introduced her.

Nancy seemed to be about forty years and talked with natural confidence; she came straight to the point.

'My nightmares are not as bad as they were two months ago; I am not taking any Valium now to sleep. This means I am not dysfunctional any more during the day.'

'That's great news. Can you tell us how you managed all this?' the chairwoman, Parvathy asked.

'Time, I guess. Also, I go to the Holy Cross Church every Sunday; the father there counsels me; he has been helpful in making me see things in perspective. He always reminds me to "look below", at people worse off than me rather than those better off than me. It seems to help me to come to terms with my loss.'

As she spoke Nancy had a far-away look as though she was seeing pictures in her mind, trying to translate them into words.

'As I started to feel better, I reduced the number of pills. From one a day to half and gradually to none. I now take the pill only on the occasional night when I can't sleep at all; I didn't take any last week. I feel good about that.'

'How are the children now? Are they less disturbed?'

'Yes, much less.' Nancy's voice was firm. 'I think it was my state of mind that perturbed them even more than losing their father. When I started becoming calmer, they also became normal.

'But I know I still have a long way to go to gain control.' Nancy turned to the group and smiled wryly. 'My in-laws are interfering a lot in my life, trying to impose decisions on me: decisions regarding my house, car, and job; I have to assert myself. I also feel they are spying on me, about where I go, what I do. My driver says they ask him where I've been when they see him on the roads.

'Control is what it is about. I find myself wondering about how they will react to anything I plan to do; it's like an invisible camera always turned on me. But they are good to my children and I don't want to antagonise them.'

Parvathy asked the group whether any one else had experienced this kind of harassment from in-laws.

A woman called Mira spoke up. She was a feisty looking person, probably in her early thirties.

'It's the taboos I mind most, so I ignore them. Can't wear rich clothes, can't go out and look as though I am enjoying myself, can't talk to men outside the family without some one telling me I am stepping out of line. Even our children expect us to turn our lives upside down.

'My sister-in-law often comes to my house to make sure I don't do anything that will bring dishonour to her family. I must dress in a subdued manner, mustn't go to parties, wear a pottu… I just ignore her. She amuses me. She's really upset when I laugh at her. Sometimes she "catches me out", according to her.' Mira laughed. 'I just giggle; this makes her walk out in a huff. But she's always back to tell me how to live my life. When she found she wasn't winning with this nagging, she got the priest to "talk" to me.' She smiled at Nancy.

'I never wore a pottu before marriage; my forehead is narrow and they just don't suit me. But I wear one when I know she is going to be around. I also wear bright colours and costume jewellery even if I am not in the mood for finery; she gets the message. I suppose she thinks all I should wear on my forehead is a streak of sandalwood or sacred ash, to show my piety. And my widowed state.

Mira pulled her sari around her and arranged it like a shawl, displaying an ornate pallu block-printed in rust and black. She has style, Thankam decided, watching her talk.

'If you are not dependent on your in-laws financially,' she said, addressing Cecily, 'they can't hurt you or force you to behave in any particular way. I work as a Marketing Officer in a building firm to support myself.'

An old woman spoke up from the back.

'I agree. If you are free financially, all other freedoms follow.

The woman looked around at the others and then wryly down at her plain white cotton sari. She was silent for a moment before she resumed, smiling.

'Anyway, we have been talking about negative things. I'd like to hear some good news for a change. Isn't there any one here who has been enjoying themselves last week? Doing something that made them especially happy? Asserted their right to have a good time occasionally, like the rest of the world?'

'I went to the Padma theatre with a colleague and saw "*Punjabi House.* Great music,' said Maya. She worked at a local kindergarten and had her afternoons free.

Parvathy responded to a hesitant hand at the back. All eyes turned to her; they had to strain to hear what she was saying.

'My husband died two months ago,' Suma almost whispered. 'Ever since then I've been getting dirty phone calls late at night. Now I am terrified to answer the phone at night; this makes me feel really alone in the evenings.' The speaker was about Thankam's age.

'Did you report this to the police?'

'No. I am afraid they'll ask me to repeat what was said; I couldn't do that, it was vile.'

'Would you like us to report it?'

'I want those calls to stop so that I don't panic when the phone rings after dark.' She sounded terrified.

Parvathy made an action-note to talk to the police. 'I'll let you know what we have been able to do when we meet next week,' she assured the woman.

Listening to all the women Thankam felt some were worse off than her. Poorer, lonelier, more traumatized and without support from family. She was grateful she had adult children who cared for her, though they did smother her at times.

Thankam had not worn a *pottu* since Unni died, partly because she did not feel like it and partly because it did not seem right. She did not have a streak of sandalwood or ash on her forehead either because she knew she was not the kind of widow who would turn to a life of prayer and looking after grandchildren. Maybe a time would come, she told herself, when her interest in her appearance would return. Then, she would start wearing all her bright clothes again, possibly even put a *pottu* on her forehead: one of those large magenta ones she used to so enjoy.

'That's a huge one', Unni says looking at her face. It is yellow and Thankam is a little doubtful of the colour, whether it will show. But she need not have worried; it is great on her large forehead framed by curly wisps of hair.

Don't you like it?' she asks, smiling.

'I think all your pottus are great. It's the shape of your forehead, broad and regular; they're made for pottus. And kondas at the nape.'

Unni comes to her and touches the get-away curl lightly. He is off to college in a minute.

'I could stay home today, do some marking.'

Thankam recognises the gleam in his eye. She laughs and touches his hand on her face.

'Can't. I've got to do something for Amma. She can't see too well; so I said I'd look at the moong dhal and remove the sand and stones. She wants to soak it now, so's to be cooked this evening.

'If you must,' he says, letting go of her reluctantly.

At five, the dabba on the road sent tea and *vadas* up for the meeting and the women broke up to chat and mingle again. Tea came, sweet and steaming, in an aluminium urn and the vadas, straight out of the frying pan were wrapped in banana leaf inside yesterday's *Manorama* newspaper. The women headed in the direction of the channa-and-hot-chilli smell and picked up their plastic cups for tea.

Thankam found herself standing next to Nancy.

'Do you come regularly?' she asked.

'Most Wednesdays, yes,' Nancy answered.

Thankam looked at her and thought, we must be the same age group, more or less. Yet her children are quite young.

'Your children. Are they quite all right now? Must be hard on them when you are not coping. I'm pleased you're better now.'

'I was worried about a lot of things, apart from the grief itself. I wasn't sure I'd be able to keep the payments on my house going, with one wage. I asked my in-laws to help out, but they made excuses. I can't ask my parents; they've given me my dowry and that is that.'

'Surely your in-laws, having taken the dowry; they owe it to you to help you.'

'That was ten years ago. You think they'd even remember that? Probably used it up on their daughters' weddings and the repairs on their house. Apart from the money, they are quite kind to me, so I don't want to take them to court. I can work to support myself.

'I talked to my boss eventually. He is a nice old man - Mr. Usman. He gave me a promotion and I'm taking another two thousand home. I think I'll manage - just.'

As the newcomer, many of the members came over to Thankam and greeted her. They talked about themselves and what they were doing now to make ends meet, have a reasonable life, cope with unreasonable in-laws and domineering children.... They did not probe too much about

Thankam; perhaps they knew she was not ready to talk about herself yet.

'Did coming here help?' Thankam asked Parvathy when she finally broke free from the group around her.

'I lost my husband ages ago. I come now for the camaraderie. I make many friends here and some of them, I meet outside of here too. I think of it as a club. Somewhere I don't have to carry around that awful stigma of being a cursed woman.

'You know, "widow" is my most-hated word in the English language. And the Malayalam alternative *vidava* sounds almost the same. A sound to express longing and alienation from life itself.'

'I know the feeling,' Thankam said. 'Some days I have to con myself in a hundred different ways to feel I still belong to the human race.'

'Who is longing for what?' Vrinda joined them. She was a pretty woman in her fifties, tall and imposing, with a bewitching dimple in her left cheek, when she grinned. She was grinning now.

'And what do you long for, Vrinda?' Parvathy asked. Looking at her, it was difficult to imagine her not getting anything she wanted. She was immaculately turned out: blue chiffon sari, very brief blue choli, with a silver border, showing comfortable love handles, and a silver necklace to match. In her ears she wore chunky silver studs with blue inlay.

'Oh, sometimes I feel I'd love to belong to someone, have a man care for me.'

'But, do you really want all that again at this stage of your life? You have an active social life, many friends; you are forever going here and there on jaunts... Are you telling me you want a man to tell you where to go and what not to wear? Think of it, he probably would tell you not to wear thin chiffons or costume jewellery.'

'I want companionship, someone to hug me tight, really tight in the night.' Vrinda hugged herself as she spoke and then burst out laughing, leaving Thankam wondering whether she meant what she said, or was having them all on.

'Go on, Vrinda, give them a shock.' Parvathy was only half-joking. 'Get yourself a partner. Time you stopped talking and started doing something about it.'

'I don't see what the fuss is about,' Vrinda added. 'If a man loses his wife, the family will start putting pressure on him, within a year, to remarry. The main excuse is that he cannot manage his household without a woman. With us, though, even if we are twenty, it is as though we've had our one shot at life and that's it.

'Some of them don't wait even a year. That Sankaran Nambiar, lives down our road, lost his wife ten months ago; he is now married to a woman twenty years younger than him. It was a quiet affair; perhaps he was ashamed of the unholy haste. I saw him recently, he can't stop smiling.'

'It's difficult, but some seem to have managed it. Forget about what others might think and get on with our lives,' Thankam remarked.

'Seems to me they are harder on older widows, like life has now ended for us,' Vrinda added soberly.

Raji, from the other end of the room caught Thankam's eye. 'Everything all right?' she mouthed. Thankam nodded. The women floated back one by one to their seats after tea, to begin the second half of the meeting.

Parvathy turned to Thankam when everyone was seated again. 'We have a working method here: every time a new person comes to our group, we ask her to identify the one thing that is troubling her most about her widowhood. Something she must face up to, if she is to lead a peaceful life.'

Thankam knew what stifled her most. 'I want to live without depending on anyone, family or friends. But, whenever I try to do anything for myself, my family and friends want to "protect" me. They'd rather I didn't go to work, drive a car, travel on my own…

'I feel stifled.'

'And do you listen to their advice?'

'No, I go ahead and do what I need to do, but I feel guilty doing it.'

Before she left Thankam talked to Parvathy.

'I'll talk to the Telecommunications office about those calls; I have a cousin working in their office.'

As Thankam drove home, she was pensive.

'Did you hear anything useful? Will you go again?' Raji asked.

'Yes, I think I will. Not because I heard anything specific, but because it made me think. All of us widows seem to be in a category of our own, as though we are on the edge of life, not in the middle of it.

'You know, Raji, there must be widows who had bad husbands, men who abused them and made them unhappy. To them it must be a relief to be single again. Are they allowed to admit that, even to themselves?

'And then there must be young ones who miss having partners, sex, all that.'

Raji laughed. 'Now you've really gone and mentioned something widows are not even supposed to *think* about. I can see you're going to get into trouble.'

'Be honest, Raji,' Thankam countered. 'Are you saying sex has never crossed your mind since Madhavan died?'

'What can I do with two small children in the house? Ask my in-laws to baby-sit while I go out with a lover?' Raji giggled at the prospect. 'Oh, I do feel miserable now and then, not that different from those yowling cats and dogs in September. I just put up and shut up.

'Can you imagine the scandal and the gossip if I go down that road?'

'Thank God Unni's relatives are not here to tell me how to live,' Thankam said fervently.

'Oh, someone else will,' Raji said. You could see she was speaking from experience.

As she drove, an image of Mohan flashed briefly into her mind, sitting on her veranda ledge, whistling a happy tune. She banished the image quickly as though it seared her.

However she told Raji about renting out the annexe to her house.

'What are the tenants like?' Raji asked.

'Oh! It's just a college student. And sometimes her brother stays as well.' She made the brother sound almost irrelevant to the equation.

Mohan seemed to be spending almost as much time at the flat as Geetha, Thankam admitted to herself, so where did that half-truth come from? And that too to Raji.

When Thankam reached home, Seetha was at the door. 'I'm just about to lock up and leave.'

'Did Anil or Manju call?'

'No, but that fat *Nasrani* woman next door, always sitting at the window, was asking me where you had gone.'

'Seetha, Nasrani is not a nice word to use for Christians; where do you get these names? She's just being nosey – anyway, what did you say?'

'I said you'd gone to a prayer meeting, so she wanted to know which temple. She was really annoying me; I'll have to start ducking when I go past her throne from here on.'

'She's just bored, in that prison of a chair all her life; we've got to make allowances for her. But ducking is good.'

Graciamma, with her lynx eyes, kept track of everything that went on in the street; Thankam knew how dangerous she was. She would magnify whatever she saw and tell the whole neighbourhood all the details of Thankam's life. Thankam's reputation would be in shreds and she would lose friends. Many husbands would tell their wives not to have anything to do with Thankam if they heard that Mohan was anything more than a tenant.

Thankam did not want to think about the consequences of her friendship with Mohan, so she changed the topic.

'Seetha, is your husband behaving himself these days? I notice the bruises are gone.'

'It's the end of the month and he has no money for drinks. It's after he gets paid that he'll get drunk and start all over again. He's not a bad man when he is sober.'

'Well, you'll just have to stay with me at the ends of months, eh?'

Thankam was amazed at how realistic Seetha could be about her life. Until the next time, she was ready to forget the beatings and the abuse.

5

Thankam was getting into bed when Anil turned up. Since the incident on Sunday she was jumpy, so she was quite pleased to have him around; she could tell him about the intruder and perhaps he would suggest ways in which she could make her compound more secure.

'I'm so glad you have come,' Thankam said. 'I am a bit fragile these last two days.'

'Oh, Mother.' Anil hugged his mother tight. 'You just have to ask and I'll be here.'

'What brought you so quickly when I needed you?'

'I've got some good news,' Anil said, searching her face. 'Though I wonder whether you'll consider it good.'

He sounded hesitant and jubilant at the same time, as though he was harbouring a secret joy, savouring it before he asked others to share in it. Anil had always been secretive and Thankam knew it would take him a while to come to the point; she was not going to rush him, so she waited as he asked about her day, her health.

'Are you driving around a lot in Kochi, on MG Road? I hope you are being careful; I know you can be a little absent-minded.'

'I could afford to be absent-minded when Unni was there to look out for me. Kochi is full of scams and I have to be careful. Do you know they change the rules about parking on main roads, from parallel parking at an angle, to line parking, one behind the other, and back again, at whim? The most recent thing is the number plate: it went from any size digits and letters, to a regulation size of five centimetres by nine centimetres.'

Thankam always talked about the car, the taxes and the insurance to Anil because she knew he thought it was his responsibility to get all this done.

'You'll be glad to know the Maruthi is insured, taxed, everything up to date now.'

'That's a relief.'

'Anil, you didn't come suddenly like this to talk about my car, did you?' Thankam realised she would have to prise his news out of him though he had sounded excited about it to begin with.

Anil pulled up a chair and sat down in front of her. He held both her hands in his as he talked, stroking them with his thumb.

'I've got a chance to go to the UK, Ammey. We are servicing some software for a bank there and I have been chosen to go. I'm really excited at the opportunity, but my father is not around and I am worried about you.'

Thankam refrained from pointing out he was in Bangalore, a good twelve hours' drive away; England was only nine hours on a plane.

'Don't worry about me,' she assured him. 'Small glitches sometimes, but Manju is nearby in an emergency.

'Don't know whether I told you, but I'm working at the school, mornings, getting about in my car.'

As she reassured Anil, Thankam wondered what it would that feel like, Anil going so far way. People she loved were dropping off from her life like ripe mangoes off a tree. She had taken him for granted: his nagging affection and his sudden visits. Since Unni died Anil had grown up almost overnight, taking on the responsibility of looking after his mother even when she would have preferred to be left alone.

Thankam's life appeared to move on, bringing new things into her life and blunting the edge of old ones. She was not sure about all the turns her life was taking, but one thing was certain: she would have to learn to be self-sufficient. She could hardly expect Anil and Manju to keep their lives on hold while she navigated a prolonged widowhood.

Anil had left by the time Manju came the next day; Thankam was drinking her second cup of tea on the balcony upstairs; Anil had obviously talked to Manju as well and she was anxious to know how it was going to affect Thankam. The little girls ran off to the kitchen to raid the pantry where all the munchies were kept; they were likely to get much more out of Seetha than anyone else.

'So you've heard the news,' Thankam greeted Manju.

'You OK with that, Ammey? He is not very sure himself, you know. He spoke to me first and I told him you could manage without him these days. In any case, I'm here, aren't I?' Manju looked searchingly into Thankam's face.

'You don't need either of us really, do you?'

'That's the rough idea, not to need you two layabouts.' Thankam smiled to take the sting out of the words. 'At the same time, what am I without the two of you? You see, my idea is that you two cannot manage without me; I have to be indispensable to someone, haven't I?'

'Gopiettan is coming on holiday,' Manju announced suddenly. She didn't sound overjoyed.

'That's great. You are beginning to look quite bored in that big house, alone, with just his mother and the children. Aren't you planning to go to Dubai when the schools close this year?'

'Oh, I don't know. I'm not sure about "great" either.' Manju was looking in the mirror on the mantelpiece as she talked, as if her pottu had taken on world-shaking importance. Thankam waited quietly for more, no point in asking her, she thought; it has to come out in her own sweet time.

The fiddling with the pottu went on for a while. 'I was talking to Pushpa the other day.'

Oh, well, all right, thought Thankam, we are to forget about Gopi for a while. 'Who is Pushpa?' she asked, playing along.

Asha and Latha ran up the stairs having got what they wanted from Seetha. Latha had sticky smears of *jaggery* all over her chin and held it up to Thankam, who wiped them off gently with the end of her sari. It looked as though Seetha had treated them to curls of coconut and pieces of dark brown jaggery, which was Kerala's substitute for brown sugar. Asha, not to be left out, climbed up on Thankam's lap and held up her face, demanding equal attention even if she didn't need it. Thankam didn't notice any smears there, but her nose was wet and she could see signs of a recent sniffle; so she wiped that with the end of her sari too and nuddled her; she smelt of milky, fresh coconut. Asha was not satisfied; she seized the end of the pallav again and rubbed hard till her nostrils shone red; what were Ammamma's sari ends for anyway?

Thankam looked from her grandchildren to her daughter; she could see the same dark brown eyes and curly lashes and the same wide, ready-to-smile mouths. The children were fair and rosy, but would probably be Manju's light brown when they grew up. Manju brought the children rarely in the mornings; today must be a holiday of some sort, or she was anxious to talk about something worrying her.

'Pushpa, who was at St Teresa's with me; she was in my group, used to come here sometimes. Don't you remember her?' Manju asked.

'Oh, you mean that lovely Brahmin girl who came here for lunch whenever she fancied a little fish or chicken.'

'That's the one; her family are strict vegetarians. I had to give her hand lotion to take the smell of meat and fish off her before she went home.' Manju laughed remembering Pushpa dabbing hand lotion all round her mouth.

'As I said, she is here visiting her parents and dropped by yesterday; made me think.'

'About?'

Manju ignored the question and went on. 'Her husband, Satyan, in Dubai, has been sending all his money to their house in Madras in his mother's name. About a thousand dollars a month, which are all his savings. Now he wants to buy some land and build his own house in Madras, but apparently the mother has used up all the money on renovating the family home and buying jewels for the younger daughter. Satyan is livid, but what can he do about it?'

And then she came to the point. 'Meanwhile Pushpa is really upset, says she feels like a useless poor relation in their house. Satyan comes once a year and in between times, the parents won't allow her to take up a job; they'd rather she stayed at home and did all the housework. She wants to come back and stay *here* with her parents but hasn't got the courage to ask.'

Thankam was getting a glimmer of where all this was leading.

'I sometimes wonder what is gained by men going off to Dubai like this and leaving remittance wives behind. In my case, at least, Gopiettan's amma does not take his money and waste it, but what is this extra money doing for us?'

'It's quick cash and the opportunity to build your house like Satyan; how do you think Gopi would have managed to buy such a lovely waterfront villa for you if he hadn't been raking it in, in Dubai?'

'But there is no husband to live in it, Ammey, you never parted from Achan for more than a week here and there. How do you think I feel in the evenings when the day is done, the children are fast asleep, the old lady is parked in front of the television and I am wondering where to go next? Gopi spent four years with me before he went to Dubai, and now, he sends money and comes twice a year.'

'Absence makes the heart grow -'

'"Detached", I'd say. I asked him about the job at the British Council the other day, on the phone.'

'You didn't!'

'He started shouting at me, put the phone down and didn't phone for two Fridays.

'I haven't mentioned it to his mother either. She's still not well and the tests were inconclusive. They said there is a blockage within her oesophagus, making the food stick.

Sometimes I feel life is going past me like an express train and I am the rooted telegraph pole looking at it speed past. I am getting so selfish about the whole thing I can think of Saraswathi's illness only in connection with it.'

'Don't you like the old woman at all, after staying with her for so many years?'

'You can't love Saraswathi; she won't let you. She is harmless, but after her two children, she is not really keen on loving any new person, not even her grandchildren. She shoos them away if they bother her in her room or when she is watching TV. They've learnt to keep away from her.'

Asha was falling asleep in Thankam's lap and Latha was beginning to fret. 'Want to go home,' she said; Manju knew this was to get attention; so she decided to leave.

'Let's see what Gopi says when he is here, but don't start this job topic until Saraswathi's tests are sorted out and he knows what the problem is.' Thankam wondered why Manju always found herself in situations where she was going against the flow of others' expectations about her; it had always been so. She put the child down and walked over as Manju got up from the chair and gave her a long hug. 'This is a banking hug, to take out when you need some extra love.'

'When I need extra love, I'll get into my car, throw the two brats in and drive straight down to you,' Manju said, basking.

'Yes, I think Saraswathi is quite restless,' Manju added, as she disengaged from the hug. 'And scared, though she won't talk about it. The thing is, there is no question of a holiday in Dubai as long as she is unwell.'

After her daughter left, Thankam sat where she was for a long time, trying to fathom all the things Manju had said in her usual oblique manner – and all the things she had not said. What exactly was the girl planning? And what was that about losing interest in Gopi's visits?

'Is Manju mol going to Dubai then? She didn't come down to see me today.' Seetha complained when Thankam came into the kitchen. She sounded peeved.

'She is far from happy, but she should have come down and greeted you,' Thankam said, placating her. 'A rich husband, big house, two nice little girls and she is discontented.'

'You've to make allowances for youth, Ammey,' Seetha said graciously. 'It can't be much fun living with that old woman. You don't need air- conditioning when you have that one around.'

'Seetha!' Thankam couldn't help laughing at this accurate description of Saraswathi, after listening to Manju talking about her.

'And then, these Dubai wives are all like that.' Seetha was in the mood for a little gossip. 'My husband's niece is in the same boat; the husband, Madhu, works in Sharjah. He has built them a little house, tiled with Calicut tiles and a bathroom inside with a flush toilet. Mind you, they don't know how to look after it; for people like them, an outdoor one is much better; at least you don't bring the stink inside.'

Seetha was in full flow now. She turned away from the gas cooker and held the spatula in her hand away from her as she talked. Seetha's cooking knives and spoons always pointed outwards when she walked around while using them; you had to dodge to safeguard life and limb.

'Every time he comes home, about once in two years, he arrives with huge plastic bags full of things, buys them at the station for the planes. You can put a large bucket of water in those bags; they are so strong; nothing like the blow-away bags we get here from the grocers.'

'Buys them from the airport, you mean,' Thankam corrected her, mildly.

Seetha wasn't taking any notice. There were important things to be said before the food in the *cheenachatt*i got burnt.

'He says there are big shops in the station, upstairs and downstairs. Though I don't know why he brings tins of milk powder called Anitha, when the powder here looks just the same.' It took a moment for Thankam to figure out Seetha must be referring to Nido. She turned aside, trying to keep a straight face.

Seetha didn't know a word of English, but this didn't deter her from adopting some English words she liked the sound of, and changing them to something totally unrecognisable when she used them.

'And *Tank* orange juice mixture,' Seetha continued. Is it any different from the *Rasna* we use here for the girls? But everyone says the Dubai things are much better. He brings chocolates also for the children; good thing too, the kids don't recognise him and he has to bribe them with sweets to get them near him, poor sod.

'He's like a money machine for his family; I think if he suddenly announced he wanted to give up the job, they'd put him in a box and send him back.'

Behind Seetha, the cabbage fry was slowly burning; so Thankam went near to have a look. Seetha took the hint and went back to her cooking, but she was still muttering about 'not much of a life…'

Thankam's mother phoned from Thalassery the next day after nine at night, when calls were cheaper; since Unni died she had broken her life-long determination to have nothing to do with the telephone and started calling Thankam once every fortnight. After this fortnightly call, she was generally so exhausted with getting the better of this new technology, the phone had a fifty-fifty chance of being put down the wrong way round, so one of Thankam's nephews had to put it back correctly in its cradle.

Thankam picked up the phone like a hot coal, ready to drop it at the first sign of trouble. Recently she had suffered some dirty phone calls – a growth industry in Kerala. Fortunately it was not the dirty whisperer. As she greeted her mother, she wondered what she would say if she heard a stranger phoned up her daughter and made lewd suggestions. Thalassery, like any other town, knew a few flashers, who pointed in the direction of some respectable veranda and jerked off, but in a country where many men parted their dhotis at the side of the road and urinated on the walls as a matter of course, flashing was hardly worth mentioning. Dirty phone calls now? Unheard of. Whatever next!

'How is my daughter then?' Madhavi asked. Thankam could visualise her sitting in the corner chair in the living room, making eyes at everyone else in the room to keep the noise from the TV down.

'Very well,' Thankam answered, but the sharp old lady picked up the faint unease in Thankam's voice.

'What happened, *Moley*? You don't sound too certain.'

'I'm OK,' Thankam repeated more definitely. 'Nothing new here. Gopi is due from Dubai soon and Anil says he is going to the UK on business quite soon.'

By Madhavi's standards, this would be a sound reason for Thankam to feel reasonably dejected, so she would be reassured. She had been quite upset when Appu, her only son, got up one fine morning and announced he was resigning his job as Circle Inspector in Kannur district and was going off to Dubai to make some money for a change.

'As a police employee, the only way I'm going to get rich is by taking bribes; I'd rather tote some sheik's briefcase and walk behind him to get rich.'

Having got that initial concern for Thankam out of the way, Madhavi started instructing Thankam about Anil's going; there never was a phone call without the instructions.

'Must get him married before he goes. How old is he now? Twenty-eight? High time then. Otherwise he'll come home with a *madamma*; no use feeling sorry after the event.'

'He's only twenty-five, Ammey. And I can't see him meekly marrying someone just to please me, before he goes overseas. In any case he's going soon, too soon to get married before he goes.'

Thank God, she added in her mind; she said 'yes' and 'yes' again to several more instructions. This was the best tactic to get through this monologue. 'Make sure you padlock the gate securely in the night, don't trust any household help, they'll steal from you…' It went on and on. Thankam switched off as she usually did around this point in the conversation, wondering how quickly she could decently put the phone down.

Why did her conversations with her mother always start well and then proceed to nagging by her mother and impatience on her part? Thankam suspected her mother was still trying to improve her: make her fairer, prettier, more successful. These calls ended up making her feel guilty and dissatisfied every time? Had it ever been different?

Thankam knows her mother has never forgiven her for being born dark and less than perfect. All her childhood Madhavi has to contend with the unkindness of family and friends and as Thankam grows up, she takes it out on her.

'The boy is so fair,' the neighbours repeat often, referring to her handsome elder brother, Appu. 'But the girl is dark; pity it isn't the other way round.'

They say it often in front of both mother and daughter as though Madhavi has deliberately withheld the gift of her fair complexion from her daughter. Thankam at five and six years old knows she has failed her family in some inexplicable way. Only Appu, her brother, unaware of the handicap of a dark complexion, has adored Thankam, calling her Neeli, "the blue one."

As Thankam grows older Madhavi starts to worry no one will want to marry such a dark girl; she buys her Cuticura powder.

'Makes you look fairer,' Madhavi insists. Thankam tries it for a few days, but all it does is take the sheen off her face and make her look as though she has smeared wood-ash on herself. She discards the powder at the back of her cupboard.

In time Madhavi buys her kohl, *but Thankam has given up on looks by then and taken to books instead. She tries getting the kohl right once or twice, drawing down the eyelid with a finger and getting the black on to the inside rim in a smooth, practised stroke, as all her friends do. It never works; the kohl gets into her eyes or smudges her face. It joins the powder at the back of the cupboard; she just does not have the persistence to learn and prefers to read rather than waste time on an exercise she considers futile.*

Thankam remembered all the things that had made a nightmare of her teen years. Bad enough being dark, she soon got a reputation for being a blue stocking.

'What's the point of all this book-reading?' Madhavi often says. 'It won't get you a husband. You're better off learning to make a good Sambar.' Thankam does not believe books and cooking are mutually exclusive.
'She's the best student in her class, Ammey; I wish I was as good at English and Maths,' Appu pipes up loyally in her defence as she folds a bit of newspaper into the book for a bookmark and follows her mother to the kitchen.
At eighteen she is a head taller than most girls around her and a little higher than a great many of the men. Too tall to marry, they say, and too educated. She frightens them a little. She doesn't care as she is having the time of her life going steadily through the Brennen College library; not many people are aware of the hidden wealth of this collection.
By the time Thankam is twenty years old, most of her peers have married and are nursing their second babies. They talk about in-laws and bottle-feed while she reads Bertrand Russell's Marriage *and* Morals *and considers whether the emphasis Kerala puts on sexual morality, to the neglect of all other moralities, is justified.*
Thankam decides no man will want to marry her, as too many irreversible things are wrong with her. How is she

to change the colour of her skin or the quality of her thinking? She makes the most of her few assets, however.

Her hair, black and wavy, is waist-long by the time she is sixteen and continues to grow. Madhavi winds it into a thick plait to go to school, and later, college. The only adornment on Thankam is a large pottu of magenta dust right in the middle of her broad brow. And the jasmine she weaves into garlands for her hair. Wherever she walks Thankam carries the faint, tantalising perfume of jasmine. All the women who have declared her ordinary now look at her, gliding past, head held high, thick black plait swinging from side to side, and murmur, 'She is not pretty, but...' Thankam's response is to square her shoulders and walk even straighter, like a queen among her subjects.

When the first precious marriage proposal for her comes her family's way, the astrologer looks at her horoscope and pronounces,'She has Saturn sitting threateningly in her seventh house.' Everyone knows how difficult it will be to find a male horoscope to match hers. Any husband will need to have Saturn in the seventh house too.

As the years go by and the proposals become scantier, Madhavi looks at her daughter with something close to impatience. 'It is the sins of my previous lives that are being visited on me,' she announces, making Thankam despair for being personally responsible for everything that goes wrong with their household.

6

The hullabaloo woke Thankam up at seven in the morning; what was that ruckus going on in the west side of her house? Normally, all you would hear at this time would be Seetha getting the day started, dropping steel pans and spoons, talking to herself. Thankam listened and she could hear several men: 'Catch… cover that end… don't let it get behind the flowerbeds…' She recognised one of the voices; it was her tenant Mohan. Some of the others sounded like boys and in that cacophony a dog yelped with excitement.

Then the noise transferred itself to the back of the house: men running helter-skelter after something, shouting at each other, and all giving instructions at the same time. Thump, thump! The sound of sticks hitting the ground. Thankam quickly pulled on her kaftan and ran downstairs to her back garden. They're trampling my flowerbeds, she thought, angrily. What are they up to that needs so much scuttling about and beating of the ground?

The men took no notice of her; this was their domain, they continued chasing something, which was trying to slither under the jasmine growing on the back fence. Thankam realised it was a snake they were after; she remembered Unni often saying to her, 'Be careful where you plant jasmine; the smell brings the snakes.'

Seetha had abandoned her half-ground coconut on the grinding stone; turmeric and ground coconut were drying on her hands, but she was directing proceedings with gusto.

'At this rate you lot won't even get an earthworm, let alone…'

'*Anali*,' she said excitedly to Thankam when she noticed her amma was watching. She wiped her hand on her sari end and explained, 'Coiled near the kitchen steps, I nearly stepped on it; the only reason I saw it was because the gods cannot be bothered with me yet. I was taking off my slippers to come in, and I thought, what's that piece of rag? I bent down a little to look closer and it moved. So I screamed and Mohan Sar came rushing down. Good thing too, because if it ran away and hid in the kitchen, I'd be scared to work in there for weeks.'

'If it is a viper, it's not going to run very fast; this is probably a harmless water snake,' Thankam pointed out.

Soon the thumping became focussed on one spot in the garden and she walked across to investigate, slowly, so she could turn and run if the snake came her way. The next-door neighbour's dog, Chessy, had somehow got into the act too and the men were trying to chase it away as it kept getting in their way and hampering their efforts. At one point, the dog got the snake in its mouth and tossed it high up in the air and it fell in an untidy heap on the ground. Thankam had to run back a little way, as the stunned snake flipped over. It was quick work after that. The newspaper boy, Densel, picked it up on the end of a stick and you could see it was now dead; he brought it over triumphantly to show Thankam.

'See,' he said, 'quite big.' No one could deny that; it was a good two feet long, probably not fully-grown yet, and it was certainly not a viper; it didn't have the viper's distinctive, smudged spots.

'Where did it come from? Is there a nest of them somewhere?' Nobody answered her.

The crowd dispersed slowly, crowing about their skill in beating it to death, one snake against five young men; Chessy who actually did the deed was not mentioned. Mohan detached himself from the group and came up to Thankam. 'It is very unlikely you'll have a nest here; I shouldn't worry. They have unloaded some red soil next door for their garden and I guess the snake would have come with it. The mud comes from the hilly areas like Mannurthi or Kakkanad and the digger tends to claw the snakes out with the soil. Then they get dumped in unfamiliar territory and scurry about for a little while ending up like this.'

Thankam observed Mohan as he spoke. He had unhitched his lungi, which had been doubled up and tucked into his waist while chasing the snake. However one side had caught around his knees, exposing a hairy leg with a dancer's calf-muscles. For a crazy moment she wanted to touch that hair, pass her fingers through it; she could almost feel its wiry thickness in her hands. She quickly looked away, confused.

'I don't like killing them,' Mohan's voice came back from a distance. 'But in a residential area like this, people just don't know how to deal with them. This one is certainly not a viper and probably not poisonous. Vipers don't run for their lives, this is the problem with them; they stay coiled and inert even when noise approaches. There is never a need to chase a viper; it is a stupid snake. If you step on it, it will sting and because it doesn't slither away, it is easy to step on them.'

'I'm glad you were here to deal with it,' Thankam said, all gracious housewife again. 'I'm just about to have my coffee, please come in and have some with me before you go upstairs.'

Thankam had never been in this situation before. Were they to go back to being landlord and tenant again? Perhaps the drive on Tuesday was just kindness and he had already forgotten about it. But she remembered the look in his eyes when he left her that evening; had she imagined it?

Seetha was quick with the coffee and while they were sipping it Thankam asked polite questions about the flat and his work.

'Is everything comfortable upstairs?'

'More than,' he said. 'It is a lovely flat and we are lucky to have found it. If you could see the dusty, broken-down rooms some of my mates live in. And, I shouldn't tell you this,' he said, smiling, 'they pay more rent than we do. No, I can't complain.'

Mohan's face had become animated talking about snakes; he has such a warm smile, Thankam thought. This was the first time she had seen him for any length of time after their drive and he appeared more relaxed and confident. Perhaps he is doing better at business and is not so worried anymore; he had appeared tense and distraught when she saw him the day he and his sister moved in. A part of her mind chided itself: she had not been too friendly with Geetha when she was upstairs alone.

'I haven't seen Geetha around for some time,' she said. 'Where is she now? Surely she has another year after this to do at college.'

'Oh, yes, almost a year. She'll be finished next April. Then, I suppose it will be time to get her married, if we can get together the dowry for her. If not, she'll have to work for a while and help with the dowry and the jewels. Our father died long ago, so it's really my responsibility to get her settled, I am putting off thinking about it, it scares me so.'

As Mohan talked, he was looking at the room and Thankam realised he had never seen this part of the house.

'This is a beautiful room,' he said. 'The pink granite and the brass together make it special. I suppose it takes a lot of maintenance.'

'Not really,' Thankam answered, disproportionately pleased he had noticed this room, which she loved. 'The light has to be right to show brass and polished floors off; this room gets the morning sun.'

'It's the smell of incense as well.' Mohan nodded towards the melted bits of incense in a small brass tray on the sideboard.

He finished his coffee and returned the steel glass to the side table. 'And thank you for the coffee. Saves me from making my own when I get upstairs; I'm really lazy with things like that. Now I should get out for work in a hurry.'

As he pushed himself up from the chair using his arm, the muscles on his upper arm flexed under his T-shirt. He stood in front of her for a minute, thoughtful, almost as though there was something left to say. He was a head taller than most men in Kerala, she registered, and his air of diffidence was no longer evident. Thankam noticed the morning stubble on his face and the way he regarded her, light brown eyes questioning, reassuring. When he looked at her like that she always had this sense of something momentous about to happen, something like an act of God, which would take control of her life and change its shape completely.

When he got up and left, it seemed the room had suddenly lost its glow.

As Thankam let the Maruthi roll out of the garage and on to the lane a little later in the day, Graciamma's curtain flicked slightly and stopped. Oh, well, thought Thankam, the old busybody has to do something with her time. She drove towards MG Road, hoping she would have an easy ride at this time, but she had forgotten how soon the town geared up for Christmas; it was creeping and crawling time. Both Christians and non-Christians participated in Christmas to a greater or lesser degree; she herself would have put up lighted Christmas stars in her house if it had not been for Unni's death in that year. New stalls had sprung up overnight on the sides of Park Avenue and Marine Drive and the alleyway opposite the park thronged with shoppers.

As always, the trade was mainly in textiles and ready-made clothes; the variety was unbelievable. But, in between, many vendors were busy selling Christmas stars, big and small, in every colour imaginable; they hung from wires strung between poles and from the trees, which lined the roads. Thankam was lucky to find a small Maruthi space in front of Hameesh Supermarket, so she edged the car in, and got out, delighted with herself that she had managed without scraping the paint. When she shut the ignition and took the key out, she heard a familiar, friendly voice. 'Quite the accomplished driver now, eh?' It was Raji's smiling face beaming a welcome.

'And the glad rags have waited a long while to come out. You look great!'

'Thank you; I needed someone to say that today. I lost some weight in the year; I guess that's why I look better.' Thankam positively glowed with well-being.

'I have to get some beef. Do you think I can sneak it into my house without the old hag next door sniffing it and cackling, "When did the Hindus start eating our beef?"'

Raji laughed. 'What are you going to do when the *Shivsena* people manage to stop the slaughter of cows in this country? They keep threatening to force the government's hands to do this.'

'What are all the Christians and Muslims in Kerala going to do is more to the point,' Thankam responded. 'This is one state in which they won't be able to enforce that. The people will go on *hartal* until the government is forced to give in.'

The two women went inside the shop and walked around the aisles, pushing their trolleys; Thankam bought beef, vegetables and bread, which again was something only Anil asked for. The maids had a healthy contempt for bread and Thankam preferred rice.

'This new generation wants bread and spaghetti and God knows what else. Have you noticed how these supermarkets have started stocking all this stuff?'

'It's called progress. But it costs a lot more.'

When shopping was finished Thankam tried to coax Raji to go home with her for lunch. 'With my decision to pander to my vanity, I need an audience. And I also need reinforcements when Graciamma notices my clothes and smells my beef. With the beef, I might need protecting from Seetha too.'

Raji excused herself, 'I have to pick up Shija from school soon, so I better not. I'll come by in a day or two. Anyway, you can drive now; why don't you come round to my place?'

'That's a thought,' Thankam admitted. 'Maybe I will, but not today'

'You look pretty in your new sari,' Seetha said, as Thankam walked in.

'Not new, it's something I haven't worn this last year. I looked at my clothes and decided I need to start wearing some of them again.'

'But you didn't wear a pottu,' Seetha stated.

'That's right, Seetha. A little at a time. I'll get round to that soon, I'm sure. You know Anil is going overseas; when he comes back we'll take Achan's ashes to the Thirunavaya seaside. Then perhaps…

'Meanwhile Gopi is in town. He always wants me to make pickles for him to take to Dubai. Must get some green mangoes and limes and start getting organised; he's only here for a fortnight.'

Seetha was unpacking the grocery bags and putting the stuff away as Thankam talked.

'This looks like beef!' Seetha exclaimed, picking up the meat; she dropped it quickly when she realised what it was.

Seetha put away the rest of the shopping and started putting lunch on the table. It was lentils-and-prawn curry today and cabbage *thoran*: cabbage shredded, fried, and garnished with fresh coconut, to go with the rice. Thankam was ravenous after the trip into town and ate with relish, finishing off with yoghurt and pickle.

Anil came home again the next week, bringing suitcases to store in his mother's house, when he went to England.

He gave Thankam an unusually effusive hug. 'You look good, what have you been doing to yourself?'

The smell of dried up perspiration on him competed with the tangy smell of aftershave, not altogether unpleasant. She touched his face lightly.

'Oh, this and that.' She shrugged his query off.

'I took a few days off to be here with you and Manju. Heard Gopi is in town too, so I thought I might as well meet him also. In fact I stopped off to see grandmother in Thalassery; slept the night there.'

'How is she?'

'The diabetes is not getting better, but why should it? You should see the way she puts away the local sweets. She brought a plateful of *jilebi* for me, but I noticed she ate most of it.

'I asked her about it and she said something crazy like, "What's the point of living if you can't eat the food in your own house?" And her tea is so sweet; it is like a watery pudding.'

'She also told me it is a pity I'm off so soon,' Anil continued, smiling. 'If only I waited a few months I could get married. Since I can't, she spent an hour advising me how useless a white wife would be.

'She thinks all these white girls are lining up at Heathrow airport to meet guys like me.'

Thankam and Anil laughed heartily at the picture this evoked.

'I tried to tell her I was only twenty-five years old and not considering marriage just now. But it was no use; I had to promise her I would never, ever, bring a *madamma* home.' Anil sounded quite amused.

Anil also looked older – he had got his hair done in an uncompromising crew cut, which took his boyishness away.

'Apart from pampering me, what are your plans for the next week?' Thankam asked.

'I was going to ask you something like that myself. I have a couple of friends to see. Then there is Gopi; perhaps we could go over tomorrow to their place. Then I am all yours, Ammey.

'I was wondering: you mentioned some tenants Vyttilla way were defaulting on the rent; maybe I should talk to them and see whether they will part with the dues.'

Thankam knew Anil had this absolute belief the tenants would quietly hand over the rent when faced with a man; she pretended to believe it too.

'They are small fry actually and their not paying their negligible rent is not making a huge dent in my budget. But, yes, we definitely should go over and see what their problem is.'

'I need a big favour from you, Ammey,' he added. 'I have to pack up my flat for the few months while I am away and I don't want to leave it in a mess. Do you think you could come over to Bangalore for a few days soon to help me?'

'You are only off in January; I'll come when the college closes for Christmas, will that do?

'I'll look forward to that.'

The next morning, Manju came early with her entire family; clearly this was an official family visit.

Gopi couldn't wait to see you,' Manju volunteered. He came bearing gifts: a new mobile phone for Thanakm and an electronic organiser for Anil.

'We are planning to go to Bangalore next week; my mother wants to visit my sister Janaki and spend some time with her. We'll come back after a day or two but I wanted to see you before we went.'

'Is your mother's health better then?

'We are still waiting to find out what is wrong with her. She is going for an endoscopy tomorrow and then we have to wait for the results of tests. She needs a little diversion anyway. Just stays in that house all day and goes nowhere; watches Malayalam serials the whole evening.'

Thankam went in, leaving them talking on the verandah, to make tea and give instructions to Seetha about food. Gopi would probably stay for lunch because he would want to talk to Anil; they were seeing each other after months.

Manju followed her mother inside and the children trailed after her.

'Are you really planning to go to Bangalore with that sick woman?' Thankam asked.

'I'm not planning anything,' Manju answered. 'This is all arranged between mother and son; I am just informed.'

'Aren't the children going to miss school too?'

'Yes, not too many days, because we are coming back in three days. Saraswathi wants to stay in Bangalore, she says. Gopi is a little disappointed; he wants her to stay here with him, but she's decided it is the humid Kochi climate that is making her sick; she'll be fine if she goes to Bangalore. What can he do? She wants him to take her there of course.'

'I'm glad you came by; Anil has been wanting to see you. We were planning to come over, but now that you have come this side, we'll visit when you have finished with all the hospital stuff, tests and things.'

'I might come over before that to have a natter with Anil; Gopiettan has a lot of visiting to do and I often beg off, pleading children's homework or something. I get thoroughly tired of their Dubai talk: exchange rates and the price of Bose speakers and mobile phones; I see he's brought you one, it is the current craze.'

'It's very useful for me, Moley; if the car breaks down on the road, I can call you or someone for help.

'Talking of a car breaking down, did I see the driver, Mani, sitting in the driving seat? I thought you sacked him because he was cheeky. What changed your mind?'

'Yes, sitting in the driving seat is the right phrase for it; I haven't changed my mind and I can't understand how he got to know Gopi was coming. He was at the airport waiting, like family. Gopi asked him along and since then, he's been hanging around like a dirty smell I can't get rid of.

'I feel they have a secret I'm not party to. Gopi was grinning like a Cheshire cat when he saw Mani, and Mani gave me a strange, arrogant look, as though he had put one over me.

'I'm going to get to the bottom of this in the next few days, watch me, Ammey.'

'Take it easy until Gopi is less worried about his mother,' Thankam reminded Manju; she knew how Manju could sail into battle, flags flying, without a thought for the consequences.

Thankam was glad she'd cooked the beef curry the previous day; as Seetha carried the hot food on to the table, the strong smell of asafoetida from the sambar mingled with that of pieces of coconut fried in ghee, the garnish for the beef. In addition Seetha had fried seer fish marinated in chilli, turmeric and salt.

The family waded into the food. Manju didn't really care what meat she ate and both the men liked their beef, though Gopi wouldn't allow Manju to cook it in his own house, because of his mother. However Thankam noticed he did not object to the children eating it. How much hypocrisy we maintain in our life, she thought.

Thankam had the two girls on either side of her, so she could take the bones out of the fish, before they ate it. She helped each of them in turn, pushing the safe flakes of fish towards their rice. In the midst of all this, she remembered Unni; he enjoyed these family feasts so much and would eat without restraint on such days, blaming the quality of the food and the company for his misdeeds.

It is soon after Manju's marriage: the time of duty visits to all members of the extended families of both parents. Manju and Gopi have been to Thalassery to pay homage to Manju's grandparents. On their way back they have bought big bags of mussels and prawns, because they are much cheaper in the north. When they get down from the car, Thankam can detect the stench of well-travelled shellfish.

She takes the parcels into the kitchen and gets the maids working on them, quickly, before they go off. Unni follows her in; he is never quite comfortable with his new, just unwrapped son-in-law; Gopi's uxoriousness galls him.

Today, for instance, Manju is wearing an enormous amount of gold jewellery; apparently both Gopi and

Saraswathi have insisted she is fully decked out for these ceremonial visits. "Like a Christmas tree," Manju says gamely, not wanting to annoy her new family.

Lunch is a solemn affair; Unni is particularly well-behaved. To compensate, he goes for the fried mussels and prawns. His stomach-ache starts at the dining tablet; he strokes his fat tummy furtively with circular movements of his left hand and looks distressed. Finally Thankam whispers to him, 'Go and lie down a bit; I'll bring you a hot water bottle and a pill in a minute.' He disappears, gratefully.

To her guests, Thankam explains, 'The doctor has asked Unni to rest a little every day after lunch; he has got high blood pressure.' As lies go, it is a useful one, because it is reusable, Thankam says to herself. Manju looks up sharply and Thankam winks at her.

A few minutes later Thankam takes the hot water bottle, filled up, and a pill for acidity to Unni. "Have they gone?' he asks hopefully. 'My stomach hurts.'

'You ate too much, what got into you?'

'That Saraswathi and Gopi together will give anyone a stomach ache. In any case, I had to eat a lot; it was delicious. And it is your fault for cooking such tasty food.'

After lunch, Manju went in search of her old music cassettes and soon the house returned to the joyous noises it hadn't heard for a while. Anil started jiving with his nieces, but, after a few minutes, declared his stomach was too full for any activity. The girls kept pirouetting about till they exhausted themselves and came to Thankam's bed, where she was resting, to climb in, either side of her, and fall asleep. Thankam removed Asha's thumb from her mouth when she was fast asleep, but she kept making sucking noises. Her lips stayed slightly parted and Thankam could get the fresh rubber smell of infant mouths. One little hand clung to Thankam's right earlobe. She dozed off, thinking there were few joys on earth to compare with this.

It was late afternoon when Manju came in to say they were leaving.

'I'll see you before I go to Bangalore,' she whispered; she made going to Bangalore sound like a prison sentence.

Anil and Thankam went out to Vyttilla the next day, late in the morning, after Anil had seen his friends in town. The house was an old one, and merely driving over the pockmarked Sahodaran Ayyappan Road made Thankam feel it was a penance for anyone from Vyttilla side to get to work. When they reached their destination, Thankam realised how dilapidated the little house had become. The rent was not much; only six hundred rupees a month, but the tenants paid for the water and the lights and Thankam could see they were living in abject poverty.

'I tried to phone you,' Thankam said to Laila, the housewife, 'but no one picked up the phone.'

'We haven't had a phone in years,' she said, resignedly. 'We didn't pay the bills one time and they cut us off. Good thing in a way, because I was forever having to shout at the children to stop using the phone to call up their school mates.'

Thankam looked around her and knew she was trying to collect blood from stone; having seen how the family lived, the whole enterprise had become quite distasteful to her. The windows and doors had rotted and rainwater had obviously leaked into the veranda during the monsoon, leaving the wall black with damp. There was only one plastic chair on the veranda, so Thankam sat in it while Anil walked around uncomfortably, looking at the alamanda creeper growing on to the roof, big yellow butter-cups in blatant disregard of the misery below it.

An old man, Laila's father, sat in the sun outside, on a rickety chair. He was a bag of skin and bones, wrapped up in a grey lungi and torn white vest, the foot sticking out gnarled and misshapen under the lungi. He wheezed as he spoke. 'Kannan has not been employed recently.' He referred to his son-in-law. 'If he had the money he would have paid you. We were really sorry to hear Unni Sar died;

he was a good man. Many a time, he has waived the rent, saying he knew our problems.' There was a hint there and an entreaty. The man ran out of breath and stopped. He gagged noisily, straining his neck back and Laila brought him a glass of water. He gulped it down greedily and sat there, wheezing steadily.

'I'll send someone to get the roof repaired and get the house painted,' Thankam said as she got up to leave.

'We won't be able to pay anything until Kannettan can get work. House prices are so low around here, all the building works have come to a full stop. He went out today hoping he could get some casual work, digging. He's a trained mason...' Laila swallowed a sob threatening to surface.

Thankam went to her and said, 'Let it be, things will get better. But don't cry.'

As mother and son settled into the car, Anil said, 'That was one fine collection of rent; you offered to do repairs instead.'

Thankam didn't answer.

On the way back Thankam saw Mohan waiting at a bus stop; Anil drew her attention to him.

'Isn't that the bloke who lives in the annexe? Shouldn't we give him a lift? I'm sure he is trying to catch a bus home.'

Anil drew up to him without further comment and asked Mohan to jump in. Thankam wanted to ask him where his car was, but thought better of it. Mohan got in and they drove home in silence.

'Nice looking guy,' Anil said after they dropped him off and walked into the house.

'You should see the sister,' Thankam said. 'I didn't think the brother was handsome, though they look alike. Effeminate, I thought when I first saw him, but something has changed. He is much more self-assured recently, I wonder why.'

As Thankam got ready for bed much later, the conversation resurfaced in her mind. Definitely something different about him now, she mused, or is it me that is seeing him differently?

She read for a while but soon put down the book, as her restless mind would not allow her to make any headway. She tried to think about Unni as she always did, during the final waking moments of her day, but his face kept fading away, not quite coming into focus. Instead the hesitant smile on Mohan's face, his quiet way of regarding her when he spoke and his confident masculine presence earlier in the day kept intruding. As she dropped off she knew there were questions to ask of herself, soon.

7

Mohan went through Thankam's front gate every day to go to work, but she had hardly noticed him before; she did not know what time he left home daily. Recently, however, she seemed to have developed an extra antenna for his comings and goings; she always found herself accidentally at the kitchen window just in time to spot him.

During breakfast, Anil surprised her by asking, 'Have you made a decision about those tenants in Vyttilla? They're never going to be able to pay their rents, you know.' He was heartily mopping up the last of the *pittu* and *kadala* on his steel plate. Thankam was slow to respond, so he went on. 'You have to safeguard your income; otherwise you'll sacrifice your long-term security.' He sounds like my bank manager, she decided.

'I'll survive. Which is more than can be said about that old man and his family in Vyttilla,' Thankam answered the first question. 'They've been our tenants for a long time and we cannot put pressure on them to pay, when quite obviously, they can barely manage to exist. And for what? The house is old and crumbling in places like the grandfather we met. I think we must give them some time, get the repairs done, and then wait to see what happens.'

'I hope you don't have too many tenants like that.' Thankam understood Anil was uneasy about her philanthropy; the new computer generation could be quite cold-blooded and result-orientated, forgetting the human factor. She hoped Anil was not going that way.

'Not really. Most of our premises are commercial properties and I have no hesitation in sending in the bailiffs if they don't pay up. But this family is different.'

After breakfast Thankam and Anil sat on the veranda with their tea still half-finished in their hands.

'I feel there are lots of things I should talk to you about before you go to the UK,' Thankam remarked. 'Your dad used to say he had to listen to about five different elders in his family and village about how he should deport himself there.'

'And did he *deport* himself?'

'I have my doubts; he was always a bit cagey about his UK days. I've heard mention of a Judith, and I'm sure there were some photos too.

'The thing is, when young people go to foreign countries where they have no family or friends to answer to, they behave in strange ways sometimes; they lose their sense of right and wrong. That does worry me.

'It's not about *madammas* and who you marry; it's what is right and fair. I think your ammamma is right in thinking any man would make it hard for himself if he chooses a partner who is from another race and country; there is some wisdom in that. God knows they have enough adjustment to make even when they are from the same race, caste and village like your dad and I.'

'So what are you saying?'

'I wish I was quite sure, but I'll see you again in Bangalore, before you go.'

As they sat talking, Mohan came down his steps in a hurry and walked past with his sister; he called out a "hello" as he disappeared down the walkway to the gate.

In the evening he came by. 'I didn't have time to greet you both properly,' he apologised to Anil. 'Geetha had to get to the bus stop on time. I felt bad later for running away like that.'

'That's all right. You know, I hardly recognised you. You have put on weight - or, maybe it's just that you look fitter. Have you been working out?'

Thankam sat sipping her tea and looking at Mohan, over the rim of her mug, as he spoke to Anil.

'It's yoga, I think,' Mohan sounded certain as he flicked his forelock back in what Thankam now recognised as a mannerism of his. 'Since I started yoga, I find I'm much healthier and happier. I am also more relaxed and have a better perspective on many things.'

That's what it is, Thankam decided. I thought there was a difference, but I couldn't put a name to it. He seems to have more bounce and purpose. Mohan addressed her, 'No more snakes, I hope.'

'We're doing a spring clean of the kitchen, store and garage, Seetha and I, next week. There won't be room anywhere near the house for snakes to hide.'

'Garlic and asafoetida will also do the trick,' Mohan offered. 'They hate the smells of both. If you want the garage cleaned out, I could lend a hand.' She supposed this was in deference to her man-less state.

'It's a lot to ask,' Thankam said, but Mohan insisted. 'It's the least I can do for being able to live in such a nice flat.'

'In that case, you should be doing things for me, not Amma. It's my flat,' Anil broke in, 'and as far as I am concerned you can clean the garage any time you like.'

On Thursday evening, Anil and Thankam drove over to Manju's villa on the waterfront. The water hyacinths had come back in strength into the backwaters with the rains. The tide was going out when Thankam and Anil reached Vaduthala. They stood at the edge of the compound and watched the clusters of hyacinths bobbing along in the slow wash; some of them looked as though they were carefully man-made: circular baskets containing polished green foliage to set out the vivid blue and violet flowers. The mild evening breeze bent the palm fronds lining the shore west to east and set up a soft, soporific murmur.

Fishermen had spread their nets just off the coastline during the previous night and were now collecting the catch near the shore. They waded waist deep in the slush of the backwaters, feet sinking into the mire with each step. Every time they lifted a foot to move forward, they had to pull them out with effort, releasing the vacuum with a plop. They had only short loincloths on them, and their bodies, dark and oily from the waters, looked like small tree stumps with stick legs attached.

The rotten egg smell of marshland was pervasive and Thankam wondered whether the fishermen ever got rid of it entirely from their bodies, even after a bath.

'What's that smell, like a hamburger fart?' Anil asked without ceremony.

'That's the hydrogen sulphide in the marshes, I am told. Horrible, isn't it?'

The paddleboats were near them as the fishermen worked in ones and twos, detaching the nets from the poles they had been tied to, and folding them into the centre. Then they carefully separated the few small fish they had caught, throwing them unerringly into a bucket of water in the boat a few feet away.

Their shanty houses could be seen near by, made of corrugated iron sheets, or thatch. In front of one, an old Chinese net was slung low, this one certainly in use and not for amusing the tourists. The lean-tos doing duty as fishermen's toilets jutted into the water near by.

The catch was insignificant: a few tilapia, small crabs and *pallathi,* scant reward for all the wading in that slush and sewage, but it was near home and they would probably sell their catch straight to the houses lining the water, without going to the market with it.

'This housing estate looks like stately Mysore rather than messy Kochi. In this compound, there are no open drains, no rubbish hillocks, no litter…' Anil remarked as he turned away from the waterside.

These were the tiny pockets of affluence in Kochi. In these housing estates of the non-resident Indians, they maintained a kind of fantasy, like they were some place else. They didn't even live here that often; most of the houses were closed up for three quarters of the year. They came at Christmas and Onam, depending on what religion they belonged to, from Dubai, Switzerland, Germany, UK and US, all the places where Indians went to make money.

A young boy of ten swept past on roller skates, wearing Adidas shorts and baseball cap, back to front; he would be at home in Dallas or Los Angeles. He called out to the girl behind him.

'Race you round the block.'

His accent was a mixture of educated Kerala and Dubai International School.

'What's the bet?' the girl asked, gathering speed as she whizzed past, hair flying. 'Good evening, Auntie,' she called out as she passed Thankam and Anil.

'That's a nice girl, but in the main, they are a lot of spoiled brats: too much money too soon and the guilt of parents who leave them in boarding schools, then compensate with expensive gifts.'

'You don't have to go overseas to spoil your brats; Indians are good at that, even the home-grown kind,' Anil answered easily.

Mosquitoes were beginning to hover and dive and soon drove mother and son inside, but the half-naked bodies of the fishermen could be seen labouring late into dusk.

Gopi was on the veranda engrossed in his laptop and they had clearly disturbed him at an inopportune moment. So Thankam went inside in search of Manju while Anil played with Asha and Latha, who threw themselves at him. Gopi quickly closed his programme down and walked over to Anil.

Manju was in the kitchen preparing *pazhampori*. She sliced each plantain lengthwise into four strips and dipped the strips in the sweetened batter, a mix of white flour and small quantities of gram flour, which would give them their slight yellow colour. She then gently lowered them into the oil already smoking on the cooker and reduced the flame.

'You're doing the busy housewife act with Gopi here, that's good. I haven't seen you making homemade sweets in ages. It looks as though we're just in time for tea.'

Manju didn't turn round or answer, but Thankam thought she heard a slight sniffle, so she moved closer. Manju's eyes were red, and her expression was angry.

'What's the matter now?' Thankam asked. 'Here, go and wash your face while I mind your plantains.' But Manju stood her ground, turning the fritters over as though her life depended on it, so Thankam found a kitchen chair and parked herself on it. A marital squabble, she assumed.

Living with Manju was not an easy business, Thankam knew; sometimes she felt a little sorry for Gopi even as she sympathised with Manju.

'That Mani is still here; I asked Gopiettan to get rid of him, but he says he needs him for the long trip to Bangalore. I told him we could take turns driving, but Gopi *must* pander to Mani. And Mani looks so smug too. Can't he see how I hate that man? I told Gopiettan that I am sacking Mani as soon as he leaves and you know what he said? "Mani and I get on; we understand each other and he doesn't give me any lip."

'What about me, Ammey? Isn't Gopiettan concerned this man treats me like a little girl who doesn't count? I hate him, I hate them both.'

'Shh...,' Thankam cautioned, 'you'll upset the children.' Gopi had followed Thankam into the kitchen and heard only the last part of it, but was wise enough not to ask any questions.

Manju drained the pazhamporis, put them on a plate and carried them out to the veranda. Thankam decided to make some tea to go with it and put the kettle on. While she stood watching the kettle boil, she thought of Manju in her youth, when every day had been a battle with her.

On their way home, Anil appeared pensive.

'Manju and Gopi - do you think they are going through a bad patch?'

'All married people have bad patches. Long ago, we used to run away to our parents' home from our in-laws in the same village. Now, with such small family units, women can't abscond; they have children going to school and so many social obligations.

'I think it's also the long absences of husbands; how can you sustain a close relationship like this? However, don't you think your sister is hard to please anyway?'

'There's that,' he said and both of them laughed, remembering different instances no doubt, of Manju's traumas.

Anil left after the weekend with several instructions to his mother: 'Remember you're coming to Bangalore during the Christmas holidays. And you have to decide what car you want to buy if your back is bothering you. I think a Maruthi Zen, but it sits quite low in the ground. Also, make a decision about those Vyttilla tenants; don't spend too much on repairs on a property which is not giving you an income.'

Thankam agreed to everything because that was the easiest way to keep Anil happy. If she disagreed, he was liable to get out of the car again and give her explanations about all the instructions and this could take forever; she needed to get to the college.

'I plan to see you at the end of December then; that's only a few weeks away,' she assured him. However, she had no intention of extracting rent from her tenants in Vyttilla.

As soon as Anil left, Thankam got the car out and headed for the college. She had taken two days off when Anil had come and she felt she must show her face there every day. Getting to the college from the centre of Kochi, she knew, could take ten minutes to an hour, depending on the traffic. This was not the rainy season, but one of the freak showers of December had swept across Kochi and there weren't too many pedestrians or animals out.

Roadside vendors were just beginning to rearrange their wares on pavements and shop fronts: buckets and plastic *kanna*s in bright rainbow hues and scoops to match.

These were for leaking roofs in the rainy season, and for collecting water when the rains failed and the Kochi water supply went into seasonal hiding. A whole host of mini packets of shampoo and washing powder, Paran's tooth-powder and *bindi*-cards, *pan parag* and Hans tobacco for the chewers, had been dismantled hurriedly from where they were hung on strings under the awnings, when the showers came. These had to be unravelled patiently, like tangled knitting, and hung out again.

Thankam drove slowly, enjoying the rain-washed air around and the petrichor, which usually brought the snakes out. This reminded her of Mohan, but she let it go; she was too relaxed, happy in the sense of here and now, something that had been rare in the last few months.

At the college, as Thankam walked into her office, she noticed the large pile of papers and files waiting for attention. She had a quick look and decided they could wait. She went looking for Jacob and found him at the other end of the building, engaged in serious conversation with Vasanthi.

'Do you share this office with Vasanthi?' Thankam asked pointedly.

'I'll talk to you later - maybe, at the end of the day,' Jacob called out to Vasanthi as she slipped away.

He looked down at the papers on his desk for a long moment.

'Anything special you wanted to discuss?' he asked woodenly, before looking up. His face had set into a stubborn mask.

'Actually, yes. We've had some complaints from parents of our students about various things. I'll need to discuss those with you.'

I'm not going to reform this man if Unni wasn't able to do it in fifteen years, thought Thankam. And if this married young woman is happy to stand around and flirt, it's their funeral.

Jacob looked completely unfazed at Thankam walking in on them. But I'm darned if I am going to pretend I did not notice, Thankam said to herself.

'You've been away; have you been ill?' Jacob asked a moment later, with an effort.

'No, I had Anil for a visit. He's off to the UK soon for his firm,' she added proudly.

Thankam forgot about the plan to clean the kitchen store and the garage until Saturday, when she and Seetha set about the task. When all the things were moved out of the store, Seetha used hot water and Lysol to clean the shelves and the floor beneath. By the time she finished, her hands were white from the chemicals in the Lysol.

'Your hands look as though you have a skin disease,' Thankam pointed out, but Seetha was not concerned. 'It feels a little itchy, but it isn't hurting,' she answered, casually. Must get her a pair of gloves, Thankam thought. She'll probably refuse to wear them, knowing her cussed nature, but I must try. Thankam, meanwhile, started poking among all the things in the room to see if anything could be thrown out; she had reached a point in her life when she was beginning to see she was carrying a lot of unnecessary baggage, her life needed a spring clean. She managed to make a pile of things to throw away, mainly old containers and plastic bags, but as she did this, Seetha delved among them and pulled out things she wanted to take home. After that, they dusted and rearranged everything they had moved out on the shelves.

The two women then came out to the garage and started moving piles of old newspapers and magazines about. Unni never threw a single copy of the *Week* magazine out, Thankam remembered, looking at the chaos.

'Achan wanted to keep all this to take to the college for the students,' Thankam explained to Seetha. 'But he never got round to it.'

Seetha turned over a big unsteady pyramid of ceramic tiles; it collapsed and a few fell down and broke into pieces with a resounding clatter.

'That's it, Seetha. If we break them, then we have a good reason to throw them out.'

Seetha was not contrite. 'We can't clean this place unless we clear out all this rubbish; looks like some of it has been here since the house was built.'

Thankam knew Seetha was right; the tiles were from that time. Both women regarded the clutter in front of them and quickly closed the door on it. They smiled to each other, in full agreement that this was not a task to be undertaken lightly.

Neither Moli, the outside maid nor Seetha came to work on Sundays and this was only one of the reasons Thankam hated Sundays. She usually got up late, had no breakfast, wandered around the house and read the papers. When she finished the interesting articles, she read all that was left; sometimes, in her desperation, she read the advertisements as well. She was doggedly looking at a huge centre spread in the *Hindu* on the *Dream House Builders*, when she heard the first strains of singing upstairs. The female voice started humming and slipped into the song. *'Ayiram pathasarangal kilungi, aluvapuzha pinnayumozhugi'* (A thousand anklets chimed as *Aluva* river flowed on), one of Thankam's all-time favourites, for its melody as well as the priceless lyric. She lowered the paper to her lap and held her breath. Then a male tenor joined while the female singer blended with his voice. Thankam had not heard anything so painfully lovely for a long time. All the sadness and longing of a woman alone welled up in her as she listened, until the short song died away, leaving her with a sense of undefined want.

This is the trouble with music, she thought; it catches you unawares, without even trying. She remembered how much a part of her life Unni's song bursts had been, occupying the house like a pleasant background theme, which she didn't notice most of the time.

Thankam summoned up a sudden flash of determination and decided today would be a good day to attack the garage. She walked over and swung the doors apart; they were rusting at the hinges and dragged on the cement floor making grinding, teeth-clenching noises, which put her on edge, but she moved the car out and waded grimly into the debris of many years. As she crooked a finger gingerly around the handle of a tin of ancient engine oil, which had practically glued itself to the floor, a big bandicoot rat scuttled past her, from behind a pile of magazines. Startled, she dropped the tin; the top opened and oil spread slowly on the floor in a glutinous mess, the kind that would take forever to clean. She hitched up her sari into her waistband and started putting old newspaper on the oil to catch it. Soon, however, it started seeping out from under the paper. She cursed and turned around as she heard footsteps from the side of the house.

'It's only me,' said Mohan. 'I heard the sounds in the garage and remembered I'd offered to help.' He looked at the mess. 'Geetha has just gone off to one of her friends for a sleepover; she gets bored with just me for company.

'Here, let me do that,' he said, seeing the oil and the frustration on Thankam's face.

He fetched some mud from the garden and dumped it on the oil; then he took a small spade and took most of the oil and mud out, and now the mess no longer looked forbidding. He soon had it under control.

'Let it dry now and we can wash it down later.'

Mohan surveyed the task. 'If you tell me what you are sure you want to throw away, we can get a start here.'

'This is dusty work; I hope you know that, the kind that makes you sneeze and cough and take to your heels.'

'I'll take a chance on that,' he answered, looking up at her and smiling as he started arranging a heap of tiles to carry away.

'What shall I do to help?' Thankam asked.

'Show me where to throw all this stuff and make payment in cups of tea when my throat clogs up with dust.'

He prodded a bag of cement with his foot; it appeared frozen solid but threw up a puff of grey dust when he tried to move it.

Thankam sat on the steps enjoying the languorous sunday morning, watching Mohan make short shrift of the debris in her garage.

He was wearing an old T-shirt and a lungi, his Sunday attire. He hadn't shaved because she could see his morning stubble clearly as he walked up to her. He smelt of just-drunk tea. She couldn't see an ounce of spare flesh on him, but what he always had, seemed to have been redistributed, making him seem more solid and sure now, whereas he had looked weedy and insubstantial in the beginning. She realised she had been staring at him and averted her gaze.

'There is nowhere in this house for builder's rubble; what we used to do when Unni was around was pack them in empty gunny bags and pile them into the boot of the car; there is a big land-fill site at the end of town where we can dump it, but it's a long way to go and a lot of work.'

'In that case, let's get the bags filled.' He seemed eager to get on with it; so Thankam found him a bundle of empty cement bags from the garden shed.

She hovered ineffectually, putting bundles of newspaper together, trying to make stacks of the *Week* magazines, but stopping so often to read some old article, she did not make much headway. He laughed at her efforts and teased her, making her feel young and joyous. It was an intoxication long forgotten. After a while she went inside and made two outsized mugs of tea and brought them out.

'That's *some* mug,' he said, laughing, 'more like a flower vase. This will set me up for three or four days!' It seemed anything could make him laugh today; seeing this Thankam realised he was as excited as she was and she was happy too.

'Unni brought a set when he went to England just before we got married; these two are all there is left of it; I don't find any this size around here.'

The tea was sweet and hot and he balanced it on the veranda ledge while he rested for a moment. He gazed around at the garden. The cannas, in reds, yellows and pinks were in bloom as well as the ixoras. 'Whenever I pass this way I look at your garden; it is quite beautiful, though it is not very big.'

'My garden gives me pleasure through the seasons - which is more than you can say of people.'

'Oh, come on –' He laughed.

Thankam felt at ease in his company; she found some of her reserve had melted.

Mohan talked about his work as he bundled the old papers. She remembered the last occasion when she had asked him about his business in Kottayam.

'Going to check on the music shop, are you?' she had asked, meeting him on his way out.

'Something like that,' he had said and made a quick exit. After that she never asked him about his affairs.

She realised it was a great act of trust on his part to talk about his business.

'That music shop,' he began. 'It is going nowhere. My cousins who manage it never actually give me any of the takings – it is always spent on new stock, repairs, whatever. At least that is what they say. I am spending more time with the estate agents these days. Must concentrate on that and make it work.'

While he talked he gathered the empty tins and cans and stuffed them into sacks; soon he had nine bags lined up at the back of the garage.

'The question is: how long are these bags going to languish here?' Mohan was teasing her and Thankam was reminded how pleasant he looked when he was not tensed up and wary. He could always make her laugh; perhaps she was more ready to laugh.

'Just you wait. They'll be out within two days,' she answered jauntily.

Mohan worked until past mid day and then decided to take a break. 'Want to come upstairs for yesterday's moong and *pittu* with me?' he ventured.

'We can do better than that. I've got fish curry in the freezer and Seetha left string hoppers for me. Why don't we warm them up and eat down here?'

Mohan collapsed on the verandah ledge while Thankam busied herself getting lunch for both of them. They sat outside and ate companionably.

I could get used to this, thought Thankam. I never realised how friendly he can be; he has always been so formal with me, perhaps it is my own fault, keeping a distance initially. She wanted the day to go on forever.

Mohan continued clearing up for another two hours after lunch and then disappeared. 'I'll come back and finish the work another day; there is quite a bit more to do and I'm beginning to flag.

'What are you doing with the rest of Sunday?' he probed, an unashamedly naughty look on his face.

'Pottering around, this and that,' she answered, suddenly shy. As if she knew what she meant to do with a dreary Sunday!

'Feel like a film? There is a good one showing. I hear Mohanlal has surpassed himself in the role of an eighteenth century chieftain in Wynad, who took the British on by refusing to pay taxes...' But they both knew that going together without a chaperone was out of the question. Thankam had not been to the theatre for nearly a year and she would have loved getting out on a sunday.

'Another day, perhaps, if you can persuade Geetha to go with us,' she suggested. If she were with them, there would be no questions asked.

'I'll have to bribe her,' he answered, laughing indulgently. 'Cheeky girl!'

Thankam was glad he had mentioned coming back - and the film. It was as if a stray shaft of sunlight had found its way into a gloomy room.

She closed and locked the garage happily and went inside for a bath. He has not just moved in upstairs, she told herself bluntly, he has moved into your heart as well.

8

From the upstairs balcony where she was having her second coffee of the day, Thankam watched Mohan go to her gate, open it and step out. Then, it seemed, he thought of something, turned and walked towards his apartment. She observed him walk back and forth, a picture of easy grace, which made her breath catch for a moment.

He was wearing his office clothes: charcoal grey trousers and a white linen shirt. A mobile phone was wedged into his hip pocket and he carried a small briefcase. Looks like a model, she said to herself.

She shook her head then as though chastising herself, but her body appeared to have a will of its own and waited for him to come out.

She tried to concentrate without much success on the bulbuls and mynahs congregating on her balcony at the birdbath; she had just finished her morning ritual of scattering birdseed for them. They attacked the food raucously, informing the whole neighbourhood of birds about the feast. Then they drank out of the bath and sat preening themselves on the jasmine bushes on the balcony.

Mohan went up to his apartment and returned with what looked like a rolled-up newspaper, but instead of going out, he walked up to her veranda and left it there. She was dying to know what was inside, but allowed a few minutes to pass before she finished her coffee and went down to see. As she reached the bottom of the steps, Seetha had the paper in her hand.

'From where did this paper come?' she asked innocently. 'Surely I brought your paper up to you with the coffee.' Seetha was ready to defend herself if anyone claimed she had forgotten her morning chore of delivering paper and coffee.

'Yes, you did,' Thankam said seizing the paper from her hurriedly. 'It looks like someone has left it for us.'

'Mohan Sar or Geetha, who else could it be? Must tell them we have our own paper.' This must have been a big conundrum for Seetha's uncomplicated mind; why would Mohan Sar give them another copy of the same paper?

Thankam noticed a small section was circled in black marker on the entertainments page. She sat down in the verandah chair and had a good look. The circled portion showed that the Malayalam picture *Smaranagal* was showing at the *Sagarika* theatre for a week.

Inside the circled bit he had written: 'Next Sunday? Geetha will come with us.' Mohan's presence in her life was enriching it like the soft breeze of *shishiram* on a parched landscape. How could she deny it? She sat in the chair and thought about it. It felt good, a little heady and challenging perhaps, overturning many of her long-held beliefs about herself, but invigorating. She decided she would go to the film on Sunday, if Geetha came.

On Saturday, Mohan came early. 'I hope you are coming. Great music, I'm told and not a bad film altogether. Geetha is home this Sunday and I've made her promise to go with us.' The new familiarity in his tone did not surprise Thankam; she was happy to let things happen, without probing anything too carefully.

Mohan was wearing rust coloured Bermuda shorts with sunflowers at the edges; who else could carry off something like that?

'Very original, those shorts,' she teased but he grinned, sure of himself. And when he stopped and turned those quiet brown eyes on her, she could not think of anything to say; she was like a rabbit transfixed in the headlights of an oncoming car.

Thankam knew she was acting like an adolescent whose heart did a sudden somersault at the sight of a lover; she did not even try to tear her eyes away from him.

Did he know what he was doing? she wondered. Does his heart pound when he sees me the way mine does when I see him? Or is he just being kind? Passing time? She was at the top of a roller-coaster ride from which she might not be able to jump off; was *he* totally in control?

Thankam composed herself and answered carefully.

'It's kind of you and Geetha to consider taking me; I'd love to come. Which show were you planning to go for?' She stressed the 'Geetha' because it somehow lent legitimacy in her mind to the enterprise. But Thankam did not have the skill of deceiving herself, so in a tiny corner of her mind, a little voice said, "You know what this is about, don't you?"

'The eight-thirty is good. Then, when the film is over we can go to the roadside teashop and eat dosha, if you are game. There's one near the theatre, which Geetha and I often go to; it claims it does over a hundred dosha fillings. Our version of Pizza Express, I think.' He appeared to have had it all planned, so Thankam agreed to go along with his plans.

'We'll take my car,' she volunteered. 'I don't usually drive in the night, but if the two of you are with me, I won't feel uneasy.' Thankam made it sound like a family event.

As he went, he looked really pleased with himself and jaunty as though a special wish had been granted. Running up the stairs to his flat, taking two steps at a time, he whistled happily.

She chose her clothes carefully for the Sunday, searching for a sari that would flatter her slim figure and dark complexion without appearing as though she was making a big effort. She decided on first one and then another, and discarded each in turn. Finally she settled on a light green *pallavi*, with a blue, flocked print; the material would drape beautifully however she wore it. The border was a pencil-thin paisley design. In her shelves she hunted down the matching blouse in green and blue and tried it on; it was a little loose on her, but she had no time to alter it. It was months since she had taken such care over her appearance.

The week went by slowly and Thankam went to the college every day and sat down with Jacob many times to plan the next year's budget. She found herself dressing carefully, even to go to work. Before she went to bed each night she would choose her clothes for the next day and put them out so that she was never hurried. She saw Mohan sometimes as he went out to work, accompanied by Geetha; he would call out a greeting to her and she would call back. She was pleased they were comfortable with her, but occasionally she wondered whether she was imagining rainbows in the horizon where none existed.

Thankam treated herself to an elaborate oil bath on Saturday, something she hadn't done for ages. She was reminded of her mother's attempts to make her beautiful in all of three months between her engagement and her marriage, oil baths had been an important part of that strategy. In her heart she had to admit that her interest in her appearance had suddenly peaked. Seetha took in all the pampering Thankam was giving her body and looked at her speculatively.

Mohan and Geetha rang the bell at eight in the evening on Sunday. Thankam opened the door on two young people ready for an evening out. For an instant she had a sobering thought: what was she doing with these two children? Mohan looked like a teenager in his *kurtha* and Geetha was in jeans and tight-fitting green, embroidered top with sequins at the neckline. Thankam shook her uncertainty off and stepped out. Mohan and Geetha gazed at her and at each other, their surprised admiration apparent in their eyes.

'You look stunning,' Mohan exclaimed, involuntarily. This time it was *he* who could not stop looking. Thankam smiled her thanks knowing her efforts had been worthwhile.

At the *Sagarika*, the curtains were just rising when they took their seats. Thankam's seat kept springing back on her when she tried to sit on it and Geetha had to hold it down; Thankam was quite inexperienced in all this. The crowd was not big for a Sunday and the noise level from the screen was too high for comfort. Thankam told herself to stop nitpicking and enjoy the event.

She settled back into her seat and followed the plot. It was the story of a successful businessman who abandons his world at the peak of his success and returns to his village, tempted by the memories of the life he had lived there long ago and the girl he had loved and deserted. The film was something of a disappointment, but Thankam was content to listen to the dialogue now and then and let her mind wander, finding nothing to hold her attention in it. The mosquitoes searched for the exposed parts of her body: toes, neck, arms and back and had a feast.

'Not as good as I expected,' Mohan leaned across his sister to remark to Thankam during intermission. Geetha excused herself and went out and Mohan moved across, ostensibly to talk about the film.

'Never mind,' Thankam answered. 'It is nice for me to get out like this once in a while.'

'This floor is not too clean either,' Mohan said, picking up the end of her pallav, which fell on the floor. He draped it carefully round her shoulders. His fingers touched her ear lobes lightly as he did so – or did she imagine that - and for a brief moment, his arms rested on her .She hugged herself, feeling cherished. He turned to her and smiled then.

'Must do this more often,' he suggested. The caress or the film, she asked herself.

When Geetha returned and the lights dimmed, he continued to sit where he was; gradually covering her hands resting on the broad armrest with his, and his fingers caressing hers. Oh, my God, thought Thankam, what is happening to me? The rest of the film was a blur in

Thankam's mind and when the lights came on again at the end, she got up clumsily to meet that sudden stark intrusion of crowd and noise like a sleepwalker in a corridor full of impediments. Mohan had to hold her while she steadied herself.

After the film, Mohan led the way to a small wayside restaurant, which specialised in doshas. A crowd from the theatre had gathered there quickly and the man at the steel-top counter turned them out with practised speed. They ordered potato and egg fillings with hot coffee. All this was new to Thankam who had never gone to a teashop like this before; Unni had stuck to regular restaurants and didn't think the little outlets were clean; Thankam could see why. The road immediately in front was quite dirty with the debris of the city: pieces of paper, banana peels and food wrapping. The recent rains had soaked into some of this and the customers were treading on this muck to reach the outlet. Some of it entered the shop floor and Thankam had to lift up her sari hem to keep it clean. The tables were primitive: a formica top with four shaky legs for support.

The doshas, however, were delicious: thin as onionskin and crisp. The potato mixture in the dosha melted in the mouth and the eggs were coddled with milk, garlic, coriander leaves and fresh black pepper. As she ate, Thankam read the certificates pasted on the wall; many tourists, probably back-packers, had written glowingly about the food.

It was past twelve when they walked back to the Maruthi. Thankam drove slowly as she had never before taken the car out in the night, but the presence of her friends made her feel secure. The crowds coming out of the theatres and restaurants were relaxed and happy, thronging the roads and ignoring all traffic rules in their eagerness to get the most out of the entertainment scene. Thankam had not been out at this time since her children were toddlers; Unni had liked to spend their evenings at home, rather than go out again after he got in from work.

Thattu kadas had sprung up on the roadside in every corner serving every conceivable local delicacy: *vadas* and *bondas*, *doshas*, *iddlis* and *pittus*... Through the glass windows of the major restaurants you could see families and couples having a meal out, but the teenagers merely congregated near the park or in front of music shops, talking loudly, determined to have a good time even if it killed them. This was Kochi after the buses had gone to sleep and Thankam was delighted to be part of the scene.

As she got out of the car in front of the house, she turned to thank Mohan and Geetha.

'We'll see you to the door, better open up while we are around,' he said firmly. He took the house keys from her while Geetha ran up the stairs to their apartment. Mohan opened the door and said, 'All right?' Then he hesitated for a moment and looked at her; something in her eyes must have encouraged him, because he leaned across and touched her face lightly, before he turned and left.

The next morning Mohan made it a point to come by, before he went to work; Thankam smiled at him, not saying much, considering how their relationship had shifted and formed overnight and how it would go from there. He did not seem any more certain than she; so he made idle chat, telling her about his workplace and his schedule for the day. Thankam was aware he had come down early to spend a few minutes with her; for the first time in months her heart sang.

'Since Christmas is nearly here, all our clients, particularly the Christian ones, are here from the Middle East and I have to dance attendance: open up their half-finished flats and villas for them to see, discuss finishing touches with them, try to get some money out of them to bolster our liquidity and – get a good Christmas bonus and commission. What are you planning to do for Christmas and New Year?'

'I don't do anything now the children have left the nest, apart from hanging up a big lighted star on the front porch. I haven't even done that this year.'

'Oh, we must do that,' he said. 'I'm not going anywhere and it will cheer me up.'

'In that case-'

'It would make me even happier if you came with me for a drive this evening.' He looked straight at her and held her gaze. What can I deny you when you look at me like that? Thankam thought.

'In the Maruthi?'

'No, this is much more fun. We'll take my Suzuki and go for a jaunt; it always makes me feel young and carefree. But you should wear a helmet; it's not safe without, though most people, especially women, don't wear them. They like to keep their hairdos intact.'

'I'll think about it,' she said, laughing. And what will Graciamma say, she wondered. And will I feel young and carefree too?

In the evening Mohan turned up with a huge magenta star for her. He fiddled about with wires and switches and put it up on her front porch in a few minutes. 'I've earned a cup of tea, I think,' he said cheekily. So Thankam asked Seetha to produce tea. They sat companionably, sipping their tea. This bit is uncomplicated, she conceded; I wish this could be enough for both of us, but in her heart she knew she wanted more

'I've got the Suzuki filled up and I've got a spare helmet for you. How about that jaunt?'

When Thankam hesitated, he pleaded. 'With the helmet no one is going to recognise you in the dark. I promise you, you'll really enjoy it. And I will behave myself: no speeding, singing songs…'

'Oh, I don't think you should behave yourself,' Thankam answered, laughing.' You're much more fun when you're not behaving. And, what is Geetha going to say?'

'She's not around - again. That girl! Never mind, I'll tell you that story some other time.'

'Okay, but I hope you realise I've never been on a motorbike ever. What if I fall off?'

'You won't fall off and it is high time you experienced a ride, anyway,' he said dismissively. 'One of the luxuries of this life. You can hold me tight if you are scared,' he added, enjoying himself already.

As soon as Seetha had gone for the day, Thankam changed into a nylon sari that wouldn't crush and dug out her one pair of strap-up sandals. The hair was a nuisance: too much and too thick, so she pulled it back from her face and plaited it tight; it came down six inches below her waist.

'Look at that hair,' Mohan exclaimed when he saw the length of the plait. 'Is it real?' Thankam merely smiled; she was used to this kind of comment about her hair.

She had a moment's apprehension as Mohan started the engine and she climbed on the pillion, but she ignored her saner self, which was asking her what she was getting into.

'Hold on tight,' Mohan said, 'and don't sway to correct the tilt of the bike when I go round corners. And tuck your sari pallav into your waist so it does not fly around. Just relax and enjoy the scenery.'

He moved off slowly, through MG Road, into Sahodaran Ayyapan Road, leading to the Vyttila junction and the national highway, number forty-seven. Thankam rode sidesaddle and watched the road, while hanging on tight to the handle in front. Other motorcycles came close sometimes; one man on a Hero Honda had all his family wedged on the bike. His daughter, about four years old from the look of her, sat in front of him and smiled at Thankam as they rode in tandem for a few minutes. His wife behind had a small bundle in her left hand while she clutched the handle with the right. The bundle, when it got close, turned out to be an infant, wrapped in a blue blanket.

After a few minutes Thankam relaxed, as Mohan drove expertly past the crowds at the junction and got on to National Highway. Once on the three-lane highway, he accelerated past the lorries and cars and started enjoying himself. Thankam moved her hand to his waist and hooked her fingers round his belt. The inside of the leather felt coarse on her fingers and the smell of sandalwood shampoo came with the wind that blew past him. Conversation was not possible because of the noise, but Thankam felt exhilarated, as though anything was possible in this world; she wanted this ride to go on forever. After a while Mohan picked up her hand from his belt, placed it around his waist and gave it an affectionate little pat.

They came home late at night and Thankam got a snack from leftovers for both of them, which they ate from trays in the living room: chappathi and mutton curry from the previous day. When the meal had been cleared away, she sat down to chat with him; she didn't want this day to end.

'Were you scared?' he asked, presently.

'Only when I got on. I loved it after that; I wanted the ride to go on forever. Thank you for taking me.'

Her scalp was pinching because of the tight plait, so as she talked, she unwound it and let her hair down; it seemed the most natural thing in the world to do this in front of Mohan. She passed her fingers through her hair, trying to massage her scalp. Mohan came over and sat next to her. 'Let me,' he said. He put the fingers of both his hands through her hair and slowly worked them down, stroking the scalp and the temples when he started at the top each time. She kept absolutely still, afraid the dream would vanish if she moved.

Mohan did this for a long time. Then he turned her face towards him and looked at her; in his eyes a statement rather than a question this time. She lifted her left hand and held his hand to her face. He touched her cheeks and lips lightly, lingeringly, with his fingers till every nerve in her body strained towards him. He kissed her then and embraced her. Then he got up from the chair, pulling her up with him, and holding her hands, led upstairs to the bedroom.

Mohan was gone long before dawn. When Thankam woke up early the next morning all that was left of him was the lingering smell of his after shave on her pillow and the memory of his tenderness.

She knew her self-perception had changed forever. By committing that one act of self-indulgence last night, she had jeopardised her reputation as a widow beyond reproach. If her friends and family came to know about her relationship with Mohan, they would turn their backs on her. She had also betrayed the memory of a loving husband.

Thankam did what she always did when she was troubled – walk out into the garden. However, she felt light-headed, once removed from the things around her. Guilt washed over her in waves, followed by the memories of Mohan's body wrapped round her.

How would her children react if they heard about her liaison with a tenant? Would they despise her? The more Thankam thought about it, the more confused she became; she who had led a transparent life this far had a secret to hide now. She could not find any answers to her predicament within herself, so she abandoned remorse and started making plans to get out of Kochi for a few days.

Thankam remembered her long-ago promise to Anil and decided Bangalore would be a good place to go right then. In spite of the feelings of guilt, the memory of Mohan's lovemaking stayed with her, like a benediction, which she carried with her every moment of the day. Sometimes she was surprised at the incredible risks she was prepared to take to be with him. Where did she get the courage to go into Kochi with him on the back of a motorbike? What if someone had seen her? She had always thought of herself as a cautious person, but she knew something stronger than her thinking self was in command right now, and discretion was the first casualty

'I've got to go to Bangalore next Sunday,' she said, when she saw Mohan on Wednesday. He had taken to dropping by late in the evening when they both knew it was unlikely a chance visitor might turn up. 'Anil is off to the UK in two weeks and I promised to go over before the New Year; so I'll probably be there at Christmas.'

'Everybody is abandoning me,' he tried to sound pathetic and did not succeed. 'Geetha is never here and though it is convenient right now for us, I am concerned she'll never complete that degree, if she goes on like this.

'Problem with her is, she's far too good looking and knows it.'

'I know one or two others like that,' Thankam said, laughing.

'I hear rumours that she has a boyfriend in Kottayam and that is why she keeps running away there.' As he talked Mohan leaned across, and with his finger, traced the outline of Thankam's lips. For a moment the rest of Thankam's world went out of focus as all her nerve-ends strained to his touch.

'One Dr Nambiar has sent a broker round asking for her hand in marriage,' he continued. 'This man has a clinic next to our house and I am suspicious as to whether they already have an understanding.

'On the other hand,' he continued, 'if she is not interested in her studies why is she wasting time and my hard-earned money going to college in expensive Kochi?'

'Nambiar? Sounds like one from my part of the world.'

'Yes, and he doesn't want a dowry. That would be a great burden off my shoulders.'

'A Nambiar from our side would not ask for a dowry,' Thankam said firmly. 'The dowry thing is not prevalent among them.'

'I've told my senior uncle so that he can consult with the other uncles and come to a decision.'

'What does Geetha say?'

'She blushed when I asked her and didn't deny she knew him.

'After making me rent this annexe for her, she's always away in Kottayam. I can see why now.'

He moved closer and started kissing her neck, in between times trying to tuck stray hairs behind her ears. It seemed he could not have enough of the feel of her and

Thankam wallowed in all the attention, feeling like a bride on honeymoon.

That evening, when they were lying in bed, after making love, Thankam said to him, 'I've opened the connecting door to your flat from my house. So you can come and go that way. I don't want Manju to walk in on us. Recently she has taken on a job at the British Council here and doesn't come on weekdays, but that might change.'

'What about that fat old woman next door who is always asking questions about everyone?' Mohan asked, teasing. 'Aren't you afraid of her?'

'That one is dangerous, believe me,' Thankam answered. 'Don't take her too lightly. There are years of venom getting thick in her veins. But the person who'll really figure this out soon is Seetha. That's a hurdle I will have to cross some time.'

'What? That daft maid of yours? Rubbish!' Mohan said dismissively.

'That daft maid is like an Alsatian dog: one master only. Where I am concerned she has a special antenna, she always knows the state of my well-being.'

Thankam felt a new sense of vulnerability she had not had in years, not even when she was young and just married to Unni. She had been confident then, in her youth and in her role in his life. She had been particularly sure because she knew he loved her without reservation.

Mohan, on the other hand, was an unknown quantity. Some days, as when he took her to the cinema, he looked not much older than Anil. Other days, she had felt him to be in command, old and wise; he seemed to have a perfect timing for all things to do with their relationship. He led and she followed. But she was conscious of the ravages of age on her face and body. She recognised the signs: the dark shadows that had appeared under her eyes in the aftermath of Unni's death had never really gone away, and when she smiled, she could see the laughter lines etching into wrinkles slowly but surely.

There were huge portions of Mohan's life she knew nothing about. Surely he was well past the age when men in Kerala considered marriage, but he was still single; what made him stay that way? He was never too keen to talk about himself, a shutter quickly descending if she asked too many questions.

It had been an idle query from her that precipitated their first quarrel.

'What did you do before you came to Kochi?' she asked.

'Oh, this and that,' he replied.

Thankam had persisted. 'Which this and what that?'

'Nothing to talk about really.'

'You can be very dismissive of me sometimes. What are you so uptight about?'

'I hate all this prying.'

'Is that what I am doing? Well, you'll be free of my prying, as you call it, because I'm going away for a few days.'

Mohan got up and walked away.

Thankam decided to make that trip to Thalassery the next week, get as far away from here as she could, may be get her relationship with Mohan into perspective.

She could see he was always keen to be with her at the moment, but would that last? Would she become the needy one, long past the time when his enthusiasm flagged?

9

If she went to Bangalore by way of Thalassery Thankam could see her mother, at the same time avoid having to stay longer than she intended; Madhavi would not put pressure on her to hang around if she knew she was on her way to Anil. It was possible that Appu, her beloved brother, would be there on leave from Dubai; she had not seen him since he came down for Unni's funeral. Thinking of him made her eager to go; he had been a strong shoulder to lean on when Unni died. As always, she thought. When had he ever let her down? Appu came the day he heard of the tragedy and stayed till he felt his sister was out of the dark depths.

She thought of the time of Unni's death; the children as devastated as she was, all of them unable to help each other. She knew that she would remember that hopeless day as long as she lived

Thankam sits inert, a heavy sagging heap in the corner of the day bed in the dining room, listening to the murmur of her family around her. A family in mourning, talking in whispers, showing due respect for Unni, her husband, her love, her safe place, who has died - is it two days or three now? She tries to anchor the idea of time somewhere where she can keep in touch with it, but it drifts away on the wings of incense burning in the room and flutters in the flames of the ceremonial lamps. She wishes the children would shout and scream as usual and in some way restore her life to the ordinariness of last week, but the parents shush them and shoo them out. It appears that death, for the moment, reigns, reducing this home of hers to a wasteland.

Many have gathered there in this house at the moment: Children and grand children, brother and mother, nephews and cousins. A few have gone away the previous night, after the cremation and early this morning, on the Kanyakumari Express *to Bangalore and on the* Malabar Express *to Kozhikode and Thalassery. When she hears them mention her home town she has a sudden longing to go back, if only briefly, and remember that other person who had travelled such a long way and arrived here, at this time, and in this urban place called Kochi. She does not care whether the mourners stay or go; it appears it is not her responsibility for once to look after the visitors to her home.*

Sometimes a word drifts to her, clear and sharp through the surrounding miasma of incomprehension that lives in her head right now. Mostly the words are about mother or father. At least that is what her ragged mind chooses to focus on. She ignores it, but she has a nagging sense of déjà vu from long ago, when her people, family like this, in another time and place, had sat around her much younger self and discussed her life. She had not been part of it then when they were planning her marriage, and she is not part of it now. Unni's death appears to have reduced her to a functionless object, something for which a comfortable place has to be found.

Appu finds her there, bewildered, and he picks up her hand, as he lowers his bulk on to the bed, to sit beside her.

He's put on too much weight since going to Dubai, she thinks; she holds on to his comfortable bulk. 'Appuetta -' she says.

'I'm here.'

'How long can you stay?' She knows she is pleading.

'As long as you need me; I'm not going anywhere.'

He stays the month, making sure she is not alone in that dark tunnel, holding her hand, guiding her to the glimmer at the end. As long as he is here she is not totally lost.

When he leaves, he says, 'You've had such a lovely marriage; it is going to be with you forever. Things like that don't die.' He has stayed with her till she is able to walk on.

When Thankam's mother, Madhavi, phoned to say Appu was arriving on Friday of that week, she couldn't wait to go to Thalassery; she booked her tickets immediately.

'Seetha, I'm planning to go to Bangalore to stay with Anil Mone for a week; I'll stop off at Thalassery for two days on the way. We can close up the house for a week. Mohan will be around, so we don't have to worry about security.'

'Won't they go anywhere for the holidays? Surely Geetha must have days off from the college.'

'Probably, but Mohan works at an estate agent's and he can't go anywhere.'

'A week off is useful, Ammey. There is a proposal for Preethi and I have to make some preparations; someone from the boy's house is coming to see her next week; I must get some sweets and stuff for them. Otherwise they'll go away thinking we're beneath them. Also, I must make some discreet enquiries about him and his family; these marriage brokers are such liars. He is supposed to be a house painter; apparently makes a good living in season. They own the house they live in, so she won't want for a roof. She's so young and cries when you mention marriage; she wants to study. But all my brothers are insisting she should marry before she is seventeen; they think girls get a bad name in the community if they marry late.'

Thankam knew that this subject of Preethi's marriage was a knotty one. Seetha's husband didn't have money to feed his family, leave alone pay for a wedding, and this proposal may come to nothing, like so many others. If he couldn't stay sober for the day the bridegroom's family visited they'd take one look at him and disappear. Time enough to think about weddings if the engagement went ahead.

Thankam sat in the train and day dreamed. In the second-class, air-conditioned compartment were seven others, all travelling to various parts of the north of Kerala. A young parachutist from the Kashmir border was coming home on leave with his wife and son, so that he could leave her behind at home; he did not manage to get home to his base in Kashmir very often and he would feel happier if she was safe. He had stopped off at Kochi to see his parents before travelling on to his wife's home in Badagara. Three men from Kannoor who were working in Kochi were returning home for Christmas after a year; they had spent the time setting up an outlet for a small spinning and weaving factory they jointly owned in Kannoor. A young Muslim couple were going to Mahe from Kochi; he sold dry goods in Kochi and this was her first visit to her home after marriage. She was noticeably pregnant and kept her head covered right through the journey.

The three men from Kannoor bought food from every vendor they could find on the way and insisted on sharing it with all the others; Thankam had forgotten how friendly people were from the Malabar end of Kerala. And how nosey.

'Where are you going to, *Chechi*?' one of them asked. She was everybody's big sister today, being the oldest in the compartment.

'Up to Thalassery.'

'Who is there for you in Thalassery?'

'It's my hometown; I'm going to visit my family; they live in the Thiruvangad area.'

Thankam tried to read a book; she had brought Bill Bryson's *A Walk in the Woods* with her, but gave up after a while: the conversation in the compartment was much more interesting than Bryson's account of his adventures on the Appalachian trail. All the men in the compartment knew every gory detail about the murder, some months ago, of the schoolteacher, Jayakrishnan, in Mokeri.

'Wait and see, there will be more killings soon to avenge his death,' one of them warned.

'So long as they don't start leaving bombs here and there as they did some time ago. A young girl lost both her limbs in a blast and she was not old enough to write CPM (*Communist Party, Marxist*) or BJP (*Bharathiya Janatha Party*) yet.'

'Our towns are always more violent than the South, we have to admit that. Long ago, it used to be Hindu-Muslim quarrels,' a third man reminded them. Then he realised a Muslim was in the compartment and smiled shamefacedly.

One of them had heard the police were not showing too much initiative in finding Jayakrishnan's killers.

'The police may have been suborned by the Communist Government in power in Thiruvananthapuram,' he surmised.

Another tried to coax Thankam into the conversation. 'What do you think, Chechi?'

'I was horrified to hear about the murder of the teacher, but what do I know about North Malabar politics? I have lived in Kochi for so many years; I know only what I read in the papers.'

After a few hours of sitting around together some of the men wandered off in search of the berths they had booked for sleeping, in various compartments. Thankam spread out her handloom sheet on the seat and put a pillow under her head, but she slept fitfully. The train swayed as it gathered speed and bumped clackety-clack over the bridges and culverts; Thankam thought of Mohan and her crippling need for him. She dreamt sporadically in between thinking, and could not distinguish thought from dream.

She is opening the door to Mohan's apartment, eager to see his welcome. He is not in the sitting room, so she walks across to the bedroom. He is lying there with his arms under his head, listening to Yesudas on tape. 'Ishwaran orunal...'

The most mellifluous male tenor in Kerala sang with that perfect mixture of feeling and melody only he could bring to a song. 'God went to the palace one day, without telling them.' Mohan looks up, but doesn't recognise her. 'Who?' he starts saying, sitting up.

A girl walks in through the door; she is young and beautiful. She is in her nightclothes and enters as if she lives there. She smiles at Thankam arrogantly and then looks at her with pity.

'Ara?' Thankam begins to ask. It is Mohan who speaks.

'I don't know this old woman.' He turns to the girl and beckons her to the bed.

Thankam struggled out of that nightmare and sat up, gulping the fetid air of the compartment. The young Muslim girl opposite was still sleeping in her *burka*. Her husband on the top berth looked on as Thankam fought her way through the cobwebs in her mind.

'Nearly there,' he said.

Thalassery railway station in the early hours of the morning - she was expecting dopey Kumaran, the cook, to be waiting with an auto, but it was Appu's cherubic face she saw; he started running along the platform when he spotted her at the window. He hand-signalled to her to come to the door; so she collected her small case and fought her way to the door, through others trying to do the same thing. The train stopped at Thalassery for only three minutes and if you didn't hurry, you could end up at the next stop in Kannoor.

'Neeli,' he shouted happily, as he took the case off her hands and helped her down. He was the only person who ever called her Neeli, a childhood teaser for her dark colour. He summoned an auto-rickshaw and told the driver where to go, then he smiled at her.

'You are all right now.' It was half question, half statement. Thankam smiled in answer; she had no need to say anything; she was overjoyed to see him.

As the auto rickshaw put-putted into life, she looked around her at the old town; nothing ever happened to it. The narrow streets were still narrow, the railway station was dirty and miserable as ever, the porters still wore their red headbands and got into arguments about the payment though charges per load were fixed. This was Kerala's forgotten hinterland, she thought, far away from the centre and punished with negligence for its violence and terrorist tendencies, even by the left wing Governments in power, who may have taught them the "end justifies the means" philosophy.

The auto sped through familiar streets, but the shops were all closed and it made good time. When it descanted the two of them at Madathil House, Madhavi Amma was at the door, waiting.

'So you have come,' she said. 'How long is it since you've come home?'

Thankam ignored the usual complaint. "I'm here now, aren't I, Ammey,' she answered, hugging her. Then she escaped inside to greet Lakshmi, her sister-in-law, who was staying back, just behind the door; they had always been good friends.

'You look good,' Lakshmi said. 'A little thin perhaps, but everyone wants to be thin these days, so that's not bad, is it? Appuettan has been jumping up and down with excitement since he heard you were coming down.'

Thankam hugged Lakshmi and got the familiar cooking smells of shallots and green chillies on her; she was forever chopping for one meal or another.

When Thankam had bathed and breakfasted, she felt sleepy, but she battled off the sleep; this was precious time and she wasn't going to waste it, sleeping during the day. So she sat with her family in the veranda, catching up on local news and talking about her children and her life in Kochi.

'Don't tell Amma,' she whispered to Appu. 'I started going in to the college last month. Seems a good idea not to let the business be entirely in the hands of others.

'And Appuetta, I drive the car nowadays. I'm managing my affairs well; you should be proud of me.'

'You always did show me up,' he answered happily. 'You beat me hollow at studies, now my affairs are left to Lakshmi to manage and you are looking after yourself. So what's new? When I come down for a holiday, I know very little about my family. How much can you find out in a Friday phone call?' Was there an undercurrent of sadness in his tone?

'I have an only son who was born after a long wait and how often do I see him? Now Jayan is starting college, I wonder whether he's made the right decisions about subjects for the eleventh and twelfth years, but I cannot advise him as I know little about his strengths and weaknesses. Still, my being in Dubai keeps this family comfortable financially and that is important too.'

It sounded as though he was persuading himself. Thankam moved closer to him and picked a long hair off his shirt.

'I bet that's Lakshmi's hair,' she said, trying to lighten the mood, but he was not fooled.

'I should ask you: do you need any help? Are you all right money-wise? That's one thing I can do for you because of being in Dubai. I don't like to think of you struggling; I ask because I wonder whether you are working because money is short.'

'I am all right, Appuetta,' Thankam answered. 'As though I don't know where to come if I need help. In any case, Anil's got a good job; surely he will help out if it comes to that. Though I doubt it will; Unni has provided for me well.'

In the evening Thankam persuaded Appu to take a walk with her to Moozhikkara to visit her husband's home, which was now closed down, with a servant in charge as caretaker. She knew she would open old scars going there, but this was a ghost she had to learn to live with, since she never wanted it to be exorcised.

'Must get back before it is dark,' Appu reminded her. 'After the murder of that teacher, Jayakrishnan, in front of all his sixth-standard students, the town is still very jittery. The communists are quiet and some arrests have been made amongst them, but the BJP is not going to let this pass unavenged. It's tit for tat here now. I'm sure some personal feuds also get settled without anyone realising this.

'It was brutal: several men came into the classroom while he was teaching and attacked him with machetes; his blood and hair splattered on the children. After that the murderers wrote, "Anyone bearing witness will suffer the same fate as Jayakrishnan" on the blackboard, so not too many people will come forward or allow their children to say anything to the police.

'D'you know something? I'm glad I'm not in the police here. I don't have the carapace to deal with this kind of thing and these killings are quite frequent in this district. Soon there will be a BJP avenge-killing of a communist; it is never- ending. Some strange rumours are going around: ministerial intervention in the conduct of the investigation, some say. No one knows what to believe; I'm well out of it.'

When she reached her husband's old home, Thankam went wandering from one disused room to another.

'Why do you hurt yourself coming here now?' Appu asked. 'Let's go home.'

She went to the back veranda near the kitchen and sat on the ledge. This was instinctive, a need to reaffirm something inside her. In her mind's eye she could see that other young person sitting here, cleaning her teeth with mango leaves. The ledge was a convenient perch looking out on the mango grove and the small vegetable patch, where her mother-in-law, Meenakshi, grew yam and banana. Thankam had loved watching the soft, dark blur of banana trees, gradually coming into sharp focus as sunlight crept into the dense, leafy mass, driving out the shadows. Now the vegetable patch had gone wild and the mango trees were big; the small mangoes were visible, hanging in rich green clusters.

Appu came over and sat next to her on the ledge, while the caretaker and his wife, Kalyani, hovered, asking whether they would like some tea made. Thankam had a compulsion to talk about this part of her life and Appu knew he mustn't stop her.

'Amma always made the coffee in the mornings; she wouldn't allow anyone else to do it; it was as though this was a responsibility that went with the housewife's territory. She said Kalyani couldn't make good coffee.' She smiled at the memory.

'It was quite hard work too in those days, no kettles, no electricity in fact; she boiled the water over a three-stone fire. She'd rake the overnight cinders in the fireplace first and heap small pieces of dry twigs to light the fire. I'd watch her carefully thinking I must learn to do this in time. Then she'd blow into it with a long bamboo blower to get the flames to rise, and place a pot of water above it. It was all so deftly done.'

Appu didn't interrupt. She was talking faster and faster with each word and a sob was beginning to form in the middle of phrases. 'She was so gentle and loving, I used to wonder what all those usual mother-in-law tales were about.' Thankam started sobbing now for Meenakshi, but Appu knew she was crying for many different things, so he sat quietly holding her close, and let her finish.

They said their goodbyes and left for their mother's house before dusk had set in. She was quiet walking home. 'You must come here more often and ask Anil and Manju to come too,' he said. 'This is a good part of your life and theirs and you mustn't lose touch with it.'

'I know, Appuetta. I only wish you could always be here when we come.'

'I'm around at Onam and Christmas, just come during those times. And send me e-mails more frequently; then I'll know what's with you and my niece and nephew. I miss seeing Manju's children, but it is impossible to get everywhere in the one month's leave. Lakshmi's mother also expects a slice of that time.'

'I'm so selfish; here I am talking about myself so much. How are things with you? I know you make money, but all the other things?'

Appu probably knew this was the only chance he would get for a long time to talk to his sister, on her own.

'You married Unni, a kind and good man, but also an educated person. You could talk to him about things. You had a good partnership there. I married my uncle's daughter, my *murappennu*, my traditionally ordained wife. My uncle demanded and my family agreed. Who was I to question their word? It was another time and another world then in the sixties and seventies.

'But, I have no one to talk to, really, about the things that interest me. Can you see me and Lakshmi having a heated discussion on the nature of the judiciary in Kerala? And I grew up talking to you.

'But Lakshmi is a good wife; she stays with my mother and runs the house in my absence. Many educated girls would have found something else to do as soon as I went overseas. I am happy with her; I just have this longing sometimes to open my heart to a partner and with that she cannot cope.'

Appu laughed. 'The other day, I said to her, "D'you believe you'll be born again after you die, according to your '*Karmam*' from this life. Do you think I'll be born as one of those prisoners I interrogated when I was Sub-Inspector here?"

'And Lakshmi answers, "In which case, I shall be born as an onion or a green chilli; I chop so many in a day." She can always make me laugh with her down-to-earth comments, they are so surprising. She goes, "What kind of nonsense are you talking about? Who is dying, when? I must go and see to the mango pickle, takes a lot of time to chop the mangoes."

'Who knows, perhaps she is wiser not to think about the things for which there are no answers.'

They strolled past looking at the new concrete boxes: low, flat-roofed houses on either side, which had sprung up from gulf money. The tapioca and red spinach fields stretching for miles, where farmers used to plant vegetables after the harvest had meekly withdrawn to the nudge and push of the new money. However, Thankam noticed, in some respects the place had moved forward: electricity supplies had reached the villages and huge hospitals had sprouted up near the main roads.

Thankam spent two days with her family, then went to Bangalore. When she arrived late in the evening, she was met by Anil, who was delighted to see her.

'Long journey from Kochi to Bangalore; you look exhausted.'

Thankam ignored that. 'Come on; take me home. I want to see this executive pad of yours.'

She liked the minimalist look of his bachelor quarters, but wondered whether it was intentional or due to lack of interest in his domestic arrangements. 'My firm has allocated this flat to me recently,' he said, almost in answer to her unspoken thought, 'and I was just beginning to think about decorating it when they asked me to go to the UK for six months.'

Anil took her overnight bag into the guest room saying, 'This bag is feather light; doesn't look as though you intend to stay long.'

'You'll be the first to complain if I stayed long,' she pointed out, smiling.

It was a neat little room with a fitted wardrobe and a small bathroom next door. Anil made some tea for the two of them and followed her round the flat while she looked around.

'Nice,' she remarked, 'and functional. No water problems, I hope.'

'Not here on the ground floor. I've heard the third floor is short of water sometimes.'

Thankam poked around in his kitchen, looking for wheat flour or vegetables; she saw nothing much by way of fresh food.

'What do you eat in the evenings?' she asked.

'I don't cook. I get a take away. Let's get something in tonight. You don't have to play housewife here; you should be thinking of getting a holiday instead.'

The next morning Thankam gave him a list of things to get: 'I want meat, vegetables and spices,' she instructed. 'And take care you come home straight from buying the meat, I don't want to end up cooking rotten stuff.' Last time she visited he had left his meat in the car while he played squash and had arrived home with a stinking parcel, which Thankam had discarded immediately.

She ate some bread for lunch and when Anil came home after work, she made rice and lentil curry and cabbage *upperi* for him. She had brought some mango pickle with her; so they had a proper Kerala meal.

'I could get used to this, there's something so simple and easy on the stomach about Malayalee food,' Anil stated, as he tucked into his mother's cooking.

'That's because it's mainly vegetables and rice, hardly anything in there to offend the stomach.'

After an early dinner, he went out to meet some friends of his, so she watched television for a while, on the big Sony Vega flat screen in his room. On the Malayalam channels it was serial time and most of them showed women weeping and trying to speak through racking sobs. Some cried silently, tears streaming down their faces, looking like well-ornamented sacrificial lambs. Sometimes the same woman was crying on two different channels in two different stories.

Thankam decided she was disgusted at this portrayal of women as martyrs stoically suffering everywhere she looked, but the Hindi serials did the same in Hindi, with the difference that the women were taller, fairer and definitely slimmer. Thankam switched over to Zee TV and watched *Friends*; she liked the feisty girls there who asked for and gave no quarter to anyone. She nodded off watching TV and had to drag herself off to her room eventually.

On Saturday Anil's friends came visiting, two girls from the office and three young men, all about Anil's age. They appeared very familiar with each other. She noticed it was a whole new language they spoke.

'So what did you do last evening?' Anil was talking to a young woman, in her mid thirties. She wore faded blue Levis and a scanty top, which was tight across her bust. No jewellery to be seen anywhere, Thankam thought; this was one thing about which Thankam wholeheartedly agreed with the younger generation.

'Chilled out at home with a book; I needed some quiet time.'

The girl was comfortable with Anil, as though she visited here often. She wandered off to his music centre and started going through his CDs. 'I see you've got the Beatles Number One,' she commented. She picked it up and extracted the CD, then went over and placed it on the CD tray. Remembering Thankam's presence, she turned around and asked, 'Do you mind if I put a CD on, Auntie?' Thankam smiled her consent and thought, wonder when they'll start calling us older people by our names. The "auntie" still reigns.

Thankam felt out of place in the sitting room; she could see her presence cramped their style though they were all painfully polite, so she went to her room by seven in the evening. She lay in bed reading, until she felt sleepy. As she dropped off, her thoughts went back to Mohan; he had turned her life around and hope had returned.

Thankam could hear the sounds of laughter and happy chatter in the sitting room as she lay in bed, mind very much back in Kochi, with Mohan and Seetha and her life there, which had become exciting again. Much later, when she surfaced now and then from sleep in the early hours of the morning, the softer murmur of conversation and the faint strains of *ghazals* were still audible.

After three days of this, she had to admit nothing was more boring than to spend a day, in an unfamiliar town, cooped up in your son's flat. However, in a secret corner of her mind she wondered whether she was eager to get away because she was pining for Mohan like a lovesick teenager.

Thankam thought of all the widows she knew who lived permanently with sons or daughters and wondered if they were as content as they pretended to be. There had been no daughter-in-law in Anil's house to make Thankam feel the outsider; yet she had not been happy there. In her mind, she thanked Unni for leaving her financially independent of her children; she could be of assistance to them when they needed her emotionally, but she need never be an adjunct to their lives.

However Thankam saw the week out; she had booked her return trip on that basis. In between Christmas came and went; it made no impact on her or Anil. On New Years Eve, he took her out for a slap-up meal at the Taj; it was by way of a good-bye gift.

'So what are all the things you thought you should say to me before I left, Ammey?' he asked, only half jokingly.

'I thought about it. What is proper in the sense of accepted by society seems to change with each place and time. I think you have to go by your instincts and your sense of fair play and justice. In the end, I think the yardstick is: don't do anything you would not want to admit to your Achan or me. I am not worried about you.

'Have a good time there, make friends, enjoy yourself. Some of my friends gave me the addresses of other Indians in London for you to meet, but I can't see the point. If you want to meet Indians, there are over a billion here, why go there?'

She continued cooking for Anil and had the flat spick and span by the time she left, all the while feeling guilty he may be forgoing his social life, because of her presence. She could hear the phone conversations sometimes.

'Sorry, can't come today, my mother is here visiting.'

Or, 'Can we do that next week? I am tied up for this week.'

In between, she packed up all the instant soups, spaghetti and noodles and such like, thinking, what a lot of rubbish this boy buys!

Anil was travelling to the UK in two weeks' time; so she put away all his residual debris in the unused top shelves of his cupboards. 'This place should be all right for your colleague for six months if you don't buy any more rubbish,' she told him.

'Give me a ring as soon as you get to the UK. Tell me what kind of accommodation they have arranged for you.'

It was lovely to see Anil, but she was eager to be back home. She reached her house at six in the evening and found Seetha had waited to see her in, before leaving for the day. Thankam felt a huge happiness to see Seetha, her home, her rain-drenched veranda, even the leak in the kitchen sink...

'It is great to be back,' she said to Seetha, 'I hadn't realised what a boring homebody I've become.'

Thankam longed to see Mohan; she listened for his footsteps on the stairway or his cheery whistle when he pottered around upstairs. She did not have to wait long.

'Mohan Sar asked when you were coming back,' Seetha said.

'I told him I'd be back today, perhaps he forgot.'

'He is always asking about you these days; maybe he wants a loan. And that girl, his sister- she is hardly ever here; I asked Sar about it and he said she has lost interest in her studies. Says they are trying to get her married soon.

'Apparently whenever he shouts at her for missing college, she runs away to their house in Kottayam. Just now she's gone for her Christmas holidays and he is free.'

Thankam teased Seetha,' If you don't get all this information for me, how would I know what is happening on this street. You'll soon qualify for becoming Graciamma number two.'

'Oh, I forgot to tell you - you won't like this: Graciamma asked me the other day why you have a young man staying here when you are a widow. So I got really annoyed. I said, "You tell me what age is appropriate and I'll tell my Amma." That shut her up; so now she doesn't talk to me when I pass her window. Great relief! I can stop ducking for a few days.'

Thankam realised Graciamma would figure things out long before anyone else, even Seetha, because Seetha had a guileless mind. Once the busybody next door knew about her relationship with Mohan, how long would it be before the whole community knew?

Mohan came bounding in immediately afterwards banishing Graciamma and all else from Thankam's mind; for a moment it was as though Seetha was not there.

'You've been away for ages,' he complained.

Thankam's smile started in her eyes and spread slowly to the rest of her face. Mohan's right arm came out involuntarily as though to touch her face and quickly withdrew. Seetha looked at that arm and back to Thankam's glowing face, then quickly walked away.

Seetha appeared to be going through a rough patch at home again. Her son, Prakash, was becoming as bad as his father. He went to work rarely and made no contribution to the household.

Prakash's wife started the traditional work of cleaning in the richer households as soon as their son started at nursery school.

'Amma, Prakash never takes her anywhere, three years married and he has never bought her as much as a pair of knickers. Sold all her jewellery and drank it away in the first year itself.

'The little one waits for me to bring leftovers from here, so that he can have a meal when I get home. You often ask me why I don't eat my breakfast. I wrap it up and take it home for him. The men in my household are useless; we women bring the food home while they drink and abuse us.'

Thankam knew enough about the Bhai community, in which it was commonplace for the women to be breadwinners and be beaten up for it; it was a very repressive community. Girls were married off early when they were sixteen so that they did not bring any dishonour to the family.

Seetha's daughter was only seventeen, but already the family were putting pressure on her parents to find a husband for her. At least no huge dowries were needed as in the case of the Christian girls. Working class Bhai households demanded moderate dowries of ten thousand or twenty thousand rupees, whereas the Christian households put the price of a casual building labourer at thirty thousand and over, in spite of the fact that the bridegroom's employment was often sporadic and uncertain. It was not uncommon for a Christian bride to end up in her own home, after the birth of her first child, sans dowry and sans the gold jewellery she had taken with her.

10

When did Mohan become an acknowledged part of Thankam's life? Not even Seetha, who served the meals in absolute silence, or Geetha, who came and went, absorbed in her own concerns, mainly to do with how she looked, could say. The household got used to bringing him tea when he came home from work in the evenings and stopped to have a quick word with Thankam before he went upstairs. If he was around at meal times they assumed he would eat with Thankam and the table was laid for two.

Sometimes he would disappear for days on end, presumably looking after his business in Kottayam, but Thankam had learned not to ask questions. As the weeks went by and Onam approached Thankam began to notice a change in Mohan: worry lines started appearing on his face.

He also became moody and taciturn. The joy had drained out of him leaving him empty and impatient. The rest of Kerala were busy preparing to celebrate their most important festival of the year, with an orgy of spending on friends and family, but Mohan was opting out.

This cannot go on, Thankam finally said to herself.

'What is bothering you recently?' she asked when he sat, almost sulking, on her veranda ledge one day.

He continued to stare into space and didn't say anything for a few moments. 'Nothing that you need to think about,' he brought out finally.

'Except you walk about these days with a face swollen up like a hundred wasps have stung you. Maybe talking to someone will help. Look at the way you answered me just now, what an effort that was!

Thankam got up and disappeared indoors for a little while. He found her a little later in the study, where she was arranging books. She had a duster in her hands, but as she rubbed half-heartedly at the spines, she had a faraway look in her eyes.

'Sorry,' Mohan ventured. 'It's everything. All coming together on my shoulders – Geetha's wedding, a bank loan from long ago, the salaries of the workers in Kottayam... I thought I could mortgage or sell some of our land in Kottayam and sort this all out. But the land is jointly owned by Geetha and me; so that's not possible.'

Thankam replaced the book in her hand on the shelf lovingly and thought for a moment.

'Mmm... Geetha is not a minor. She can sign too and you'll be able to sell. If that is what you want.'

'I *don't* want Geetha to know any of this.' Mohan was vehement.

Of course, Thankam thought. The girl was Mohan's Achilles heel. She had to be indulged and protected all the time. Like giving her this flat in which she hardly stayed now that she had found a boy friend in Kottayam.

'I might be able to help, if you are stuck,' Thankam offered, wondering whether she would embarrass him.

Mohan did not answer; indeed he seemed not to have heard. Thankam did not repeat the offer.

Thankam had forgotten all about this brief exchange when Mohan brought the subject up again a few days later. He was driving her Maruthi and she was in the passenger seat; his face seemed cast in stone and she knew there was no point in starting a conversation.

'Did you really mean what you said the other day?' Mohan suddenly asked. He continued to look grimly out of the car.

'And what was that?' Thankam asked carelessly.

'About helping if I got stuck. With the bank and everything.'

'What I was offering was some money to tide you over. A loan till you got your business sorted out. How much do you need?'

Anything to lift the clouds, she thought.

'I need two lakhs in the next month,' he murmured. He was still staring straight ahead.

Thankam did a quick mental calculation. Two lakhs! A whole year's housekeeping money! She could find some of the money if she broke into her deposit account, but it was daunting.

'I can give you one, if that will help. Two, I can't make.'

'Thanks. That would help a lot.'

Thankam quickly changed the topic after that and started telling him about Jacob and his peccadilloes, hoping to bring a smile to his face, but the smile did not appear. Mohan went on looking out, clearly not wanting to meet her eyes.

A few days later, as Thankam was about to go shopping Mohan reminded her about the offer of a loan.

'Would you be going to the bank, by any chance?' he asked. 'I'll come along; you could get that cash out for me. Then I can go straight to Kottayam and pay the workers.'

When they reached the bank Thankam noticed the huge queue at the tellers; she was half inclined to come back another day.

'Long wait,' she said to Mohan hoping he would be willing to come back the next day. She turned to him, but the look on his face was stubborn, uncompromising. Like that of a spoilt child who wanted his toy *now*.

'I really need it now,' he insisted.

So she planted herself in the queue while he stood to the side. For an odd moment she thought he looked like a dog-handler with his dog on a leash, making sure the animal would not run away.

When her turn at the counter came she signed the necessary papers and asked for one lakh rupees in cash. Nearly enough to buy that new *Maruthi* car, she thought. Suddenly she wanted to finish the transaction and get out of the bank.

'Large amount,' the girl at the counter murmured. 'Shall I make out a draft instead?' Thankam looked at Mohan questioningly.

'Cash,' he answered, shortly.

The cashier darted a quick look at him and then at Thankam. I've seen all this many times before, her look seemed to say.

As soon as Gopi went back to Dubai after Christmas, Manju had begun to work at the British Council. She seemed to be full of new life and joy after she started, but Thankam did not see as much of her or the children as she used to; she had to be satisfied with talking on the phone more frequently. Sometimes Manju breezed in and out after a few minutes; she was always in a hurry. It was two months before Thankam had a chance to sit down with Manju for a proper gossip.

'Don't tell me your mother-in-law intends to stay with her daughter permanently; she doesn't like her son-in-law very much,' Thankam commented, hoping to know what had transpired with Gopi. She couldn't imagine Gopi agreeing meekly to his wife becoming a working woman, with his kind of ego, and his mother had been his trump card for a long time.

'That's mutual, between son-in-law and mother-in-law,' Manju volunteered, smiling. 'But don't you want to hear about my job?'

'Actually, I'm more curious to know how you blackmailed Gopi into letting you work.'

'You didn't hear about the humungous fuss I made? Well of course, you didn't. You were in Bangalore then. I had a real ding-dong with Gopi soon after you went off. The security guards, cleaning woman, Mani, everyone within a radius of about a kilometre were provided free entertainment. I think my dignified lord and master was hugely embarrassed.'

'I know *you* can put on a convincing show, but even you have to have a reason of some sort.'

Manju sat down and leaned back luxuriously in her chair. 'I hope you have a long time to listen to me,' she began. 'because this story has plots and subplots and events and scenes...

'On Christmas day, Mani is hanging around - again. Now, he is Christian and I can't figure it out. Why isn't he with his wife, kids and mother instead of irritating me? Gopi tells me to give him breakfast and the maid feeds him. That annoys me as well; he is forever turning up at meal times and expecting to be fed.'

'Don't tell me you grudge the driver a meal,' Thankam remonstrated.

'It's not the meal, Ammey. Anyway, after a while I don't see him and I forget all about him; I assume he's gone home. Then Asha takes a tumble from the swing and comes running in, tears streaming down her face. She has taken the skin off her right knee and it is bleeding slightly.

'So I run upstairs to my bathroom and who do I see in my bedroom? Sitting on my counterpane, knees drawn up, laughing about something with my husband, is that insect. He has what looks like a huge wad of money in his hand and as soon as he sees me, he stuffs it willy-nilly into his shirt pocket. The pocket is bulging out by the time he has got rid of all of it. Gopi is looking a little nonplussed.'

Manju was trying to make all this sound like a joke but she was not succeeding; bewilderment showed in her eyes.

'So I glare pointedly at the pocket and say to Mani,' she continued '"Do you not have Christmas in your house? I know of distant villages where Christmas and Onam never reach, but I thought you lived near here in Cheranellore."'

'The man gets up and makes his escape.

'After he went, I pitched into Gopi. I shouted and screamed at him; I think I really scared him.' Manju sounded joyous at the thought, but was there a hint of desperation in the laughter?

'Finally Gopi admitted it. Mani has been supplying him with what he calls "a harmless smoke, now and then." I suspect it is *Ganja*; I know nothing about it, so I am guessing. I've noticed, recently, Gopi is lost to the world after seven in the evening. He sort of disappears to his bedroom and stays in, watching TV, whatever else may be going on outside.'

'Not much of a life for you from the sound of it,' Thankam admitted, sadly.

Manju continued, ignoring the comment.

'I insisted on his coming clean. He said he had started the habit in college; apparently, it was quite easy to get it at the gates where it was sold openly. Then he started working and stopped. He insists - and I don't know how true this is - he doesn't need it when he is busy and happy.'

She looked questioningly at Thankam, looking a bit lost and Thankam's heart went out to her. She wanted to go over and hold her close, banishing all the doubts.

'He blames it all on Dubai. There he found himself alone in the evenings with nowhere to go and not many friends; I think it was sheer boredom that made him start again. He claims it was only an occasional smoke.

'This cleared the air a bit. I think Gopi was quite ashamed because the whole of Gulf Stream Villas stopped whatever they were doing to stare at our house during this performance. I, naturally, took the opportunity to get some mileage out of this; a girl has to look after herself.'

'But, naturally-'

'And the long and the short of it is: he has allowed me to work, provided I make adequate arrangements for child minding. The argument being: if he is bored there, with a full time job, how much more bored I must be doing nothing at home, with the children at school, Gopi in Dubai and Saraswathi in Bangalore?'

'More to the point,' Thankam insisted, 'how is he dealing with his smoking? Has it stopped?'

'I think so,' Manju answered. 'Mani wasn't allowed into the house after that, but what do I know about how he lives, or what he does in Dubai? And, in any case, how *dare* Mani sit on my bed?'

'That's sad,' Thankam said, 'that husbands and wives lose touch and don't know much about each other. This Dubai thing!'

'Yes, this Dubai thing. I agree.'

'And I also see you've been spending a lot of money on your wardrobe recently,' Thankam added. Manju was wearing a beautiful cream salwar-kameez outfit, which flattered her pale honey complexion and light brown eyes.

'You didn't seriously think I was going to work to add to the family fortunes, did you?'

Thankam noticed how well work suited Manju. Her eyes sparkled with mischief and wit and she had a lilt in her voice, which Thankam had not heard for some time. Thankam had enough question marks in her own life to have to worry about children now, but where was all this going to end?

Anil phoned most Sundays: he had settled down in digs in the Earls Court area. Apparently three others were sharing with him, but he didn't mind; he seemed busy with work and getting used to the place.

As Manju learned her job at the library and became more competent, she also became busier. She phoned most days, but rarely made the journey from Vaduthala to Carrier Station Road, unless she had a holiday. At Easter, she got a week off.

'What have you been doing with yourself, lately?' Thankam asked when she came by, trying to catch up on three months at one go.

'With two children of school-going age? For heaven's sake Ammey! Asha is in the first standard and she has monthly tests and term exams. I have to sit down with them and do their homework daily; it takes forever. And the worry when they don't do well! Teachers making silly comments in the reports like, "Must try harder." What does a five-year-old know about rank and marks, I ask?'

'Hey, hold on. I was only asking a casual question.' Thankam had nightmare visions of herself becoming one of those mothers who were scared of their children, being snapped at when they opened their mouths. She was determined not to let that happen. So she added, 'You are really short-tempered recently. I don't quite know why, but you mustn't take it out on me.'

Manju quickly came off her aggressive tone. 'I know,' she said. 'I am sorry. Everything in my life ends up on your doorstep.

'And who else is there, anyway?' she added, looking penitent.

'I know Gopi is not here the whole time, but don't you think you should be talking to him if something is making you worried or stressed? He rings up every Friday, doesn't he?'

'I am busy - which is not worried and certainly not stressed. Talking properly to Gopi is easily said, but impossible. When he phones, it is always about his instructions to me as to how to run this house of mine, my children, my life. I generally switch off and think of democracy. He tells me in detail what to do with the draft he sent; how to get the gutters repaired and details about who to phone for that and how much to pay; what I should be doing to make the children first in their classes…. First in their classes at five and seven years? What for? We always seem to end up on the wrong note.

'The other day, I had a bad migraine and just lost it with him, but he didn't seem to think I was being reasonable.'

'When is he coming home next?' Thankam asked carefully.

'I don't really know. And I'm not sure his coming solves anything. I just have him *here* giving instructions. He doesn't seem to understand I have work to do. Though he allowed me to start work, and I enjoy my job, he thinks of it as a time-filler. When he is here, he'll probably want me to neglect my work, take time off, come home early and be full-time wife. I am new in the job and have to watch my step. Last time he was here, he was upset because I had a year-group get-together of old college mates and had to be out for a whole day.'

'He's been good to let you work at all, don't forget that.'

'That's the attitude of *your* generation; I don't go with any of that. Dave, at the office, was telling me the way women are in the UK today: independent, making their own lives the way they like it.'

'Who's Dave, then?'

'He works at the head office in Delhi. Comes down once every two or three months to check the library accounts and the running of the library generally.'

'Maybe. But you're here and when in Rome…'

When Manju left, Thankam had this uneasy feeling that there were still many unsaid things. And who was this Dave? He came up in conversation a lot recently. But Thankam also had started working on developing the spoken English curriculum at the school and did not have time to pursue will o' the wisps. In addition, she had taken the library in hand and started getting it up-to-date; it was a neglected part of the college.

Jacob had reluctantly accepted Thankam as a colleague and employer after a long period when he had treated her as a dilettante playing at a career. On her part she was determined to understand all aspects of the business and make sure Jacob did not make all the decisions on his own. She was now beginning to enjoy her role at the college. Thankam wondered whether she would have been so confident at work if Sister Cecilia at the convent had not singled her out for special attention, and put pressure on her family to let her go to college.

I am forty-nine and I have two adult children who need me now and then, Thankam reminded herself, something she did quite frequently these days, like a penance. But strangely enough, I don't consider myself unattractive any more. At twenty I thought I was ugly; I have to thank Unni for this self-confidence, and Mohan, perhaps. But I could come down with a big thump where Mohan is concerned.

She finds herself watching all the time, when she is with Mohan, to make sure he does not notice the ravages of age. Recently he has been a little detached and this makes Thankam wonder whether this is due to her.

Neither had mentioned the loan since that day at the bank, but Thankam occasionally thought it stood like an invisible third party between them, making conversation stilted, not quite coming to the point ever.

None of this helped Thankam's confidence. She kept the lights dimmed when they made love.

'I like to see your face, when I am this close to you. I want to see your eyes open and look at me. Gasp and scream and clutch at me.' But she was not sure of herself, so she continued to keep the light down. One day he turned it up without warning, walking back from the bathroom, just before getting into bed. He noticed her confusion and came to her side of the bed.

'You don't realise how beautiful you look lying there, waiting for me. I am a lucky man.' But when he had got into bed, she still turned round and dimmed the lights.

Thankam felt reassured for the moment, but the doubts tended to resurface when she was not with him. She remembered how secure she had been in Unni's love. When Unni and she made love, there had never been any inhibition. Their bodies were fine tuned by habit, unthinkingly doing the right things, fitting into each other like well-worn garments.

And she had to admit, what she felt for Mohan could hardly be sanctified by the label of love.

How could it be when she knew so little about him and every bit had to be prised out of him? Why was he so reluctant to talk to her? Did he think of her as a sexual partner only, never on the same side of the fence with him?

Was she just a "time-pass" between now and marriage?

Thankam also knew that this was an extremely unequal relationship and she was the pauper in the pair. One of these days I am in for a jolt, she admitted, but meanwhile, she carried on letting her body lead her. He came through the partitioning door between their quarters every now and then; strangely she never went into his apartment.

Initially, it was because Geetha might come in at any moment, or might be there already. Gradually it became apparent that Geetha came very rarely. Still Thankam stayed on her side of the door. She never summoned up the courage to open that door and go through.

This told her who led and who followed in the relationship, but she was too consumed by her need for him to question it. Eventually it was too late to change anything.

However, she never forgot the dream she had in the train, travelling to Thalassery a few months ago; was her subconscious trying to tell her something? So one Sunday evening she made up her mind to change some things. She chose a moment when she was sure no visitors were next door; Mohan had gone out in the morning to Kottayam and had just got back.

'You've been away a whole day, I missed you,' she said as she opened the door and walked into his apartment.

When she glanced around, what she saw was a place to sleep, not a home. Not many books or magazines, no scatter cushions on the sofas; the place looked stark and dismal. They could have done better with this apartment, she thought.

Mohan was sitting on the long sofa in the sitting room, going through what looked like accounts. Papers were strewn about the floor and she had to step over some to get to the chair next to him. She tried to identify the strange smell in the room;

it took her awhile to realise this was the smell of stale takeaway food, and rotting fruit long past its eat-by date.

Mohan greeted her briefly and carried on for another moment. Then he put the papers down.

'I went to Kottayam, as you know. We are doing some repairs to our house to get it ready for Geetha's wedding. The engagement will be quite soon, now that all the elders have agreed. I'm shattered.'

Then he got up and went to the kitchen to get some tea. She followed him through. The kitchen was a total mess with unwashed plates and pans on which food had dried up and congealed.

'God help us-'

'I don't have servants to do my washing-up for me,' he said, sounding defensive.

Thankam set about doing the woman thing; she moved the dirty dishes out of the sink and took the sponge and Sabena out. This seemed to irritate him. He left the kitchen and walked through into the sitting room and put a CD of Pankaj Udhas on. Thankam found him there ten minutes later, fast asleep on the sofa, when she brought the tea in.

Now I'm putting him to sleep, she thought wryly, and left, tea undrunk, closing the door softly behind her.

It was still only seven, so she wandered around in her garden for a little while. The water lilies in her little round pond were in flower, holding up yellow and violet blooms proudly. An orange carp surfaced and went under and a baby shark swam up and dived between the leaves of the lilies in a quicksilver flash, sensing her presence. She took some bone meal out of the garden shed and sprinkled it on the water.

The garden was still showing a lot of colour, before the monsoon set in; huge spiky orange and yellow *Rajamalli* trees stood a head above the others, asserting they were not bushes. Under her feet the grass was a springy green carpet; she kicked off her slippers and walked barefoot, enjoying the feel of her feet sinking into that softness. The birds congregating in noisy chatter near the birdbath dispersed with a flutter of many wings when she came round the corner.

Just there, on the other side of the low wall, which separated their houses, Graciamma waited, many arrows in her quiver; Thankam had forgotten all about her.

'So many days since I've seen you in the garden.' The statement held a question.

'I've been a bit busy.' Thankam's tone did not encourage further comment. However, she had not reckoned with Graciamma's thick skin.

'I have known about how busy you are,' and in case the barb had not found target, 'That girl is no longer there, is she?'

'I've got rice on the boil.' Thankam excused herself and hurried in.

What did she expect with all the comings and goings, Thankam chided herself. Who else knew? she wondered.

Inji came trotting in through the doorway and purred, rubbing his whiskers on her feet. 'I know you are hungry,' Thankam said as she bent down and picked up the kitten. He leaned towards her and sniffed at her nose; the smell of the sardines he had eaten for lunch was strong on his breath. 'Phew!' Thankam exclaimed, as she held him away from her face. Satisfied it was his own person, Inji relaxed into the crook of her elbows as she carried him into the kitchen and opened the refrigerator to take out milk. He jumped off then with a "meeaow" and waited patiently by his saucer until the milk came.

Thankam still had the whole evening empty in front of her, but she was not in a mood for watching despairing women shedding tears on the TV soaps, so she decided to read the book she had left half-read by her bed, some time ago. Pre-Mohan times, she thought, when I did read. It was Penelope Lively's *Moon Tiger*.

As she walked up the marble stairs to fetch the book, the large cast-iron Ganeshan on the landing looked at her impassively; she stopped and stared into his elephant face. What am I doing with my life? she asked him. Tell me what to do, give me my life back so I am not at the mercy of my need for this man . She touched Ganeshan's head in the age-old gesture of worship and carried his blessing on her fingers to her forehead. To this have I come, she thought, I who uncompromisingly believe this is a beautiful image but not God, never God, if indeed there is a God.

That's where I am, Thankam admitted, not sufficient to myself any more and I have to gain my emotional ground back, whatever it takes.

Next morning, bright and early, Mohan was at her doorstep. Thankam was still in bed and Seetha was taken aback; her surprise showed on her face; what was Mohan Sar doing here at this time? She ran up the stairs to call Amma.

'Ammey, Mohan Sar is downstairs, wants to see you.'

'Ask him to sit down and give him coffee while I make myself respectable.'

Thankam studiously avoided looking at the mirror when she walked past it; he could take her as he found her.

'*Entha*?' she asked when she saw him.

He did not look comfortable. 'I'm sorry about last night; I was really tired.'

'I could see that, never mind.'

Seetha came with the tea making it unnecessary to dwell on the incident.

That evening Mohan came early, with his spare helmet. 'Please come with me for a ride'

'Sure,' Thankam said. As usual, she enjoyed the ride, which lasted over an hour. When they got back, she warmed up the iddli and sambar left over from breakfast and they ate it on the veranda. Thankam noticed Graciamma's curtain flicking but she knew the damage was probably already done, so she ignored it.

Mohan made love tenderly afterwards, as if he was making up for a misdemeanour. Making love is not about compensation, Thankam thought, while he was still on top of her, so she stayed detached, an outside observer, and without her collusion, he could not take her with him. She was alert, but passive, and eventually he reached his unsatisfactory climax.

He stayed unusually long in bed with her, dropping off to sleep after a while. She had to wake him up late at night, before she fell asleep, to send him off to his quarters.

As the days went by it became more and more apparent to Thankam that she knew very little about Mohan's life when he was not with her. What was he doing hanging around his sister, instead of cherishing a family? She decided to throw away restraint and ask questions the next time she was with him.

They had spent a companionable Sunday morning reading the papers, planning an evening out, when she brought up the subject.

'Where is Geetha these days? Thankam probed as he daydreamed, with sheets of his *Manorama,* half read, spread all round him.

'She is often in Kottayam these days now they are planning to marry,' he answered after a moment.

'Why is your face like you have a severe stomach ache, then?' Thankam persisted. 'It is a good thing, isn't it?'

'Yes, if they'd just leave me alone.'

'What do you mean? How are they not leaving you alone?'

'That Nambiar's family want an exchange marriage for him and his sister.'

Thankam knew all about exchange marriages; they were common in her part of Kerala. A brother and sister from one family would marry the sister and brother from another family. In this way both families would feel they had gained from these marriages.

'But this is a love marriage. Surely…'

"Love-and-allow"' he answered shortly, scattering the sheets of paper as he sprang up to leave.

So much for asking questions, Thankam admitted to herself woodenly. He was always going to get married to some nubile young thing. And he will deny his sister nothing; he will marry that Nambiar woman to please her.

She sat where she was for a long time thinking of what was certainly to come, sooner rather than later. She had been an old fool to think anything but grief would come out of this relationship. For a few months she had forgotten she was a widow; she had had something to look forward to each day.

Why then the sharp pang of physical jealousy when she thought of him marrying some one else? Why did her stomach cramp and her throat muscles constrict as though poison had been injected into her? Jealousy must be a kind of poison, she concluded finally; she had to get rid of it.

It was amazing how, where Mohan was involved, Thankam took each indignity and tried to make sense out of it. She sat at her desk at the office trying to concentrate on the accounts Jacob had put in front of her. But her mind darted away like a heat-seeking missile in search of Mohan; she knew there was much to consider about her relationship with him.

When the phone rang and she heard Mohan's voice at the other end, she thought it was only an extension of her thinking.

'Can you spare another one lakh rupees?' He sounded hurried.

'I am quite busy just now. Can't it wait till tomorrow?' Even as she said it she knew she was going to give him the money. Why couldn't she just say *no*?

'Can't wait,' Mohan said curtly. 'Need it now.'

'Right,' Thankam said. I'll meet you at the bank in about half an hour.'

'Half an hour? You're only five minutes from your bank.' He put the phone down.

She met Mohan at the bank; he seemed rushed and harassed.

'Can I drop you off and take the car for an hour or two?' he asked as they came out of the bank. His car was still at the workshop and now she knew why it would take a long time to come out - he would not have the money to pay for the repair bills until all the other demands on his purse were met.

As it happened Mohan – and the car – disappeared for the weekend. When he returned he was quite casual with his explanations: Geetha had needed to do a lot of visiting and shopping in connection with her forthcoming marriage and he was held up in Kottayam.

Thankam knew that by giving Mohan money she had stepped into territory, which she should never have gone near. But now it was done. For a while, Mohan kept saying he would be able to repay her when he called in his own debts. After a while, he did not mention the loan at all; it was as though it had never happened.

More than the money, his easy way with her time and her belongings, like the car, began to nag at her. She had to admit that since she lent him money she sensed resentment in him. What was that about?

11

Thankam lived opposite Susheelamma, had done since she first arrived in Kochi. At that time Susheelamma's husband was still alive and Priya, their daughter, was a little girl in pigtails, who treated Thankam's house much as her own, running in and out as she pleased. She often ate lunch with Thankam, insisting the yoghurt was much sweeter there, and slept in Thankam's bed in the lazy afternoons, while Thankam read a book beside her. Susheela helped Thankam to settle down in Kochi, showing her the various shops where the best brown rice was available and taking her down to the fish market in Kadavanthara and the supermarkets near by.

In the complicated social milieu of Kochi, Susheela had always been simple and uninterfering. Thankam was sorry to hear she was planning to leave Kochi for good and emigrate to live in England with Priya, whose husband was a doctor, working at Guys and St Thomas's Hospital, in London.

'Do you *have* to go? I am going to miss you, you know,' Thankam announced as she walked in for a neighbourly visit.

Susheela sighed. 'I have gone past the point of no-return,' she said, trying to smile, but she sounded tired and uncertain.

'I have collected the pre-paid tickets, my resident's visa is here, suitcases are packed and ready; all I have to do now is get on that plane and forget all my worries.'

And worries had multiplied with each month. She had been telling Thankam about her sorry plight for some months now:

'The interest rates have fallen to below half their value over four years; my income has plummeted. From a woman with money to spare I have become one trying hard to make ends meet.'

Priya had come in the summer for a holiday, with her husband in tow. Narayanan didn't stay long; he had only four weeks off for travel, for being with his own parents, for shopping and for making obligatory visits to his relatives in the village. His parents, like all other parents who had sons and daughters in the developed world, were reconciled to these tiny morsels of time with their children. He spent most of the four weeks with them, resenting the time needed to do all the duty visits, and the holidays always went by like a video on fast forward, leaving a sense of discontent at the end.

'Priya insists I should not live alone in my old age,' Susheela explained. 'I know my spondilosis has resurfaced and sometimes I am weary and lonely. But leaving everything I've always known? I'm petrified.'

Thankam could not find anything consoling to say, so she went over to sit next to her troubled friend. She picked up Susheela's hand and stroked it gently with her thumb.

'If you don't like it there, you can come back, can't you?' she asked.

'I've lived in Kacherippadi, in Kochi, all my married life; when Priya's father died, I still had many friends nearby and my brothers visit whenever they can, though they are also getting old. Will I ever see them again? I wonder, going away at this age.'

Susheela went into the kitchen to make tea and Thankam followed her, getting the spoon and mugs out when the water boiled.

'I shall miss my morning visits to the temple and all the festivals I attend every year.' Susheela got the tray ready to carry into the living room.

'The rummy group too - we meet every Friday,' she continued. 'Eight of us belong to this group; we cook a potluck dish each, meeting in a different house each time. We play for a stake of one paisa, which won't impoverish anybody; I really have a good time on those days, stepping out in one of my crisp cotton saris, laughing and joking with my friends. A whole way of life will come to an end. What friends will I have in cold Bilathi?'

'But Priya is there. You'll love being with her,' Thankam reminded her. 'I know how excited you get when she is expected.'

'Her coming here is great. But me staying with the two of them also worries me. Narayanan is a nice enough person, but will he be able to tolerate a mother-in-law for long periods? I have moments of sheer panic when I think of the two of them fighting because of me.'

Thankam kept quiet because she knew Susheelamma was leaving because she had no other choice.

Susheela accompanied Thankam to the gate.

'I'm sorry I have not seen too much of you lately; I've wanted to come over to have a chat with you. It's a bit awkward.'

Susheela gathered her sari pallav in her right hand and covered herself with it. She looked up and down the road and continued.

'You mustn't misunderstand. You've had some bad times recently; Unni was a good man. But don't let your grief make you do things harmful to your family.

'I wish there was an easy way of saying this: I hear things about you and I say they cannot be true. Please tell me they are not true.'

A little shiver of apprehension ran down Thankam's spine. 'Don't worry about me,' she said.

Susheela stretched out her arm and touched Thankam's face.

'Don't do anything that will bring shame upon your children and your family.'

'No – never,' Thankam called out as she turned her face away and made a quick escape.

As she walked back to her house she wondered how many in that street were talking about her. She looked up at the windows on either side of her and for a moment she imagined they were merciless, spying eyes. She quickened her pace, rushing to get safely indoors where no one could find her.

What would Manju say if the rumours reached her? And Anil? Would he feel ashamed of her? Who would be her friend when the whole house of cards came toppling down on her?

For Susheela's leaving do, all the women at the Widows' Association were dressed up and in a party mood; they had raided their wardrobes for happy clothes. Thankam, a frequent visitor there now, was greeted by many friends as she walked in. She had spoken to her cousin working at the exchange and the dirty phone calls had been traced. Those calls had stopped and Parvathy was grateful.

Thankam wore a large magenta pottu on her forehead and looked trim and elegant in her yellow printed silk sari. For this occasion she had banished all the monsters in her head. Glancing around at the people in the room, dressed up for the occasion and happy, she felt this was the way they should be all the time, not inhibited by their widowhood.

She listened to some of the wo[men about] their experiences when they went to visit [their children] overseas.

'Dubai is for shopping,' one of them declare[d. 'Once] you've bought all the things you want, what is there [to do?] Also, I feel awkward about my son spending so m[uch] money; I wonder what his wife will think. They went there to make money so as to build a house for themselves, but every time they come home they bring expensive gifts for all of us; I wonder whether they save anything. And their children go to school here; they are growing up wild, with too much money and gadgets, but not enough discipline.'

'Yes, a friend of ours lost his only son, recently,' another lady interrupted. 'Fourteen, he was. They bought him a moped last Christmas and he overturned at high speed somewhere on Mount Road, in Chennai. Imagine, a moped at fourteen; I got my first watch only when I got married,' she added, looking self-righteous.

Rathi had something to say too. 'The main problem with living with children overseas is the complete pointlessness of your life. Your son and possibly your daughter-in-law leave home for work, at seven in the morning. You clear up, clean the kitchen, and then you are staring at the wall, wondering what to do next. You are not interested in their TV, you need *Asianet* and *Doordarshan*.

'I used to sit there and wonder what happened to the various characters in the soaps here. Did Hassan marry his childhood sweetheart? Was the old woman in *Sthree* who caused so much mischief still round, still doing the same things? My daughter got me Malayalam videos sometimes, but you can't watch videos all evening, every evening, can you?'

'And that is not all,' Sreedevi interjected. 'To go out, you need to wear an overcoat over your sari, you feel ugly and fat. And your feet are always cold because you don't like wearing socks and shoes.'

'Yes, then your children get tired of you,' Madhuri offered, 'because you are not the same person, whom they

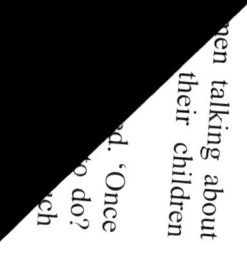

:rala. You are miserable and they [w]ith you.'

[...]ping at you and whispering with [...] onder whether they are talking about [...] was Elizabeth. She had done one [...] d to as 'house arrest' - in the US, and [...] do it again.

[...] it out on the steps and watch the rain [...] ver the fence, wander around in the compound [...] s into town without feeling I may get lost. They don't even understand the way I speak English, it is as though I am speaking another language.'

'You are, we all are,' Nirmala said, giggling. 'We don't sound at all like them when we speak English, you must admit.'

'I hope Susheela knows what she is in for. She'll soon find out if she doesn't.'

Many women had contributions to make to this dialogue.

'Everyone has to find out for themselves. Nobody takes it from someone else.'

Susheelamma had obviously put aside her doubts for the day, but she probably knew they would come back in the early hours of the morning. In her heart-of-hearts perhaps she knew the score: she simply could not cope with her bills. However, today she appeared happy and smug; *her* child wanted her and was putting her money where her mouth was. Which is more than could be said about many young people these days.

Raji came in late. 'I had to pick up the children from school before I could come.' She went to Susheela and greeted her. 'You look pretty and happy.' Then she noticed Thankam on the edge of the crowd.

'Talk of pretty, if I didn't know you, I'd say you were in love. I see the trademark *pottu* has returned.'

Thankam apologised for not meeting up with Raji for a long while.

'I'm supposed to be working part-time, but I end up carrying work home too. I don't seem to have too much time to meet anyone.'

'I rang you a couple of times, last week; nobody answered the phone. I assumed you'd gone to Manju's.' Raji was looking away, with that last bit.

Thankam had begun imagining evasion and reproach wherever she looked; she needed a friend who would not be judgemental, but she postponed telling Raji the truth. Instead, she said, 'High time we had a gossip. Why don't we meet for lunch in my house tomorrow?' In her heart Thankam admitted the need to talk to someone about her untidy life and where it was taking her.

Raji, however, was not free the next day. 'I have to stay in tomorrow; the computer man is coming to do some repairs. If you don't mind something basic for lunch we can talk in my place.'

They agreed to meet in Raji's house just after one.

Raji had already fed her children and was waiting for Thankam when she arrived at two in the afternoon, apologising profusely. So they ate first and talked of incidental things during the meal.

'Work seems to suit you,' Raji, said, as she removed the bones from the fried fish on her plate. 'I think you are getting your bounce back; you certainly look good.'

Thankam came straight to the point. 'I came today because there are lots of things I want to talk to you about, though it is quite likely you will disapprove and throw me out when you hear what I have to say. Actually, I don't feel too good about them either.'

Raji looked straight at Thankam.

'This town has no secrets. Maybe I have an inkling of what you are about to say.'

Thankam knew from Raji's face she had heard something.

'Whatever you do or don't do, Thankam, I know you are a good person and my friend. If you have something to say to me, I know you will say it when the time is right.'

'So what have you heard?'

Raji hesitated and then took the plunge. 'They say the widow is having a good time - with her tenant who plays the field anyway.

'Sounds terrible! Is that how it looks to you?' Thankam's hands flew to her mouth as though she had been slapped in her face.

Raji was moving things about on the coffee table as she talked, so Thankam could not see her face properly. Look at me, her heart begged, but no words came out.

'I can't sit on judgement on you, Thankam. You have to live the way you like. But, since you ask - you do realise how vulnerable you are, don't you? I wouldn't be your friend if I did not say that to you. I know he is not married. How long is he going to hang about? Soon his family will arrange a marriage for him, and then what happens to your relationship? Are you confident you can manage when he ups and goes?'

Raji stopped her fiddling with the things on her table and stood still to make her point; Thankam saw pity in her eyes.

'And when he goes, the whispers and laughter won't go away,' Raji continued mercilessly. 'You would have made yourself a laughing stock for silly people like that old woman next door.'

It was an unhappy meal for Thankam, but she knew everything she was hearing was true. So she listened without saying a word.

After that conversation, anything else seemed irrelevant, so she drove home, thinking about her predicament. Many times, she had told herself all these things Raji had said to her, and possibly no one else would, to her face. She had often decided she must put a stop to the affair, but the next time Mohan came round, she wanted his arms round her, she wanted the excitement of his lovemaking.

She also knew something Raji had not thought of mentioning: if Manju and Anil found out about this, they would be ashamed of her. Could she deal with that? Anil was far away, but there'd be enough willing people to inform Manju about her mother's pastimes. How could she risk the alienation of the two persons closest to her?

On Friday, Thankam phoned Manju and invited herself to lunch; it was half-day at the British Council and she would be home early. Thankam wanted to be reassured of her daughter's love.

'This is a pleasant surprise,' Manju exclaimed. 'The mountain visits Mohammed.'

''Well, you hardly get time to come *my* way, so I thought I must try to come here more often. What's the point of driving if I don't get out and see my daughter?'

'I was planning to come during the weekend with the girls, but now you're here...

'*Samosas* for lunch,' Manju said and the two women set about frying them and getting pickles and sauce out to go with it. Manju had already prepared a tomato and cucumber salad.

Thankam ate sparingly; her mind was scurrying about without direction; the resident lump in her throat got harder by the day.

'You are pushing your food around on that plate. What's the matter? Are my samosas not good enough?' Manju teased. Thankam wanted to tell Manju about the monies she had given Mohan, about the relationship and how it had deteriorated, but the words would not push past that lump clogging her throat.

'And you've lost masses of weight; you are not coming down with something, are you?' Manju added. Her concern was obvious.

Thankam's secret sat like an undigested banquet in her body, threatening to nauseate her whenever she thought about it, which was often.

'No, nothing wrong with me but discontent,' she answered with effort. 'But, let's talk about you. How's work, and Gopi and the children?'

'Work is interesting. There might be an opportunity for me to do a three- month course in Library Management in the UK. Dave thinks I should get properly trained and make a career out of it. I don't know whether I can leave the children for that long. And what will my lord and master say?'

Thankam did not like the sound of any of this: Manju was complicating her life further when it was already a mess in some respects.

'You'd be pushing your luck there; Gopi will explode. The children are not a problem for three months; Seetha and I can take care of them, but I'd watch my step with Gopi.'

'The girls would love that - being with you, I mean.

That Dave again, Thankam thought as she drove home after lunch. She pushed the thought away from her mind hoping it would not be significant. She had too many troubles of her own to worry about her daughter's traumas as well.

On Sunday, Thankam was surprised when she realised Mohan was not coming down to spend the day with her. He had not mentioned going to Kottayam; where was he? She always knew if he went out, because her mind would register the sound of his steps on the staircase and the clang of the gates opening, whatever she might be doing at that time. She felt desolate.

Walking round in the garden seemed a good way of spending some surplus time. Who said time could be measured in equal minutes and seconds? Thankam mused. Time is measured in pulses of joy or sorrow, waiting or suffering. How she missed Seetha's happy presence on

Sundays. Mohan had filled that empty space, but today he was not to be seen. She walked under the stairway leading to Mohan's flat and out at the other end; it was a bright day and all the hibiscus bushes were in flower. She picked the yellowing leaves off some of them and looked for worms: none yet, thank God. Her feet went unthinkingly back to the orchids hanging at the back of the stairway. Admit you're being nosey and wanting to know what he is doing, she chastised herself.

The orchids grew in the outer shell of coconuts, roots twisting themselves into the soft fibre. She looked for and found the bunch of big, mauve-tinged, white sprig she had noticed some weeks ago; some of the buds had opened into unbelievably lovely white flowers; the mauve almost indiscernible, but a few blooms had been eaten up by ants and only jagged tufts showed. She could see the ants crawling up and down the stems busily, so she fetched the ant powder from the garage and sprayed at them viciously. As she did so, she heard people talking upstairs. Geetha is back, no wonder Mohan is missing, Thankam thought, momentarily reassured, and took the long route back past her garage into the kitchen.

She put the kettle on and stood near it staring out of the window. As she watched, an auto rickshaw put-putted its way to the front gate and a girl stepped out. A young woman, quite fetching in a rust bandini-printed salwar-kameez, put out one dainty foot and then the other from the auto-rickshaw. Mohan shouted 'Nalini,' and rushed down to her. He darted a quick glance towards the veranda but did not appear to notice Thankam at the kitchen window. Now I am spying on him, she thought miserably.

They unloaded some pots and pans and what appeared to be mats and cushions. The happy excited noises continued as more and more people arrived through the morning. Soon the music started; these were not melodies from yester-year; this was the music to which the young of the town gyrated in private clubs and empty houses when the parents had gone for a holiday. Thankam sat on the veranda listening to the chatter upstairs, feeling alone and older than her years. It occurred to her as she drank her tea on the veranda that it was more appropriate for Mohan to spend time with the young people upstairs than with her middle-aged self. She could see herself in the years ahead sitting on that veranda and drinking tea. It occurred to Thankam she had never heard Mohan laughing and talking as happily as he was doing upstairs with his friends.

In the evening, after the lunch guests had gone, Mohan came downstairs.

'Did you have a good party?' Thankam had not meant to ask, but the question seemed to have a life of its own. In spite of herself a nagging edge had appeared in her tone and she cursed herself.

He was picking thoughtfully at a speck on his T-shirt and when he came near, smelt of lynx after-shave and mutton curry. He abandoned the T- shirt and looked out of the window.

'It was my birthday today. I didn't tell you; indeed, I didn't tell anyone. That lot descended on me without warning,' he answered, clearly wary of Thankam's reaction.

'I never got you a present.' Thankam smiled apologetically.

'You mustn't buy me presents,' he said, almost vehemently, without saying why. He pushed his hair back from his forehead as he always did when he was thinking. Did his friends mock him about the older woman and the expensive presents he might be getting from her? Or was it because he couldn't reciprocate with his unreliable income? Here were things quite beyond her understanding, after twenty-seven years of a secure marriage.

'It is unlucky to ask your age on your birthday, so I won't,' Thankam said, 'and don't ever ask mine,' she added, scratching at the wound.

He came to her and while she poured the milk and stirred the tealeaves; she was excruciatingly aware that he was near her, his fingers playing lightly with the hair at the nape of her neck – this was always a favourite activity of his.

Sometimes she imagined it was calculated to silence all questions on her part.

'There, that looks much nicer.' Mohan had picked up her coil of hair and was holding it up high on her head.

When had she last felt this amazing feeling in every pore of herself? Certainly not with Unni. This upheaval she experienced every time Mohan touched her carelessly, was mortifying and exhilarating at the same time; she knew the guilt would come later.

He was gone as quickly as he came with a smile and a wave. Except the smile was casual, the wave almost a rejection; Thankam felt a sense of anticlimax. She wandered on to the veranda, biting her lips and trying to think coherently of what she must do.

The Onam holidays were around the corner and it was fortunate she had a fair bit to do; Thankam was trying to keep quite a few balls up in the air together. Anil had been asked to extend his stay in London, but would come back at the end of the year. Appuettan was expecting her in Thalassery and she should try to persuade him to come to Kochi instead; she didn't see herself being able to get up and go anywhere just now. If she were honest she would admit she was uneasy about leaving Mohan on his own for a long period; she no longer trusted his attraction for her.

Then again, Seetha's daughter, Preethi, was now definitely getting married and the worry lines on Seetha's face were getting deeper with each day. She must salvage that marriage proposal from lurking disaster or it would die a natural death. How did the husband agree to a dowry of fifteen thousand rupees when he didn't have *one* rupee saved up? She had jewels to buy too. She must also get the Onam gifts of clothes for Seetha, Manju's girls and all her minions, like the boy who collected the garbage, the part-time gardener and the ironing man.

She wanted to organise a trip somewhere with Mohan, some quality time spent together before he disappeared to Kottayam, for a holiday at Onam. It seemed they saw less and less of each other these days; Mohan himself had gradually become more casual with his visits, coming and going as it suited him. He disappeared for days on end to Kottayam, without ringing or making any excuses, his attitude being that no concessions were to be made to this hole-in-the-corner relationship. During those times, Thankam was painfully aware she listened for his footsteps on the stairway and the sound of his keys in his front door.

She realised how ridiculous she was becoming, cooking food for him, when she did not know whether he would turn up that day or not. He was never a great eater and increasingly, he made her feel he was doing her a favour by eating her meals. Seetha also was beginning to ask questions about the food that seemed to vanish overnight from the refrigerator when he *did* eat. Did Manju turn up late in the evening with the children? 'I threw it out, didn't like the look of it,' Thankam would answer. But Seetha never dwelt too long on any one thought and it was easy to be vague and put her off.

The need to spend time with Mohan became so acute in Thankam's mind she began planning ways of going on a holiday with him. As she showed more and more needy, he seemed to withdraw into himself, often giving her the impression this whole thing was getting beyond him. She began to hate his methods of circumventing her demands; some times she hated herself for making them.

'I am going to Guruvayoor, next Monday,' Thankam offered one morning. He did not appear enthusiastic. He used to love going out with her, driving her car and acting protector; why was he so distant now?

'I thought you could drive and we wouldn't need to take a driver,' she added, hoping for some enthusiasm.

'Isn't it easier to go by train; take some of your friends with you?' He sounded blunt, careless.

Thankam knew Mohan was not into pilgrimages, but her desire to be with him made her ask these ridiculous favours.

Eventually he agreed, somewhat ungraciously, she thought. She had imagined she could restore the relationship to its former intimacy by enjoying a day together, away from familiar territory, but in this instance, he obviously was not so keen.

They set out early one Monday morning so as to avoid the commuter traffic to Kochi. Mohan was very quiet. Thankam wondered whether it was having to wake up early that had put him into a miserable mood, and whether the whole trip was going to be like this.

'Did you not have coffee before you started?' she enquired. She had asked him to come down and share coffee and iddli with her, but he had turned that offer down quickly.

'Didn't sleep too well,' he answered with an effort. 'I had a few friends in last night to watch late night cricket, and they didn't leave till two in the morning.'

They stopped at a wayside dabba and had morning tea. They must have been the first customers; the tea was scalding hot and sweet. *Pittu* and dosha would not get going for another hour or two.

Thankam paid for the tea and got back into the car. She had taken to paying for most things when they were together; he never had any money in his pocket. He paid the rent for the flat regularly, first day of each month, but recently, she had got into the habit of doing odd bits of shopping for him. A loaf of bread, bananas, milk … In the beginning he would offer her the money for the shopping and she had waived the small amounts aside, but now that he had ceased to offer, she had begun to notice it. In a corner of her mind, a tiny worm of resentment was beginning to uncoil itself and lift its head. She told herself she was being petty, she could afford these little expenses, but his general moodiness made it worse.

It was as though there had been a significant role reversal in their relationship: in the beginning he was the one always seeking her out, jealous if her family took up a lot of her time; now, she went looking for him. Sometimes, soon after they started sleeping together, he had brought her small gifts, a tin of talcum powder one time, smooth-tipped hairpins another time for her hair. Once he came with an embroidered *chikkan* blouse piece. 'I bought a length for Geetha, so I bought you one as well,' he had said, and she had felt ridiculously happy he had, in some manner, included her in his family.

'Now I just have to find a sari to wear it with,' she had said, smiling.

'When my ship comes home, I shall buy you that sari.'

As the months went by, she became the person buying gifts, spending money, seeking the lover. The respect he had shown her disappeared with familiarity. He kept her waiting, sulked when she said anything about it, and generally punished her if she made any claim on him.

She knew all relationships, even with her own children, were unequal; whoever loved more was the loser in this equation and the old always lost out to the young.

'They have all the cards,' Unni used to say. 'You will never win taking on the children. You always love them more than they love you; they have another future, you are merely their past.' Mohan would disappear for days on end and then turn up suddenly, expecting eager welcome and food. Once she made the mistake of noticing a stain on his shirt collar.

'Needs a good scrub with *Omo*, that collar,' she had said. A huge mistake as it turned out. 'What's stopping you then?' he had quipped. She had been silly enough to wash the collar for him, in her bathroom sink, as she could hardly ask Seetha to do it.

After that, he often left things for her to wash. One day, Seetha came upon her washing his shirt in her bathroom.

'What are you doing, Ammey?' Seetha's eyes appeared to hold not only a question mark, but also compassion. 'Give it here.'

Thankam couldn't look into Seetha's eyes. 'What's the point of me being here, if you do things like this?' Seetha asked, kindly.

She took the shirt away, washed it and hung it out of sight in the spare bedroom. Now Seetha was part of the deception her whole life had become.

Thankam would steel herself to show more self-respect with regard to Mohan, but the joy she felt when Mohan did turn up let her down. He always had a good reason for being away: the boss asked him to go somewhere, Geetha's wedding preparations… He knew exactly what would make her melt towards him; if she tried to keep a distance, he would play with her hair, kiss her ear lobe, draw circles in her palm with his fingers, until she did not have any control over her reactions.

On Monday morning, when she took the Maruthi out, she noticed Mohan waiting at the bus stop. What had happened to his trusted motorbike? She stopped the car and he got in, smiling.

'I've sold the bike and the car is still in Kottayam,' he declared, as he settled his long legs. 'It was becoming expensive to maintain.'

'Are you getting another, then?'

'When I can afford one. Geetha's marriage is going to make me a pauper. I'll have to find a fortune for her jewels and trousseau.' His face did not invite any further questions.

Thankam dropped Mohan off at Jose junction and went to the fish market at Kadavanthara. After that occasion, he would wait at the bus stop every day until she came by. Why make this pretence, she would think; why can't he just get into the car when I start up?

Thankam realised she was beginning to prevaricate a great deal to many people to hide her affair with Mohan; being a naturally honest person this made her acutely uncomfortable. And rumours were beginning to surface like mosquitoes out of the open Kochi drains, but she ducked and dived and held on to Mohan. When she found herself lying to her closest friend, Raji, she realised how far she had travelled down that road of deception.

Raji turned up on Wednesday evening, hoping to drag Thankam off to the Widows' Association. 'Come to the club,' she said. Thankam was sitting on the front steps looking sorry for herself.

'You look depressed, what is the matter?' Raji asked, as she came up the steps to the house. She plonked herself down on the steps alongside her friend.

'I suppose you could say I'm beginning to get disgusted with myself.'

'So what have you done now that you disapprove of?'

'I made up my mind to take myself in hand, cure me of my madness before Anil came back and Manju found out and everyone got humiliated - including myself. But he knows exactly how to play me and I fall for it each time.

'Raji, we've been seeing each other for a year now and he still keeps me rigorously on the other side of the fence. I want to get out of this and I can't see how.'

'Easy. Just ask him to get up and go.'

'There must be a more civilised way than that.'

'Is there ever? We just pretend there is. Wrap it up in silver foil and attach good wishes. But why this sudden angst if it has been going on for a while?'

'I think it has reached a point where he has no respect for me. And I think he is exploiting me in many little ways. I might feel bad for a while, but eventually, it will be a relief not to think about him at all; it's a kind of disease and I must heal myself.'

As she talked she could imagine her life without Mohan: the emptiness, the absence of something to look forward to. What would she put in its place?

'I'll be pleased when that happens,' Raji said fervently. 'I am scared for you; you have to get this sorted out, and soon.'

Thankam was in no mood to go anywhere, so Raji went off to the club as she called it, on her own. Thankam continued to sit on the steps thinking, till her legs went to sleep. When she got up to put the lights on, she was so numb she nearly toppled.

Manju phoned as usual, on a Friday evening. 'How come you are not checking your driving skills out on Chittoor Road?' she asked. 'I was hoping you'd come by; I need to do some early Onam shopping for the minions and for the children. It appears Gopi can't come this year because he has to go to the States for some business for his firm; so you'll have to hold my hand.'

'We could do that any day of the week, after working hours. Why don't you come over next Tuesday, after dropping the children off at school?

'Have you any idea when Anil is coming home?' Manju asked. 'It feels like he's been away a long time. I'm beginning to wonder.'

'Wonder what?'

'There's a girl called Sarah, crops up a lot in his e-mails.'

'He's coming home this Onam for two weeks; we'll soon find out.'

'Ammey, I ran into Mallika recently; she's Saraswathi's niece, if you remember. She said something strange to me. "And who's looking after your mother these days, with you going to work? I hear your mother really needs looking after." I didn't like the sound of it; what on earth did she mean? I didn't like the look on her face either; I felt like taking a swipe at it and wiping off that smirk'

'Can't be worried about every bitchy comment, can we?' Thankam dismissed it, but a fiercely insistent alarm bell started ringing in her mind. Her sins were returning to visit her with a vengeance and she did not know how to dodge.

12

Mohan was not to be seen on Sunday – again. Thankam was dejected as she thought of Sunday as their day together. When evening came round, she decided she was not going to sit waiting for Mohan; instead, she would be adventurous and take the car out to Jew Town. Mattanchery and Jew Town, at the west end of Kochi, seemed far away; she hadn't ever gone that far on her own, but she knew the roads would be comparatively empty. Also, this had been a favourite jaunt of Unni's and hers in the past. When Manju and Anil were small, they would often go there on a Sunday to watch the snake charmer and his basketful of creepies in the open space next to the beach. After that they would drink tender coconuts from the ridiculously expensive stall near it, where it was assumed that everyone who came that way was a foreigner.

      She drove slowly, taking in the sight of families enjoying a day out. Near the Naval Base, the porcelain vendor had all his tall vases and stands arranged on the side of the road. A young couple haggled for what looked like a shallow plant pot; the two little boys with them were pointing to the vases and getting excited.

Immediately after, the huge entrance gates, *Kataribagh* on the left and *Vembanad* on the right, announced the hallowed precincts of the Kochi Naval Base. Armed security men stood guard at the wrought iron gates; however, as she drove past, Thankam was able to sneak a glimpse through the iron bars at the gracious lawns and well-tended gardens inside.

Once on to the old *Thoppumpadi* Bridge, which connected the old and new towns of Kochi, a fleet of naval ships came into view. They flew the orange, white and green Indian pennant with the *Ashok Chakra* in the centre. After that, it was a short distance to the new *Vendurthi* Bridge, with its panoramic view of Kochi, across the waters, apartment buildings and business houses towering in the background above the lush green coconut trees that lined the coast. In the harbour, small boats and trawlers rested after the night's fishing. Thankam drove slowly, in no hurry to reach anywhere.

It was a good twenty minutes' drive through Mattanchery and into Fort Kochi and her favourite street: Church Road. She parked in front of the ancient St. Francis Church and decided to take a look inside, as she had done many times before with Unni. In front of the church, the pavement peddlers had laid out their wares: wood carvings, bronze images and sheaves of greeting cards, with paintings on gauzy, dried banyan leaves, inside.

This was Kochi's tourist land and a few white faces were bargaining for the knick-knacks on sale; one tired looking man, his face burnt the colour of boiled prawns by the Kochi sun, riffled through the cards.

'How much?' he asked.

'A hundred-and-fifty rupees.' The price asked was exactly twice what Thankam usually paid for it.

Inside the church, a guide was disclaiming in English to a group of tourists, sitting in the front pews.

'You can see the old tomb of the Portuguese explorer, Vasco da Gama, on your right, cordoned off with brass rods.' He pointed towards the spot. His voice was fractured by the poor acoustics and the tourists grimaced as they strained to hear him.

'He landed in Kozhikode in North Kerala at the end of the fifteenth century and arrived in Kochi in 1502; he died here on Christmas Eve in 1524. Subsequently, his body was removed to the monastery of Jeronimos in Lisbon. Just behind the church is Vasco House, where he lived, when he came to Kochi.'

She wandered about reading the inscriptions on the plaques, wondering about the men and women who came here to work and died in this distant land, often in the prime of their lives.

Henry Bidewell Grigg, born at Theberton, Suffolk, died in Bolgotty, Kochi, at the age of forty-four, in 1895, his plaque said. What could have killed off that young man? Malaria, plague, snakebite? C I E, M A (Oxon), it was recorded under his name; he had been the Queen's "Resident in Travancore and Cochin and Director of Public Instruction for twelve years in the Madras Presidency." More plaques like his adorned the walls, put up by grieving relatives.

When Thankam walked down towards Bastion Street at the back, she could see that the family who owned the Vasco House now, still lived in it, surrounded by shabby rooming houses and antique shops. This dilapidated building, with its crumbling façade and glass windows from another age, looked as though it could use a lick of paint. Does anyone do anything about preserving this house? she mused.

Thankam returned to the car and drove down the road. Further on, she stopped in front of the tender coconut vendor and bought a coconut; ten rupees was a good price and she did not bother to bargain. He cut the top with a machete and handed it over; it was a long time since she had enjoyed the pleasure of the clear, sweet drink.

'Do you want the flesh inside, madam?' the vendor asked, when she handed the shell back.

'Yes, please.'

The young man broke the coconut in two with a practised swing of the machete and scraped the inside with a small knife, so that the albumen-like flesh could be scooped up and eaten. Thankam took one of the plastic spoons he kept for this purpose, thinking, I must do this again, come here on my own with my thoughts, venture further than the shopping centre in town, so I can feel more confident with my driving.

She always saved the best bit for the last: a walk through the narrow Jew Town Road to the little, white-walled synagogue at the end. Turning into the parking lot, she thought she saw a girl who looked like Manju, getting into a tourist taxi, a swirl of green kameez and *duppatta*, while a young, white man held the door open. By the time Thankam parked the Maruthi and looked for the taxi, they had gone. She decided she must be mistaken; why would Manju be here with a foreigner?

Thankam walked down Jew town Road - or Jew Street, as it was locally known - lined with antique shops and old Jewish houses fronting on to the street. At the back of some of these antique shops, it was said, antiques were being busily manufactured for the gullible tourist.

As she entered the synagogue, Thankam removed her slippers, as required by the instructions on the wall; expensive walking shoes from all over the world mingled here at the door with cheap plastic rainwear from Kochi and leather *chappals* and sandals from all over India.

This, one of the two oldest synagogues in the Commonwealth, was built in 1568; the large murals in the room next to it depicted the history of the Jews in Kerala. Thankam spent some time admiring the murals and reading the story of the Jews in Kochi. Some of them had migrated to Kerala from Palestine when the Romans ransacked the second temple of Palestine in 70 C E.

Sadly the settlement of jews in Kerala was gradually dying out. Few Jewish women were left for the young men in the community to marry and they were moving off, emigrating to the States or to Israel. Soon, not enough Jews would remain in Kochi to carry on the rituals of their festivals.

The older generation hung on to their heritage, taking care of the synagogue, making sure that the blue-and-white Cantonese tiles on the floor of the synagogue, every one of them unique, were cleaned and polished to perfection. Ezekiah Raban, a Jewish merchant, had donated these in 1762. We don't take care of our heritage, Thankam thought again; who will look after this synagogue after this generation? The thought depressed her.

When she got home, she found Seetha had finished up and gone. As she let herself into the empty house, she was assailed with memories of the trips she had made to Fort Kochi and Mattanchery with Unni; he had loved the old part of the town and would spend hours in Spice Street, taking in the pungent smells and looking at the multi-coloured hillocks of turmeric, coriander, chilli powder and other spices on the floors of the shops. However, the street always made her sneeze; she would escape from there as soon as possible.

'What is so entrancing about these heaps of spices?' She is grumbling and bad tempered, after another hour spent, wandering around. The sweat is soaking through into her bra and the urchins following them around are getting on her nerves.

'Can you imagine the trade here long ago?' Unni exclaims. 'All those catamarans and boats bringing men from Arabia and China with their wares: cheenachattis *and silks to sell just to take back all this coloured stuff?'*

'Yes, and the streets are still as narrow as they must have been then and the Corporation does nothing to make this place attractive to visitors. Look at the number of North Indians here, and the back packers. Yet there are no decent, low-priced coffee shops or lunch places, and every year, there are outbreaks of rat-fever and cholera. The drains on the sides of these roads are clogged up and disgusting.'

'Why don't you go and check out that old Jewish embroidery shop, while I walk around here a bit?' This is Unni's gentle way of getting rid of her so he can wander around these streets.

She walks towards the synagogue and does some window-shopping. She covets the exquisite, cut-worked, linen tablecloth that would look ideal for her dinner table, but when she goes inside and asks the price, it is a cool four thousand rupees, more than it takes to feed the two of them for a month. So she buys some organdie runners and handkerchiefs instead.

These will sit around and I won't even use them, they are that dainty; however, I can't resist them, she chides herself. At the end of the road, she walks into the small, almost empty bookshop; there are never more than two or three customers about. She spends a lot of time looking at the books on Kerala art and culture, but buys nothing.

'I knew I'd find you here.' Unni has come looking for her. He glances at the small plastic bag she is carrying. 'Another lot of runners and napkins to fill up our linen cupboard?' he asks indulgently.

'They'll come in handy for gifts. Manju or Anil might want a few too.' He takes the bag from her and they walk back to the parking lot.

'Would be nice to have a cup of tea around here and watch the tourists, but this part of town is so unhygienic.'

When Thankam returned home from an outing she always missed Unni most acutely; it was as though he was at her shoulder, through the front door, asking for attention, prompting her on, but she could not see him or touch him.

Will I ever stop missing you? she said to his benign presence in her mind; she had this habit of talking to him whenever something good or new or even completely puzzling happened.

After walking from room to room aimlessly, Thankam gravitated to the phone. When she got through to Anil, he sounded busy.

'I just wanted to hear your voice,' she said.

'Mother, you sound really sad. Please don't be. I am in the middle of a meeting; it's afternoon here. I'll call you as soon as I get home. Meanwhile, why don't you ask Manju to come around?'

Late in the evening, Thankam rang up Manju; she needed someone to talk to, to get rid of the blues. However, no one answered; the ring tones sounded desolate in the empty house. The answering machine clicked on after the tenth ring, '...please leave your message after the beep.' How she hated the blasted things!

It's only me,' Thankam spoke awkwardly, always a little tentative with answering machines. 'Nothing special to say, just...'

When she walked into the kitchen, she noticed Seetha had left iddli and coconut chutney for her supper. She looked at the food without feeling any inclination to eat. Now that she ate alone she ate less and less, and sometimes not at all; it did wonders for her figure, but nothing for her morale.

Late, in the night, Manju returned her call.

'I was out all day today. Just got back.' She did not volunteer where she had been.

'Took the children with you, no doubt; I assumed you had gone with them somewhere when no one picked up the phone.' Thankam did not mention her desperate need to make contact with some one she loved, to fill the emptiness within her.

'No, they spent the day with a friend; I picked them up just now, on my way back.'

'You know, I thought I saw you near Spice Street. Wasn't you of course. There was a young white man with that girl.'

'I *was* in Spice Road today, actually. Took Dave to the synagogue; he wanted to see the place and buy some knick-knacks for gifts to take home when he goes on leave. It could have been us.'

'What did he buy?'

'Carvings and things. I told him they were much cheaper at Gift House or the Northern Emporium in town, but he insisted he had to buy them then and there. Tried to buy me a Pashmina shawl, but I wouldn't let him.'

After the call, Thankam went out to the verandah and sat there a long time, in the dark, her mind going round and round in circles.

When Manju arrived the next day, Thankam had this peculiar feeing that her daughter had something to say, and would not be comfortable until she said it. Nothing unusual about that, Thankam thought; Manju was uneasy if she had a secret in her head and she had not been totally honest with her mother. Thankam remembered the time Manju had come home from college in Madras for Christmas one time and announced she had something to tell her mother; it had to be prised out of her in agonising bits.

'You're going to shout at me, I know. I wanted to tell you something for a long time now, but you will be really annoyed, and I'm afraid.' Manju is asking to be let off lightly before Thankam knows what she has done, so Thankam stands her ground.

'I don't know how annoyed I'll be without your telling me what I am supposed to be not annoyed about.'

'You'll really hit the roof, I know.' Manju is still playing for time, angling to be treated gently, but Thankam will not make any concessions yet.

'You'll have to tell me if you want to know how I feel. You haven't been going out with boys, have you?'

'Nothing like that, you know me. When have I ever shown an interest in boys?'

This is true; Manju has been remarkably uninterested in romance up to now.

Finally, it comes out: 'I started smoking, but before you explode, I have stopped now. It was long ago.' Long ago, for her, was six months.

Thankam shouts at her as expected. 'I can't believe how stupid you are; can't you see the gigantic health-risk you are taking! You of all people should know how your father has been suffering with his smoking.

'And I think my children are reasonably intelligent. You simply do not know how to say, "No" when your friends put pressure on you.'

'I knew you'd react like this,' Manju whimpers. She had expected to buy grace by volunteering the information, and by doing so only after she stopped smoking.

Thankam is so enraged she cannot stop herself from berating Manju. 'Wait till I tell Anil this.'

'If you tell Anil, I won't feel able to tell you anything in the future.'

Now this is a serious threat, so Thankam quickly backs off. Manju has this exquisite skill of putting her mother on the defensive when she has misbehaved. This never fails to amaze the whole family, but it always ends like this, unsatisfactorily, with Thankam feeling she has been too hard on the girl.

'So what's with you today? I hardly get to talk to you these days,' Thankam remarks a little later. 'When you come during the morning, I know you are in a hurry and there won't be time to relax.'

'I've been quite busy with work. No time for anything after ferrying the children up and down and doing all the paperwork I take home from the office. 'What's Gopi going to say to all this?' Thankam has this sense of impending conflict. And Manju's conflicts had a way of devastating all round her for some time afterwards.

'Ammey, things are getting too messy in my life. There is Gopi and this driver; I never know what to think of those two. I think they meet up when Gopi is in town even if he doesn't come to the house.'

'What for?'

'You tell me. I am beginning to wonder whether Gopi is into men or something. He is certainly not interested in me any more.

'He hardly bothers to come near me when he is here. You'd think, after months of celibacy a man would want his wife. Recently, he buries himself in his laptop and the rest of the time he is watching TV.

'I'm wondering whether the drugs story was just something to put me off.'

'You better not mention this to *anyone*. Give it a little time and see what happens; I still hope there is nothing in what you are saying. If this town gets a whiff of scandal like that it will be buzzing along wires from here to the Himalayas in no time at all. Do you know, most people here pretend there are no bisexual people at all India? It's meant to be a totally foreign aberration. Idiots!'

'Don't you think this going to Dubai has pretty well destroyed my marriage?' She sounded bitter.

'You're not helping either, if you are seen about town with other men.'

As soon as she said this Thankam realised she was being hypocritical.

'That's not fair. I don't make a habit going out with men, do I?'

'All I'm saying is, be a little circumspect. This community will turn on you if you don't watch out.'

'The community is too busy looking at you and making up stories to bother with me.' It came out without forethought and then Manju gasped as she realised what she had said.

'And what are they saying?'

'Your friendship with the tenant is the story,' Manju said, looking penitent. 'Please forget it. I wanted to ask you something; that is why I came today.'

Here it comes, thought Thankam, and now I'll have to dig it out of her and apologise for it. She pretended she was not eager to hear.

Yes?'

'This Dave; I have been seeing a lot of him, really.'

Thankam kept quiet.

'He treats me well, like I count. I know you are going to hear sooner or later and I'd rather you heard it from me.'

'Hear what?' Thankam had a premonition of disaster.

'I think we want to be together. Dave wants me to leave Gopi and go with him.'

'Dave, Dave, you say. You've mentioned him before. He works with you, doesn't he? Is he not married?'

'Divorced, I think. He doesn't talk too much about that.'

'And the children?'

'He wants me to take the children too, get a divorce from Gopi.'

'What do *you* think? He's a Westerner; it's very easy for *him*.'

'I don't know, Ammey. I am confused; I come here and you confuse me more.'

There you go, thought Thankam; she's got me on the defensive again. So she went for the jugular. 'Have you been sleeping with him?'

'No. But I've thought about it. I'm not yet thirty and my husband is not with me, he is not interested in me; he acts like a stranger most of the time.'

'How does going off with some foreigner help?'

'I don't think of Dave as a foreigner; he's just - Dave, I guess. He cares for me, has time to listen to me; he wants to spend time with me. I simply don't know what is best.'

'If you go with him, you are burning your bridges here; no one will blame Gopi for anything; it's you they'll crucify. If it turns out there is a problem with Gopi, you should talk to him first, see what can be sorted out. Don't act precipitately.

'You are not a free agent when you have two little girls to think about.'

'I know. The other day, Dave came home to collect some papers; he didn't even come in to the sitting room. Asha took one look at him and burst into tears; she has never seen a blond white man before. And Latha hid in her bedroom until she was sure he had gone.' Manju laughed a little ruefully.

'Now you've told me this, you have given me something to worry about. All my petty problems have vanished from my head. How many others know about this?'

'Not too many, but the office people know, or guess, I'm sure. Dave comes to Kochi a lot recently. This kind of thing is hard to hide; I don't think he makes a great effort either.'

Manju got up to leave. 'Go carefully,' Thankam said, 'and don't do anything rash.'

Manju came over and hugged Thankam, 'All my life I have been a problem daughter and now I am one again. And you've always been there for me. What do I ever do for you?'

'Oh, I'm sure you'll get your chance one of these days. Never a dull moment with you, but this, what you have said to me today, is in another league altogether. I must admit I am petrified for you.'

13

Thankam walked into Meena's tearoom to buy some cakes for Raji who was coming for a visit in the evening. As she entered, she saw Mohan with a group of his friends, all young, nubile girls, probably from his workplace. The only other person with them was another man, slightly older than the group. The morning's shopping was at their feet in plastic bags and they were halfway through their cokes. The girls were talking excitedly and their laughter rose above the murmur of the crowd.

Snippets of their happy small talk reached her over the din of cups and cutlery. 'That last film of Dhanraj was a flop; I went last week. The same old formula again: Rich man loves poor girl, family objects etc. Wish they'd address more immediate problems.' She had the tone of someone who had got used to being listened to.

Thankam cursed her luck for walking into this room just then. It was too late to make a quick exit.

'Like what?' This was Mohan responding to the young girl. Clearly he had not noticed Thankam yet.

'Like, I could do with another piece of chocolate cake,' the girl turned the full battery of her young gaze upon him. She was a pert looking creature with a short bob and a much-practised pout.

'All right,' he said and got up, pushing back the plastic chair as he did. He glanced at all the others questioningly. The older man shook his head, but all the girls decided they wanted more cake. He took his wallet out from his trouser pocket and that's when he saw her.

She could see the indecision on his face: should I, should I not? Thankam hesitated and looked around her. It was close to Onam and all the youth of Kochi seemed to have congregated there, sipping cokes. Obviously this was the place to chill out.

Thankam walked towards the group, smiling.

'My landlady,' Mohan said, briefly, reluctantly, not bothering to look up.

'The name is Thankam,' she volunteered, as Mohan did not appear to think of mentioning her name. The noise and banter had come to a full stop as they waited for her to move on.

She had a moment to look at the people in front of her – a moment in which time stood still and shut the rest of the world out. The girl was pretty in that new in-your-face sort of way. Long silver earrings touched the collar of her pale blue T-shirt. A face devoid of makeup – a face that did not need makeup. And then it struck Thankam – the T-shirt was one she had given Mohan some months ago. So this is where it ended.

All of them had their gazes fixed on Thankam, except Mohan, who was still fiddling with his wallet. 'Must buy some cakes,' she added unnecessarily, trying to escape, while the chatter picked up again, where it had left off. Thankam took a few steps away from the group, then turned back deliberately, stopping that chatter again.

'Lovely T-shirt,' she called out to the girl. 'Looks great on you.'

She left the cafeteria section and walked across to the counter where the cakes and sweets were displayed. Her mouth felt dry; all she wanted was to finish her business and get out of there. For a brief moment, she could not remember exactly what she had intended to buy. A hard coil of anger unfurled itself in her mind making her momentarily blind.

The girl at the counter stared at her impatiently, slicer poised to cut the cake.

'Which one, Madam, and how much?'

Thankam concentrated on the cake counter with an effort.

'Five slices of the chocolate cake, with the almond icing, please,' she finally brought out. 'Five small slices.' The girl cut the cake, weighed and passed it on to her colleague to wrap up. 'Please pay at the counter and collect,' she added. Thankam did so, then hurried out of the shop, studiously avoiding looking in the direction of Mohan and his friends.

When she reached her car, she realised she had not felt this dysfunctional for a very long time. Both my mind and my body are clumsy, she thought. It is as though they have slowed down and cannot manage the simple act of getting into the car. She threw the parcel into the back seat and crawled in to drive home.

Raji came at five; both Ramu and Shija, it appeared, had gone for break dancing practice at the school and need not be picked up till nine.

'I'm all yours,' Raji said, walking in with a huge, happy smile on her face. 'What kind of mischief have you planned for us?'

Then she noticed Thankam's face. 'Don't tell me you are in one of your moods. What's he been up to now? Since that man came into your life, you have never had a really peaceful day; it's all ups and downs. And for what?'

'No, don't tell me,' Thankam said quickly, 'and he makes even that look like a favour to me.'

Raji stared hard at Thankam. 'You and I need to have a long talk; so let's ask Seetha to make a huge pot of tea and you can do one of two things: you can cry on my shoulder and I'll do my best, or - and this is what I would prefer - we could have an honest discussion about where all this is going and why, and we come to some difficult decisions.'

'I don't feel like crying; what I feel is furious, mostly at myself.'

However, Thankam's face slackened and collapsed into age, almost as though hope had left her.

'That's excellent,' Raji answered. 'Now I know we can get somewhere. Nothing like a good bout of honest-to-goodness rage to fuel the mind.'

'I feel I've reached an all-time low with my self-respect, and that's what disgusts me about myself.'

Thankam's voice no longer held its usual bounce and optimism.

'Hey, hold on. We are all allowed to make a few big mistakes in our lives.'

'What's yours then?' Thankam smiled at last.

'Ask me when you have an hour or two to spare.'

She makes me feel normal, no more, no less, which is what I need, Thankam thought.

'I'm so glad you came. You shall have chocolate cake for being such a loyal friend.' Thankam smiled but it needed an effort.

Seetha brought out the tea then and Raji addressed herself to the cake.

'Mmm,' she muttered, 'melts in the mouth. Perfect for tea. Where did you get this from?'

'Meena's Tearoom. And guess who I walked into there?'

'Our Don Juan, no doubt, with his usual bevy.'

'Usual bevy?'

'He's always got this girl with him, trendy looking teenager, shortish bob, henna highlights and a headful of air. I see them in town sometimes when I drive the children about. There's generally an older man with them, spectacled guy, with another girl.'

'Why didn't you tell me all this, Raji? I walked into all of them today.'

'I didn't think you were ready to hear it; you are today. And he's nothing special, Thankam; there are a great many lounge lizards in Kochi: manipulative men who don't do much by way of work and live off various women: sisters, mothers, girlfriends…'

'I see. Except this one's got it made. It's really my fault. Recently, whenever he took his purse out to pay for anything, I used to feel bad, because his business is doing badly; now he doesn't bother. The only thing he pays for is his flat; he generally pays the rent every first of the month, on the dot. And then I go and buy him expensive gifts – such as T-shirts to give his girl friends.'

'You haven't!'

'I told you; I've been every different kind of old fool you can think of. And today, he didn't want to acknowledge me when he saw me, but I went up and greeted them. I felt about thumbnail high, after I left them.'

'The question is: what do you intend to do about all this?' Raji looked hard at Thankam as she spoke. 'He'll come round again with his soft words and probably even softer touch and if you don't know how you are going to respond, you'll be lost again.'

'For a well-behaved Malayalee lady you seem to know an awful lot about all this.' Thankam was trying to avoid saying anything definite about what she intended to do.

Raji finished the last of her tea and gazed longingly at the one remaining slice of cake.

'Go ahead, finish it off,' Thankam encouraged her. 'I have no stomach for cake today. If I was a drinking person, I guess I'd be going for a stiff whisky.'

Raji seemed to be contemplating strategy. She searched for cake-crumbs in the gathers of her sari and dusted them off.

'You don't want to end up in recriminations; that is untidy and undignified. And if you are anything, you are a dignified person.'

'Still?' Thankam laughed, disagreeing, but the laughter did not reach her eyes.

Raji ignored the interruption. 'So you've got to make sure you don't let him get near you; that's the first given. Then, you need to find some hidey-holes. A day with me, a day with Manju and so on; don't wait here like a sitting duck. After that, you could go away for a few days if possible and let him stew in his own juice. When you come back you can give him his marching orders.'

'Marching as in out of the apartment?'

'That's the general idea,' Raji said firmly. 'You can't have him up there and forget about him.

'He's bad news in the long run, Thankam, admit it. Anil is coming back for a few days soon, you said; what if he gets to know all this? And then there is Manju and her in-laws. No, you want this behind you as soon as possible.

'Now if he is a caring and loyal man that is another matter. But you say he is unpredictable and makes you feel small quite frequently. Why give someone a stick to beat you with, as my mother used to say?'

Thankam sighed. 'You make sense; I want to get rid of this cloud hanging over me. However, he wasn't always like this. I think I might take you up on that offer to spend a day with you sometime.'

'Now I must go and do some late shopping before I pick up the children. Don't let this get you down too much,' Raji said as she left with a wave and a smile.

Where did the good times go? Thankam agonised. Was this relationship always doomed? Perhaps a relationship always needs a setting to flourish: the regard of other people, like the grass around the flowerbeds. And we couldn't have that; it always had to be clandestine

Thankam did not see Mohan at all for two days. In the evenings, she furiously chopped the heads off the cannas that had finished flowering and took the dead leaves to the compost bin at the back. She weeded the ixora beds and trimmed the yellow duranda borders that were getting out of hand after the monsoon. Then she collected some long-stemmed bird - of - paradise blooms for the tall vases in the living room and arranged them lovingly.

When she looked around, she realised she still had much to catch up on inside the house. She'd run out of *Dhara* for the brass; so she rushed out to Gift House and bought a few cans. When Moli, the outside maid, had finished her sweeping and swabbing for the day, Thankam sat down with her on the dining room rug and polished most of the brass. After that, she opened her corner cabinet and rearranged her Ganeshans. 'You are supposed to look after me; look at the way I care for you,' she said to the small ivory one, as she cleaned it gently with soft rags. 'You didn't do much of a job, did you?'

Moli had a good giggle at her mistress talking to the statues.

The frenzy of domestic activity tired her out early in the evening; so she went to bed with a book at ten, after listening to Star News. But before she switched off the lights she bolted the door to Mohan's apartment from her side; she found something final about the act, which was deeply satisfactory.

Thankam guessed Mohan was embarrassed at the way things had been going between them recently, particularly the sorry scene at Meena's, so she knew he would take a few days to summon up the courage to show his face.

He finally turned up two days later, by which time Thankam's white-hot anger had evaporated. Her resolve to end the relationship, however, stayed strong.

He walked in through the front door while she was sitting at the dining table looking at some bills.

'I went to Kottayam for a few days,' he said hesitantly. 'Lots to do for Geetha's wedding.' Thankam knew this already; Inji was around these days and when he greeted Thankam by sniffing her face, his breath stank of the dry fish Seetha fed him. When Mohan was upstairs, Inji would flick his tail disdainfully at Seetha's food and go upstairs for the titbits Mohan kept for him.

'You're back then. How is it going?'

'Getting there slowly. There's no dowry, thank God. But the jewels will cost a fortune. And of course, once she's taken them off after the wedding day, they'll sit in some bank vault. Such a waste of money.'

Mohan seemed to gain confidence as he talked; perhaps he had expected her to be confrontational. But Thankam was determined no drama would be attached to this breaking up.

'Yes, I haven't seen Manju wearing any of her wedding jewellery either for years; she's into beads and baubles most of the time.'

'Once she is married and gone, I have to think of what to do with myself. It was useful for me to be here when she said she was going to college in Kochi, but that was short-lived.'

This was a topic Mohan raised periodically when anything threatened his mental equilibrium: this, 'where shall I go, what can I do?' thing. Thankam had learned to ignore it over a period of time, as it was often a warning to her not to get too close.

She got up from the dining chair and walked to the veranda; Mohan followed her. Sitting down on the ledge, she looked squarely at him. 'Sit down,' she said. Thankam knew she was about to do something irrevocable, so she steeled herself to continue.

'I don't know what you intend to do, but one thing is obvious: we have come to the end of the road for the two of us. Don't you think so?'

Mohan did not try to deny that. 'About the other day at Meena's,' he said, 'I was with my boss and I didn't know what to do.' He seemed acutely uncomfortable.

'No, Mohan, you did not want me anywhere near there for some reason; I haven't figured out why and I don't care. Do we ever have a happy, uncomplicated day together, as we used to, anymore? We are on our guard with each other. It's all got too messy and I don't believe in untidiness.

'According to society I am that wretched person - a widow - and you are the covetable object: a single man. Let's look at that equation; in the long run it is a lose-lose situation for me.

'Also, we are getting talked about. Which would matter less if there was any real affection between us. There isn't these days.'

'That isn't true,' Mohan started to say, but Thankam went on as though he had not spoken. She needed to get through this without any stutters.

'What people will say is, I am buying it, from my captive tenant. I used to think I wouldn't care what people said, but I do, because it will hurt my son and daughter. And they will despise me.

'You see, without them I am nothing; even you must see that.'

Thankam thought about the time two years ago when they had first started seeing each other. 'We've never been a unit, ever,' she continued. 'Maybe there was a chance at the beginning, but it got lost on the way.

'Now don't get me wrong; my ambition is to grow old as disgracefully as possible, but this, you and I, it feels all wrong now.'

Mohan listened without saying a word till she came to a full stop.

'We had some good times together; that must mean something,' he ventured, half-heartedly.

'It does - and I hope, for that reason, we can be friends.'

'I'm sorry to hear we are getting talked about.'

'Inevitable in a town like this; I'll have to weather that one. But the sooner you can move out and have a life of your own the better. Please try to find somewhere to live. And let me know how I can help.' She smiled.

There, it was done now.

When Mohan had left, Thankam felt a sense of anticlimax; it had been easier than she expected. He had not come near her or tried to touch her; she was glad of that – or was she? She had not been sure whether she would be able to withstand the magic of his touch. Being out in the veranda had proved a good ploy. But as he left, her eyes followed him. She was going to miss him dreadfully.

Appu had come down to Thalassery for Onam and it would be fun to be there with him for a little while; Thankam started making plans for a trip. Anything to erase Mohan from her wayward mind.

She phoned Manju the next day. 'How about you and I take the children and go off to Thalassery for a little while? A week or so? I need a break from this place and some thinking time. So do you. Also Appuettan is home and I must see him.'

'I've got some things to sort out, Ammey. Maybe I will go with you, but I'm not sure yet. I'd love to see Appu *Ammaman* too. But shouldn't we wait till Anil has come and gone?'

Thankam sat on the veranda and thought of her time with Mohan and knew she had never really talked to him till today; it had always been a physical relationship. But she knew he had a kind heart except when he felt threatened in some way; how did she manage to make him feel he needed to ward her off? Perhaps it was this girl Beena he was after. Inji was going to miss him when he went; he had got into the habit of going to Mohan's house frequently to sleep on his bed.

I mustn't forget all the good things, Thankam reminded herself: motorbike rides and cinemas with Geetha and him and *thattukada* snacks late at night. I have learned a lot about myself in the last few months, and about love too.

Love is what Unni and I had and it never dies; it is like the theme of a story, threaded through my life. I always have that to fall back on.

I was a virgin when I married him, a little scared of things to come. I don't think I was his first woman either; I suspect there was an English girl from his student days in London. He didn't say much about it, but I think he loved her too. He had a lot of love in him; some men seem to have too much. Others appear to suffer from a kind of congenital deficiency; maybe some women are like that as well. I have been lucky: I adored my husband and he had so much tenderness for me.

When Thankam marries Unni they are practically strangers. Madhavi, her mother, has instructed Thankam on what would be expected of her in her husband's home: 'You must get up at the same time as your mother-in-law and be bathed and dressed to help her with the early morning chores in the kitchen. Take coffee or tea to the men; it is not seemly to lie in bed late.'

The first morning Thankam wakes up in Unni's house, she creeps out of the room early when Unni is still fast asleep, hugging his pillow. She collects a change of clothes from her suitcase on the floor and makes her sleepy way to the bathroom downstairs. Meenakshi is already halfway through her morning ablutions by this time.

She looks around the unfamiliar kitchen and wonders what she should do. She rakes the fireplace and removes the dead ash to prepare the wood fire. The ash, she knows, will not be wasted in a farming household; it will be used for manure for the coconut trees.

Soon Meenakshi is with her.

'You can have your bath now,' she says. 'The coffee will be ready by the time you come out of the bathroom.'

When Thankam comes to the kitchen after her bath, she has wound a thorthu *round her damp hair, it will take ages to dry. The kitchen smells of burning firewood, coffee and dosha sizzling in hot gingelly oil. A growing pile of doshas is heaped next to the hearth on a stainless steel platter.*

'Shall I do the dosha for you?' Thankam asks, tentatively.

'No,' Meenakshi says. 'The first thing we do is have a cup of coffee together. I have hardly had a chance to talk to you since you came yesterday.'

She spreads another lot of dough on the flat dosha-pan and comes over to talk to Thankam.

'Are you all right? If there is anything special you need you must tell me. It must be hard for you to come from town and live in a rural house like this.'

To Thankam, it seems the old lady is genuinely happy to have a young woman around. When they have both finished their drinks Meenakshi gives Unni's cup of coffee to Thankam.

'Here, go and wake him up. He will sleep the whole morning away if you don't.' Meenakshi is obviously trying to give the newly-weds an excuse to be together now and then.

So Thankam carries the coffee upstairs. The fresh smell of new-brewed coffee wakes Unni up and he sits up in bed a little blearily.

'I'm not a happy sight at this time of the morning.' He smiles, testing his stubble with his fingers.

'Have you had your coffee?'

'I drank mine with Amma,' Thankam answers. He has a child's happy smile, as though the world has always been kind to him, she thinks. They have a long way to go before they really knew each other, but she is grateful for the morning smile

'Well, in that case, come and sit by me and tell me what else you have been up to while I have been fast asleep. You two women are ganging up on me, I think.'

Thankam sits down on the bed near him; he put his hand out and touches her hair. His touch is casual, friendly and without any nuances. 'Still wet from the bath, I can see. How long does that take to dry?'

'Ages. I'll dry it when breakfast time is past.' Thankam removes the thorthu and lets it down. It falls down in a swirly, heavy mass that gives off a whiff of coconut oil and channa powder.

'There is such a lot of it. Like black silk. I think I shall get a hair fetish soon.' Unni sounds as though he is looking forward to that.

That evening, when they finish their duty-visits, he takes her to the riverside. A small boat, with the paddle still in it, is tethered to a tree on the bank.

'This boat belongs to Madhappan, the local fisherman; it is always here in the evenings. We often use it to go across.'

Unni takes Thankam across to the opposite bank. The boat sits low in the water and Thankam trails her fingers in it. The water lilies have closed their blue and maroon blooms for the evening and the Anthoni hill is beginning to turn purple in the failing light. She can hear the distant, muted voices of mothers calling children home from play. Pie dogs bark half-heartedly, hurrying the sedate cows into their sheds for the night.

By the time they get home, Meenakshi has lighted the nilavilakku *and is in her place on the footstool, next to Raghavan Nair's chair, pounding his pan. Thankam is surprised at how easily she has been absorbed into this household.*

'I want to show you my favourite place in the small maidanam,*' Unni announces another day; it is his way of finding time for themselves. He finishes their obligatory visits early in the evening and takes her to the bus stop at the end of the village.*

The town bus takes them to the Civil Courts stop where they get off. The maidanam is empty when they cross over to it; the stray goats are still trailing their ropes, waiting to be shepherded to their homes. The cement benches are hot from the day's heat and the smell of human excrement rises in a fetid steam. Piles of dried-up shit can be seen below the seats, testimony to the absence of latrines in the huts that ring the seashore, towards the north.

'The rocks are not much better,' Unni says to Thankam. 'But, I have my special rock which no one uses for this purpose. It is hard to get down to, but once we get there, it is squeaky clean. Possibly because they'd get doused in salt spray if they squat there for any length of time.'

Unni guides Thankam to the southern end and helps her down to the end of the little promontory, shaped like the snout of a hippopotamus.

'I call it my Hippo-corner,' he says. 'Soon the sea will eat this bit too.' They sit on the flat stony ledge for a long time. From there they can see the big maidanam and the remnants of Tippu Sultan's old fort, a long way away, across the waters. Behind are the Catholic Boys' School Appu had attended as well as their church and cemetery.

The waves beat relentlessly on the rocks below, churning up the waters and blowing salty spray into their faces. When they recede, the blue shine of mussel and green, drifting tufts of seaweed near them become visible.

An immeasurable distance away, the sun slides slowly into the waters, leaving an ominously glistening swathe of darkness, where there had been shimmering oranges and pinks a moment ago. Unni puts his arm round his wife and hugs her companionably; Thankam can see he is suffused with joy. She settles herself into the contours of his body trustingly and looks out to the horizon, so far away it makes most human concerns seem minuscule.

That night, for the first time, they make love.

14

Thankam went into town to look at the festive Onam shops and buy odds and ends for the household. It was a Saturday and perhaps not the best time to go out, because there were only nine days left to Onam and the streets were jam-packed with shoppers eager to part with their money.

She looked at saris in the Style Centre; Manju needed cheering up and a wastefully expensive garment, which she couldn't wear for more than one occasion in the year, would definitely lift her spirits. Inside the special hall for pure silk saris, even standing room was hard to find, let alone counter space; obviously Kerala had decided to push the *vallom* fully out for the clothes festival of the year. So Thankam stood back a little and watched the others at the counter.

A wedding group was taking its time, choosing the wedding sari for a young bride; her family and her bridegroom's family had congregated in force for this major buy. The girl was tiny, hardly five foot tall and Thankam looked on in disbelief as they got the salesman to pull out saris with more than six inches of gold work on both borders. The men displayed each sari by gathering the dazzling pallav and draping it on themselves exactly as it would look when worn. Sometimes the women insisted on seeing the colour in daylight; then the men folded up the sari in question and went to the window to show it in true light. The salesmen and women worked with infinite patience, pulling out heaps of saris to satisfy the customers. When the customer had rejected a sari, it remained splayed out on the counter; soon the counter was a potpourri of purples, reds and greens, with splashes of gold in between.

The girl would be lost in the heavily bordered ones, she was so petite, but she did not seem to have too much of a say; the bridegroom's sisters rejected one sari after another saying it looked too cheap or the colour wouldn't suit her. Thankam edged a little closer to see what too cheap was and found it was twelve thousand rupees: Seetha's wages for eight months. Suddenly she couldn't bear to be there, so she left the section and went down one flight of steps where daywear was sold. She bought two nylon saris for Seetha and blouse material and sari skirts to match. For Moli she got material to be made up into long skirts and blouses, which were her preferred costume.

Thankam made up her mind she was not going to buy another rich sari to languish in her daughter's wardrobe, so she went to Laila's Ready-mades instead and looked through the salwar-kameez outfits, which she knew would get worn. She bought three sets that Manju might like for office wear.

After that, she looked at the children's garments; she picked out two cotton dresses for her grandchildren. Then she decided to go to Ramanathan's Sweets to get some Onam goodies for them. As she stood at the counter waiting to be served, she watched the people coming in; some conspicuous consumers were in such a hurry they did not even check the prices before they ordered the goods. One huge, bespectacled man towered over all the others at the counter, his stomach spilling to all sides of his waistline and on to the counter on which he was leaning; clearly he was a frequent customer here.

'Can you make up the fifteen packets while I go next door to the post office and return?' he asked. He gave a list for each packet: a kilo of *sone pappadi*, half a kilo of *badam halwa*, a kilo of yellow *jilebis* and ten *ladoos* in each packet.

The shop hands were more than willing; they set about organising the green gift boxes and measuring out the sweets.

Thankam meanwhile moved to the counter and asked for her meagre order of eight ladoos and eight orange jilebis. After the previous customer, the counter hands were clearly happy to handle a simple order. 'I'll have tea at the cafeteria while you make up the order,' she said, as she moved towards the café on the premises; she had spotted an old friend, Devaki, with her three grandchildren. They were all busy licking their ice cream cones.

Thankam walked up and greeted Devaki. 'Haven't seen you in ages,' she said. 'Nice to run into you like this. Do you come here often?'

'Not really,' she said. 'I'm looking after Rekha's brood, as you can see.' The children greeted Thankam enthusiastically; she had often babysat for their mother when she went out of an evening. Thankam was good at making up stories and some of her friends took advantage of her single status to meet their babysitting needs. Recently, however she had been too enmeshed with Mohan to do any such favours for her friends.

'Auntie, tell us the story of the motor car with three wheels,' they cajoled.

'Did Rotor get better?'

This was a story she had made up for them a long time ago; it featured a courageous motorcar called Rotor, which lost a wheel, and how it managed to get over this handicap.

'Didn't I tell you? He learned to run on three wheels, and he could go faster than anything with four wheels,' Thankam answered.

'She turned to Devaki, 'I've been quite busy with-'

'Yes, I've been hearing about how busy you are.' Was there a nasty edge to that comment? Devaki busied herself with her ice cream and did not ask Thankam to join them.

'I've started working part-time,' Thankam added.

'Yes, of course.' Devaki did not bother to ask where she was working; she was not meeting Thankam's eye either.

She asked the children to gather their things together and left hurriedly. Am I seeing snakes in every string? Thankam asked herself, as she walked back to the counter. The joy had gone out of the day's shopping, leaving a sour taste in her mouth. She felt snubbed comprehensively by Devaki's behaviour? As if there was this magic circle from which she was now excluded?

Thankam reached home to find the inhabitants of the entire lane at the entrance of Graciamma's house. An ambulance was wedged into the side of the empty road and four men were manhandling a stretcher towards it. Seetha had climbed up on a tree stump to get a better view and was in serious danger of toppling into the open drain next to it.

'What happened, Seetha?' Thankam asked.

'It's Graciamma. When the nurse came to bathe her, apparently she found her unconscious. They say she is in a comel.'

'What? Oh yes. Thankam interpreted Seetha's attempt at "coma" accurately.

'Is her daughter not here?' she asked.

'They've phoned her and she's on her way, I hear. Meanwhile they are taking her to the hospital. Two men tried to lift the stretcher and they couldn't; they had to call two more.'

Poor old woman, Thankam thought. Now the neighbours collect to see her carried out, but we never had time for her when she was in that chair. She antagonised everyone in the lane with her gossip and her prying, but what else could she do?

Thankam went home and Seetha followed. Devaki's behaviour had sickened Thankam and now this; she refused lunch and asked for a cold drink. Seetha must have guessed something was wrong, so she hurried in and squeezed some limes into a glass. She added cold water and dropped some ice cubes in them. When she came out, she saw Thankam staring into space and something suspiciously like tears glistened in her eyes, but she kept her face averted.

'Why are you feeling bad for that diabetic old woman? It was just a matter of time before her illness brought her to this point.'

'I am not feeling bad for her,' Thankam said, tears really flowing now. 'I don't know for whom I am feeling this way, Seetha. For me, for her, for everyone, I simply don't know.'

Seetha knew her Amma too well to let that go without comment. 'Did someone treat you badly? What is it, Ammey? You are not one to get upset so easily.'

'That's what I thought,' Thankam said standing up. Thankam looked deflated, as though all the bounce and energy had drained out of her. Today she showed her age.' I am going to lie down for a bit,' she told Seetha as she left the room.

Thankam woke up at dusk; she had slept through the afternoon and early evening. She knew Seetha would have left supper for her and hunger was catching up with her, so she went into the kitchen. What she found was Seetha busy making doshas and *aloo masala.*

'I thought you would have gone home by now, Seetha; it is late.'

'I decided to sleep here tonight, it seemed a good idea.'

'It is a very good idea, but what will your husband and children say?'

'I was going to ask you, Ammey. Can you phone the small shop near my house to tell them I am staying here tonight? They'll take a message to my children.'

Seetha fetched a biro from the living room and wrote down the number for Thankam laboriously, on the back of an empty paper bag. Her writing skills must have died of attrition long ago.

Thankam called the shop, gave the message and made the man promise to take it to Seetha's house immediately. 'They'll be worrying about her, so please go now.'

When she went back to the kitchen, Seetha had put the hot, sizzling dosha on the table and was waiting to make tea. Thankam felt almost human after she ate; the traumas of the day now looked much smaller.

'I'm so glad you are here, Seetha; I'd have hated to be alone tonight. Now should you not be making some doshas for yourself?'

'No. I want proper food,' Seetha said, smiling. 'There is rice left over from lunch in the refrigerator; I'm going to warm it up and eat that with the remaining potato masala.'

Late at night, Mohan came to the front door; it was Seetha who opened the door to him;

'Is Amma around?' he asked.

'Yes. I'll ask her whether she wants to see anyone.'

'No, I don't want to see anyone; I had a bad day today,' Thankam called out.

'Have your dinner quickly, Seetha; there's a good Malayalam film on *Doordarshan One*,' she added, as Seetha closed the door after Mohan.

Early in the morning Seetha said she needed to go home briefly to check whether everything was all right there.

'I never know what is going to happen when my man comes home drunk, and it is happening more and more frequently.'

'Have your breakfast before you go,' Thankam said.

'I don't eat breakfast this early. In fact, we don't make any breakfast at home, so I'm not used to it. All of us leave home quite early for work.'

'So do you have coffee or tea then?'

Seetha smiled as though she found this amusing. 'We don't buy tea or coffee in our house. Or milk either. Where is the money? My husband and my son generally grab a cup from the wayside tea shop near by; they open at six in the morning and it's only two rupees.'

'Do you eat late at night then?'

'I don't eat much when I get home; I eat enough here, don't I? Preethi cooks rice and a curry in the afternoon and in the night, she makes what is left into a conjee and we eat it with some kind of chutney, or fish, if the men bring any home.

'Sometimes I feel bad I eat better than my whole family, because I eat here. When I take food home, I give it to my grandson; he's only two years old, but he knows I'll bring something for him.'

Thankam drove down to Vaduthala to Manju's house with the sweets and the garments; college had closed down for ten days and she had time on her hands. When she arrived there, she noticed a white Land Rover parked in front with British Council written on its sides. Wonder what it is doing here on a Saturday, she thought as she walked in; perhaps they had sent the car for Manju because she had a lot of paper to take in.

As she walked into the living room, she saw a young white man seated in one of the sofas, long legs stretched out, reading the day's *Hindu.* He saw her and stood up.

Tall and lanky, she observed. A blond thatch, the colour of straw, and a generously freckled face.

'Where's Manju?' she asked. 'I am her mother, Thankam.'

'I thought as much; you look very alike. I'm Dave Woods. She's with the children, I think.' He seemed perfectly at home in the room and went back to the paper as soon as she started walking inside.

Thankam checked in the bedroom and tested the bathroom door; then she peeked into the kitchen; not finding her daughter anywhere, she opened the back door and looked in the garden. There she found Manju sitting on the wrought-iron bench, contemplating the edge of her duppatta. The faint drizzle that came and went had started again, but she seemed unaware of it. Thankam sat down next to her and picking up the free end of the duppatta, draped it lovingly on Manju's head. She then covered her own head with the pallav of her sari.

'Are we both going to sit here and get wet?' she asked, after a moment. 'You have a guest, Moley; shouldn't you be attending to him?'

Manju lifted up her face and Thankam saw her daughter had been crying. 'Dave wants me to go to Delhi for a conference of library trainees. Ammey, what shall I do?'

'When is this conference?'

'It's two weeks from now, but he says he has to finalise the list of participants in three days' time. I think he wants an answer now.'

'Buy time. Tell him you have to think about it. There is more than a conference involved here, don't you think?'

'Yes,' Manju answered simply. 'Much more, I think, and I am frightened.'

'Go and look after your guest now; there are certain civilities to be observed even when problems arise.'

Manju went to the kitchen sink and dashed water on her face; then she turned to her mother and tried to laugh, but it came out as a sniffle. "I do get into all sorts of impossible situations, don't I? I have two children to worry about; I should know better.' It seemed she was talking to herself.

Thankam thought it prudent to avoid the sitting room for a while, so she went up to the children's bedroom; Asha and Latha were oblivious of the world, eyes riveted on the TV screen, watching a video of *Hansel and Gretel*. Thankam dropped her bags on the floor and sat on the bed to watch along with them. She had never seen the video, but a long time ago she had read the book. This was a horror story, Thankam remembered. What were the Grimm brothers thinking of when they wrote it for children? It used to give her nightmares and it was now going to give her grandchildren nightmares. As the girls watched the two children in the forest, after they lost their way, they started feeling uncomfortable; they noticed Thankam on their bed and came over for reassurance.

'I know a better story than that,' Thankam said firmly. Why don't you watch that video later? If you switch it off, I'll tell you the story. I don't like that one, it makes me scared.' Asha already had her thumb in her mouth for solace; they climbed up on either side of her and snuggled into her.

'These Onam holidays you have now, do you know why you get them?'

'For Mahabali,' Latha answered from her superior position of being the elder sister. 'He comes to Kerala on the two Onam days.'

'That's right, but why did he go away?'

Asha confessed to having forgotten, but her teacher in lower school had indeed told her.

'There was once a ruler,' Thankam started, in the time-honoured manner. 'His name was Mahabali and he was the best ruler in the world.'

'Why?' Asha asked, taking her thumb out briefly. Asha was into the 'why' year.

'Because he was just and fair and he treated all his subjects with equal love and kindness. He used to disguise himself as a pauper to go to his people's houses, so he could see first-hand how they were; he didn't trust his courtiers to tell him the truth.'

The why popped up at that moment again. Latha got a bit fed up; she wanted the juicy bits quickly. 'The why is only at the end,' she said, inventing a rule instantaneously, to suit the moment. Asha knew she was being treated with scant respect, so she put her thumb back in her mouth and settled to some serious sucking. Thankam hugged her close in the crook of one elbow as she continued.

'He was generous and compassionate and the people loved him above all things. In fact they loved him so much-'

'The gods got jealous,' Latha said triumphantly. Asha had fallen asleep and all that came out from that end was a faint sucking noise once in a while.

'So what did the gods do?' Latha had forgotten that bit.

'They sent Lord Vishnu to sort it out. He disguised himself as a three-foot dwarf called Vamanan and came to earth, to the ruler's palace. Now Mahabali had the reputation of granting any reasonable wish that his subjects asked. Vamanan asked him for three strides of land; he was so short, his strides would not amount to much, the courtiers thought. They laughed derisively when they heard this request.

'Mahabali told him he could measure out his land. Vamanan now became the great god Vishnu, and immediately grew to his full height and stature. With his first stride he measured the whole earth. With his second he measured the entire heavens. For his third stride he had nowhere to go. So Mahabali said, "O God, put your venerable foot on my head." With this third step Vishnu sent Mahabali to the nether world, *Pathalam*, where the demons live.

'Mahabali was very sad to leave his subjects in this manner, so he begged Vishnu to allow him two days in the year to come back to earth and visit his beloved people. The two days of Onam: *Uthradam* and *Thiruvonam* are the two days when Mahabali comes back to earth to walk amongst us.

'On this day, all of us celebrate his coming. We welcome him with flowers and everyone, even the poorest, wears his new garments. People exchange gifts of new clothes and greet him with song and dance.'

When the story was over, Latha got curious about the bags on the floor.

'What is in this bag, Ammamma?'

'Can't you guess?'

'Dresses for me and Asha,' she said with confidence. What else could it be at Onam time?

Thankam lifted up the plastic bags from the floor where she had deposited them when she first came in.

'Let me see, let me see,' Latha insisted excitedly. She took out a pair of denim trousers and a hand-embroidered, white muslin blouse. The neckline was smocked in pink and within the smock, tiny rosebuds had been embroidered in French knots.

'You bring the bestest clothes in the whole world,' Latha said, hugging her.

Asha was still fast asleep, but when Thankam tried to put her down on the bed, she woke up and started rubbing her eyes. 'All the crumbs were eaten by the animals,' she said, and started crying.

Thankam picked her up. 'No, actually their friend came back and put down some other things for Hansel and Gretel to find their way back, things no animals would eat.'

'What?' Asha insisted on knowing.

Plastic bags and cigarette wrappers, Thankam was tempted to say; instead she said, 'Macdonald's chips. You know no self-respecting animal will touch MacDonald's chips; only human beings eat that stuff.'

'Why,' Asha asked. She was back to normal.

'I'll tell you another time, but now we are going downstairs to see what your amma is doing.'

'A man with an old man's hair came to see Amma; he came in a huge truck, so she put the video on for us, so we wouldn't disturb her. He's from her office,' Latha offered.

'He's another Uncle James,' Asha was certain. Uncle James was a white man who owned a house in the same housing complex. He had an Indian wife and came to Kerala for holidays, twice a year; so all white men had to be Uncle James.

Thankam did not correct her. 'Now it's time to bother your mother.'

The children tumbled down the stairs eager to get to their mother.

The Land Rover was pulling out as Thankam and the girls reached the living room. Manju had accompanied Dave to the vehicle and stayed outside while he smiled and waved and accelerated out.

'Come over and look at the clothes I've got you for Onam. Work-a-day clothes because expensive saris get an airing perhaps once a year. Sometimes it's literally an airing, on to the clothesline to take the musty smell off, and back again.'

Manju came over dutifully and admired the salwar-kameez sets, but Thankam could see her thoughts were elsewhere.

'They are just right for work, Ammey; I'm glad you didn't buy me another *Kancheepuram* sari; there are so many gathering dust in my wardrobe.'

Thankam went to her daughter and touched her lightly on her arm. 'I was going to buy one of those and then I saw a family in the shop; they sickened me, so I changed my mind. They were buying a wedding sari for a girl and the whole retinue were there. The bridegroom's family were bullying the bride's family; they were practically instructing the girl what to buy for her wedding. She had no voice anyway; she was a tiny mouse of a creature. Her brothers were there with their bulging money belts, standing back, and there were these sisters of the bridegroom dictating terms. They pronounced a twelve-thousand-rupees sari too cheap; they can do that only because we set such a high value on a girl getting a husband, almost any husband.'

Thankam hung around for a while, reluctant to leave her daughter, who was so obviously stressed. When teatime came round she went into the kitchen and made tea and drank it with Manju. A little later, she fed the girls; it was getting on for six-thirty in the evening. Thankam coaxed Manju to walk round the housing estate with her. 'Clean the cobwebs out of your head,' she said. Manju was docile, allowing herself to be led as she dwelt deep within herself.

On the water's edge the small fish glided about on the surface. The tide was coming in, bringing with it the morning's cargo of water hyacinths that had bobbed out with the tide when it receded. Egrets were perched perfectly still on tree stumps, wings spread out as if on deliberate display. Manju and Thankam stood watching the sun, which was beginning to turn pink in the west.

This was walking time for the health-conscious occupants of the houses on the estate; many had come out for their evening strolls. The men had not come home, indeed may not come home from work till after eight, but wives and children had spilled on to the playground and paths. Some women sat chatting on the wrought-iron benches under the coconut trees while others talked over the low walls of their houses, in between the flower pots on them. In the children's playground the toddlers were wallowing in sand. Older boys played cricket on the tennis court while the younger ones were commandeered to do the fielding.

Manju and Thankam did two rounds and came home. 'I must go now,' Thankam said. 'Seetha would have locked up and gone by now. Our street has seen a lot of burglaries recently; can't leave the place empty at night.'

'I was hoping you'd stay the night.' Thankam could hear entreaty in Manju's voice. This was an unexpected request and Thankam had not come prepared for this; she took a moment to consider what to do.

To hell with the house and everything in it, Thankam decided. 'I'll stay if that is what you want.'

Manju was not a person to admit need in this manner and Thankam was concerned for her; she can talk to me if she feels like it, she thought, but she's between a rock and a hard place at the moment and she knows it.

Going into the kitchen together and having a tray in front of the television was almost like old times. They watched an old Malayalam movie for a while, but most of the time, they talked; the movie was simply a ritual noise in the background.

'Ammey, I have still to tell Dave my decision about the conference. How can I tell him when I don't know the answer myself?'

'I know you are distressed, but isn't this all rather sudden? You've only known him for a few months.'

'That's the bit I am sure about; how I feel about him. I have never felt like this about Gopi even when I first married him and things were going well between us. But then, I never knew there was anything different. Now I know what loving is and I am terrified to think Dave will go and I will be left with a husband who does not care, for the rest of my life.'

Thankam made an effort to imagine her daughter with that lanky youth who had uncoiled himself from the sofa earlier on to greet her; it seemed surreal.

'How is all this going to affect Asha and Latha? Have you thought about that?'

'I think of nothing else. They don't even think of Dave as belonging to the same human race as the rest of us; he looks so alien to them.'

'The conference is neither here nor there, provided that's all it is. But if you decide to leave Gopi, the courts will award custody of your children to him after the age of five. Kerala courts are hard on wives who leave their husbands; you could lose them for good.'

The phone rang and Manju picked it up; it was Dave. This end of the exchange sounded as though he was reassuring her in some way. When the conversation finished, Manju came over to Thankam and sat, resting her face on her mother's shoulder.

'Dave says he doesn't want to put pressure on me to make any decisions right now, but to go to the conference. It will give us an opportunity to spend some time together without me getting talked about.

'Could you look after the children for a week?'

'Yes, of course. But you mustn't do anything hasty.'

Manju appeared disoriented; she put the TV on again and started flicking through the channels. Thankam found her mind wandering, thinking about love and the way it came upon you unawares, leaving no room for anything else while it ruled.

Manju woke Thankam up from her reverie a few minutes later. 'You are meant to be talking to me, but you are far away, in some other world. This Malayalam film was pretty useless too and now there is nothing else worth watching.' She switched it off.

'Whatever did people do before the coming of television, I wonder. Look at me now: the children asleep, normally no one else in the house. If you don't read, what can you do?'

'I used to read a fair bit before I got married,' Thankam offered. 'In fact I've started again recently. We sat around and gossiped a lot in those days. I was considered a spoilsport because I often wandered off with a book. There really was nowhere to go and nothing to do for the women, unless you call paying the odd visit to a neighbour's house doing something.

'And then of course there was the fraternal activity of searching for lice.' Thankam smiled at the memory. 'Women would sit on the back steps in the long afternoons, picking lice from each other's heads, when they weren't helping mothers in the kitchen. Lice, in the days before shampoo, were a common hazard for us girls with long, well-oiled scalps. If a particularly fat, juicily transparent louse was cornered and caught, we would place it between two thumbnails and squash it with a satisfying plop; the blood sucked from our own scalps would burst on to our nails.

'Surely middle-class people didn't have lice in their hair,' Manju exclaimed in horror.

'Well, I did consider it-'

'Consider what?'

'Telling the lice we were middle class and to keep out of our hair, but I couldn't think of a way.'

'Ammey!' Manju laughed, knowing her mother was pulling her leg as usual. For the moment, she had forgotten all her worries.

Mother and daughter talked late into the night until Manju started flagging; the day's excitements were catching up with her.

'Come, Moley,' Thankam said. 'Go to bed now.' Manju, in response, snuggled deeper into her mother for a few minutes, then she dragged herself off to bed. Thankam knew no beds had been made up in the spare room, so she climbed in with her daughter after closing up the house. However, she stayed awake for a long time.

She listened for the familiar noises of the city winding down as in Carrier Station Road, but what she heard instead was an eerie quiet. When she listened carefully, she could hear the crickets and the frogs from the waterside. Birds called out security details to each other late into the night, and across the waters, at the computer institute, the lights stayed on as evening students worked at their screens doggedly, finishing assignments, which could not be done without the equipment and customised software available at the Institute.

When Thankam woke up and looked out through the window, she could see the tide slowly flowing out to the sea. The girls were still fast asleep and no morning noises could be heard from the kitchen; Thankam opened the front door and walked out into the garden, barefooted.

On the perfectly manicured lawn the dew had settled and the silvery grass was wet to her feet, but not enough to stop them from sinking into the rich tufts. The young *Rajamalli* bushes were in extravagant bloom at the back of the flowerbeds: pink, yellow and red on the ends of thorny spikes, reaching out for the light. On the bottlebrush tree, the sunbirds and mynahs had just begun to congregate for their turn at the birdbath, but the crows were having their noisy ablutions still, beating their wings and calling out raucously to their mates.

Thankam went tiptoe to the fishpond hoping to see the carp, but they managed to detect her presence and swam away quickly to hide behind the plants in the pond, only the odd orange tailfin showing outside. She breathed deep, enjoying the fresh morning air, so different from the polluted city atmosphere where she lived.

Thankam felt somehow more alive, wanting to stretch and flex her limbs, so she walked out of the gate and through to the security post at the main road. In the narrow lane outside, morning devotees from the Shivan's temple down the road, mainly housewives and old men, were returning home virtuously; streaks of sacred ash and sandalwood paste on foreheads bearing witness to their exalted state.

The old men lifted up the corners of their dothis, hawked and spat luxuriously, as they passed the rubbish hillock encroaching insidiously on to the lane. The women held their breaths, briefly, and turned away as the familiar rancid smell of rotting vegetation and wet mud threatened to reach into their throats.

Thankam turned back when she saw the state of the lane. In Manju's house the maid had arrived, but everyone else was fast asleep. Thankam wrote a quick note for Manju and got into her Maruthi.

15

At Nedumbassery airport, Kochi, early in the morning, the usual crowd was thronging the security barricades put up near the arrivals hall. Hefty men nudged and elbowed their way to the front, while women were forced aside in the mêlée. Whole families had come to meet one visitor; some had been camping there overnight and were feeding babies from bottles or eating breakfast from tiffin carriers. The *tea-wallah* was doing a brisk trade in small plastic cups of tea, for which he charged four times the outside price, though he carried the urn across from a restaurant at the edge of the airport grounds.

Most of the returnees would be casual labour on holiday from the Middle East, so much so that the Emirates planeload could have been mistaken for a Malayalee excursion returning home. Nobody was allowed inside the actual arrivals hall because of a recent high security alert; so everyone had to wait around the barricades; after Nine-Eleven, airports in India had become paranoid.

When Anil walked out from the air-conditioned hall, pushing his trolley, blinking in the glare of the Kochi sun, the first thing Thankam thought was: he looks like a man now, not the boy who went some months ago. He had filled out and the face seemed stronger, more confident. He had become much fairer too in England, with two rosy patches on his cheeks, and his resemblance to Appu was stronger.

Thankam went up to him and put her arm through his. 'My *ponnumone*,' she said, my golden son, and it was enough. Anil held her arm close to him as he wheeled the trolley to the car park outside and loaded the bags in quickly, eager to reach home.

'No driver for the long journey, I see,' Anil remarked, questioningly.

'It's only thirty minutes on a good day and I have been driving for a long time now.'

Thankam drove without saying much, comfortable in the knowledge of his nearness; she hadn't realised how much she had missed him. He put his head back and dozed. 'Didn't get much sleep on the plane,' he remarked, before he dropped off. 'Some of the men on the plane couldn't fill up their disembarkation cards in English; I had to do many of them. They kept waking me up when I was trying to sleep.

'Where's Manju?' he asked a little later when he surfaced briefly.

'She's got to go off to Delhi for a week soon and I think she's finishing her back log of work this morning.'

'Manju working, you driving around like a veteran, the approach road to the airport completed... What other transformations have you in store for me?'

When Thankam and Anil arrived home it was breakfast time and Seetha was on the veranda, smiling broadly.

'Anil mone is looking like a big man,' she said to him, as she took his overnight case from him. 'You went to the land of the *saive* and you have become fair like them.'

'I'm ravenous,' he answered her. 'Hope you've got one of your big breakfasts ready for me. And I could do with some hot tea right now.'

Seetha went off to the kitchen happily to do the tea.

Anil had a substantial breakfast of iddli and chammandhi. As he attacked his seventh iddli, Thankam smiled. 'I can see I have to take a night job as well to feed you.' She hadn't been so happy in a long while.

Manju phoned as he finished.

'Have to show my face at the office and tie up some loose ends. I'll see you in the evening. And have you brought any madammas with you?'

'I'm planning to; I was just waiting for your permission,' he said lightly. 'But what's all this going off to Delhi and playing the executive? I thought I was the one in this family designated for that role.'

'Oh, we've overtaken you long, long ago.'

'The women in my family!' he exclaimed.

'What's wrong with the women in your family?' Thankam demanded to know.

'I never know what to expect from either of you; you are always surprising me.'

In the evening, Manju came with Asha and Latha. Anil was quite dejected when Asha pulled away from him and hid behind her mother's sari-end. Manju kept pulling the ends away from her, but this merely made her retreat even more, so she gave up.

'Silly girl's forgotten you. See what happens when you leave us for too long. I am surprised your firm lets you get away with this.'

'That's one of the things I'm here for. And then there is-'

Thankam picked the uncertainty in his tone.

'What is it, Money?'

He regarded the four females who were his closest family. 'I'm glad we are all here together; I've got my four favourite women in front of me. Now I want to add a fifth.'

Thankam knew he had trouble finding the words, so she helped him out. 'About time too,' she said. If she had any reservations, she managed to hide them.

'Ammey, her name is Sarah. I met her soon after I went to the UK; I know you would have wanted to choose a nice Malayalee girl for me and it seems I am cheating you and Manju out of that privilege.'

Anil looked anxiously at her, making her realise how desperately he needed her approval.

'It's not an impulsive decision,' he continued. 'I've thought about it long and deep. I came primarily to tell you and Manju that.'

'You are going to live in England? It seems so far away.'

'It's not so far really, Ammey. Just nine hours on a plane. Yes, I *will* have to leave the firm in Bangalore and find work in the UK, before my work permit runs out.'

Thankam put down the flex of the iron she had been fiddling with and came over to sit near him. Strange both her children should fall in love with English people. Would she end up alone in Kochi, with the two of them far away?

When Thankam thought about something important, a time lag ensued before she said anything; this one went on for half a minute.

'I'd like to know more about this girl, but I'm apprehensive about what this will mean to all of us.

'I know you have good taste in everything; otherwise you'd have been in the clutches of one of those man-eaters from Bangalore long ago.'

'Hey, hold on.' Anil laughed. 'I didn't know any man-eaters in Bangalore. I just did not meet anyone I fancied though I have some close women friends there.'

'You want to know about Sarah.' Anil appeared to have trouble putting his image of Sarah into words. He hesitated for a moment, then took the easy option of a physical description, 'She's red-haired with freckles all over her face. She is doing her professional year to become a solicitor and I think, has been offered a job in a firm in London.

'Her family are people like all of us: middle-class, liberal and reasonably educated. They welcomed me into their fold without reservation. What else do you want to know? And oh, yes, she's about twenty-three years old and has a wicked sense of humour. I'm sure you two will like her.'

Thankam saw the dream in her son's eye as he tried to summon a picture of Sarah to his mind and knew this girl was indispensable to him.

'Whoever you marry is part of this family. She sounds like an interesting person, but the main thing is, you have chosen her. There is nothing more for anyone to say, except wish you the very best of luck.

'And, I hope she can adjust to all the circumstances in Kochi when she comes here: the uncertain power supply, water shortage, *hartals*... Manju added.

Thankam was relieved he had not gone for a barmaid; many people had told her that the only English girls who ever married Asians were "cheap barmaids". Hard to believe; in any case many Asian students served behind bars to make some extra money. Did proximity make them choose barmaids? Or were the barmaids students just like them?

However, the problem remained: she'd have a tough time explaining all this to her mother. After all the times Amma had told him not to come back with a madamma!

'I'm going to Thalassery straight after Onam. Why don't you come with me? I'm taking the little ones with me as Manju is off to Delhi. We could drive, instead of going by train; make a proper holiday trip out of it. Maybe stop at Kozhikode on the way and see some family I haven't seen in along while.'

'I know you are going to drop me in it, Ammey,' Anil said. 'Ammamma will kill, quarter and eat me. But, never mind; I have to get it over and done with.'

'Appuettan is there; so we have to go now, before he leaves,' Thankam explained. 'He has scarcely got a fortnight left.'

'And I am only down for a fortnight myself. Why don't I do a quick trip to Bangalore tomorrow? I must see my boss.'

Thankam agreed that Anil would go to Bangalore the next day, as soon as he had slept off his jet lag.

Meanwhile she would phone Thalassery and organise their journey.

Thankam was standing outside in the sun after her bath, letting sunlight into her hair and drying it by passing her fingers through, when Seetha came out of the kitchen. She had been mixing and kneading the roasted rice flour with water and a pinch of salt to make it into a crumbly, moist heap for pittu. Later she would fill the mixture loosely into the narrow pittu cylinder with grated coconut breaks, before steaming it. Now she covered the flour with a steel lid and left it for a few minutes for the moisture to penetrate through, before she started getting the steamer organised. She washed her hands at the kitchen sink and came in search of her mistress. On the sides of her palm and on top of her fingers, the flour had dried hard; she scratched at it while she talked to Thankam.

'Haven't seen Mohan Sar for a few days. No noises from their flat either.' This had all the signs of a well-disguised, leading question; Thankam did not fall for that one.

'Must have gone to Kottayam for his holidays.'

Seetha turned back towards the kitchen. Thankam relented and called out. 'He's also looking for another place to say. I'm going to take back that apartment, maybe stop renting altogether. I could even use it as an office for myself.'

'That is very good; you can do your work at home. And when Anil mone comes, he can stay there too.'

'I think it is very unlikely Anil mone is coming back to stay there, ever.

'Seetha,' she called out as she walked towards the kitchen. 'Anil is going to marry a woman from England, so he will probably live there in future.'

'*Ayyo!*'

'No point in us "ayyo"ing. He is of an age to marry and he has found his own wife. After all, Achan, not his family, chose me, so I must trust his choice.

The only thing that worries me is, how often will I get to see him?'

'That's not the way to look at it, Ammey. He's been away for a few months, hasn't he? You know you have managed without him. We can't keep our children like chickens, under a safe basket, can we?

'You speak the language and you are healthy. And most importantly, you can afford to travel. You can go and see him and his wife whenever you feel like it.'

This woman is wise and fair, Thankam thought. 'You're right,' she responded, 'I shouldn't be selfish. I do hope he'll get married here, though. And I can't wait to see his girl.'

'Hasn't he got a photo?'

'He said he'll find one when he comes back from Bangalore, after he's unpacked properly.'

Thankam phoned Appu almost as an advance warning.

'Appuetta, there is some news this side; Anil is home for a fortnight.'

'Isn't his term in the UK over yet?'

'I don't think it is ever going to be over. There is a girl-'

'So what's wrong with that? Now, if it was a man, you'd have to think a little.' He laughed. 'Don't tell me you object. Unni married you against the wishes of many people in his family, do you remember? They thought you were too dark.'

He has a gift of making all problems look small, Thankam thought.

'It's just that he'll live so far away.'

'Not any more, Neeli. Look at a homebody like me; I'm forever shuttling between Dubai and Thalassery, two or three times a year. Amma sees a lot of me. It's not ideal, but London is only an overnight flight.

'In fact, now you're on your own you should travel more, see the world; don't sit on all your money.'

'We're coming over in two or three days' time, when Anil gets back from Bangalore. Probably on Friday, since Manju is off to Delhi on the same day for some office business. You better prepare Amma, or she'll say all the wrong things and upset him.

'The other thing is-'

Appu must have picked up the hesitation in her voice. 'Go on, Neeli, say what you started to say; it is only me.'

'It seems a lot to ask. I was wondering. Is it possible for you to find the keys to Unniettan's house and get the maid, Kalyani, and her husband to open up the place? Amma has the keys. However, you have so little time with your family; I hate to suggest anything, which will take you away from them.

'Kalyani could get the rooms aired and clean the cobwebs. I want to spend a couple of days there.'

'Is this what you are making a big thing of? It's a small matter; I'll sort it out.'

'We're bringing Asha and Latha also and coming by car. I'll let you know times later.'

Thankam drove over to Vaduthala in the evening to make sure Manju was not too dejected; she greeted her mother warmly.

'I'm glad you thought of driving this way; we had such a good time together last week. And I can't leave here for a variety of reasons.' She involuntarily looked at the phone as she said that.

I know one of the reasons you don't want to leave home; you have an invisible string keeping you close to that silly telephone, Thankam surmised. Never mind.

'I think we should discuss arrangements. Shall I pick the children up on Thursday evening? Anil and I are hoping for an early start on Friday. Who is taking you to the airport?'

'The office is sending a Land Rover'

'You be careful,' Thankam warned her. 'There is no one there for you in Delhi; don't do anything you'll regret later.'

'You say that because you don't know Dave. Even if I wished, he wouldn't let me do anything I would want to forget. He's a good man; sometimes I think he's so like Achan in his attitudes, that's why I am attracted to him. I will never, ever, come to harm when Dave is around.

'Still, let's forget me for a bit; perhaps I'll have answers when I return from Delhi. I hope.' She didn't sound too certain. 'How do you feel about Anil's news?'

'I can't really make any kind of judgement about her, can I? I have yet to meet her. But he seems so sure.'

'Ammey, she sounds like a good partner for him, definitely his equal and perhaps more. He's made up his mind; if we stand in his way, we'll lose him, that's all.'

'I've no intention of standing in his way; Achan taught me that. He always said not to fight with children about things that would drive them away from you. "In a disagreement, we need them much more than they need us, because we love them more than they can love us."'

Thankam laughed, remembering. 'Once I had a huge brawl with you about your hair. You wanted to cut your hair, paint your nails purple ... Do you remember? You were about fourteen then and pulling at the bridle. So Achan came in on this.

'"Hair, nails.... These can grow again. Why bother to make issues out of them? Pick your battles carefully or no one will heed them."'

'I was quite a handful then, wasn't I?'

'Then? Still! I never know what you are going to come up with, next.'

'As if *I* knew.'

The family celebrated Onam in style at Thankam's house on Tuesday, which was *Uthradam* day, the first of the two Onam days. Seetha and Thankam had cooked all the traditional Onam dishes: the hot red-and-brown *sambar* with okra, drum sticks and tamarind; *elassery,* the colour of mustard, with green plantains and plenty of ground coconut and cumin; sunshine yellow *kalan* and *aviyal* in thick yoghurt and coconut sauces; *olan*, the colour and consistency of coconut milk in which chunks of cucumber floated ... It went on and on. No meat or fish dishes were prepared as the Onam feast was always a strictly vegetarian meal in this household. Seetha herself would not be in on Thiruvonam day, the second day of Onam; she would be with her own family, so many of the dishes which would taste better a day later, such as kalan and sambar were prepared on the Monday. After lunch on Tuesday, Thankam gave out their new clothes to Moli and Seetha, so they could wear them on *Thiruvonam* day.

Seetha was very pleased with her clothes, but she said she was going to give some of them to her daughter and some of them to Prakash's wife. 'Who will give them anything otherwise, Ammey?' she pleaded.

'These are yours to do what you like with or give to your children. I'm glad you like them.'

Manju brought a basketful of flowers with her and made a huge traditional *pookkalam* design on the veranda; she had been doing this in her house for eight days now and would complete the event with a final flourish on the two Onam days. Asha, Latha and Anil got into the act, so it turned out a little differently from what she may have planned; Thankam diplomatically called it an asymmetric design, so the little ones wouldn't be upset; Anil insisted he'd seen nothing in any book that said Onam flower designs had to be symmetrical.

Palada was served after the meal; Asha and Latha knew Ammamma was making their favourite dessert, because they got the smell of rice cooking in milk as they entered the house. They wouldn't eat much of their rice and curry.

'We are saving the space in our stomachs for the palilada,' Asha announced

After lunch the family sat around and talked, replete not only with the food, but also the joy of being together after a long while.

'I shall miss this when I live in England,' Anil said. 'However, my boss, Jagjeevan, was kind; he has arranged another six months' work for me in England; that will give me almost ten months to find a job.'

16

When Anil got back to Kochi Manju abandoned her vigil by the phone and came round with Asha and Latha, early in the evening. She had packed a small bag for a week for them and they seemed quite excited about the trip to Thalassery, though they could not have fathomed Manju was not going with them.

'So show us a photo of this dream girl of yours,' Manju insisted with Anil. She was in one of her brattiest moods: teasing, demanding.

He took his wallet out, searched in it and closed it. 'This one doesn't do justice to her; I stole it out of an old album. She hates it.'

'Let's have a look.' Manju got up out of her chair and made to snatch it from him; Anil held it away from her and managed to put it back in his wallet. He went upstairs and came back in a few minutes with a larger snapshot of both of them together and gave it to Manju.

She went back to her chair and sat down with it. What she saw was a slim, long-legged girl with her arms casually round Anil's waist. Definitely red hair, taken back carelessly and tied at the nape. Some of the hair had worked itself loose and come down on her face, on both sides. She wore a tracksuit and running shoes and Manju could see the freckles on her nose. Pert, pixie features to match the smile on her face.

They were standing in a garden, with the light in front of them. Anil was looking at her, as though about to say something. Manju had never seen him before in clothes like this: turtleneck jumper with an overcoat on top. He had his left arm in the pocket of his overcoat and the other, gloved, on Sarah's shoulder.

'Why are you wearing winter clothes when she's in her jogging outfit?'

'I don't think she ever feels the cold too much. She's trying to coax me into running with her; she says I am getting fat.'

'She's right and she looks a real charmer, I'll admit. I must show this to Amma.'

Manju ran off down the stairs.

As Seetha and Thankam walked up the stairs they were jointly inspecting the photo of Anil's future wife.

'Ammey, has she put red dye in her hair? Strange colour.' Seetha sounded upset. 'What's the point of dye when she is young?'

'That's not dye; that's the colour of her hair,' Manju said.

'You are pulling my leg, Manju mole.'

'No, I'm not. Ask him.'

'Anil mone. Does this girl have red hair really? Don't you have girls with black hair in that country?'

'You do; she's going to come here soon and then you can see her properly.'

'In any case, she's very fair; so she's a pretty girl. Has she got a job?'

Thankam knew fair was the paramount criterion for Seetha; it overrode everything else.

'She's a lawyer,' Anil said. He looked as though he didn't quite know what to expect from Seetha next, but she was walking back towards the stairs.

'I've got work downstairs.' And as a parting short, 'Is she a lawyer without any brief like so many you see hanging around the High Courts in town?'

Thankam and Manju burst out laughing. 'You'll have to dye her hair black when she comes over,' Manju added solemnly.

'I like that picture of the two of you; it's a good one. But I must see her soon. When do you think she might be able to come over?' Thankam asked.

'I don't know, Ammey. I'll ask her when I get back. Before I go, I need to get her an engagement ring; could we go down to Broadway and have a look, when we get back from Thalassery?'

'Yes, we'll go to Broadway and you can pick the ring. And when you get married, you can have Achan's wedding ring.'

'I wonder what Achan would have made of all this?' Anil pondered.

'All what?'

'Me marrying an English girl, you working, Manju rushing off to Delhi on her own…'

'I can tell you; he had his favourite words for change of any kind. "The moving finger writes and having writ, moves on." It was a much-used quotation of his. Achan would have been happy for you, I know that.'

Manju was supposed to leave for the airport to catch the early morning Delhi flight at eight, on Friday, while Thankam and Anil were leaving Kochi at six, before dawn; it was all happening at the same time. As she dropped the mobile into her handbag, Thankam thought of Gopi, far away in Dubai, like so many young men of the day, with little idea of what was happening in their families. This was one thing he did right, getting her a mobile; she noticed she was beginning to feel sorry for him.

The two little ones were only half-awake when Anil carried them and put them down on the backseat, with cushions under them. When Thankam got in, she put two extra pillows on the floor, in case they rolled off the seat. The car had seat belts in front, but Thankam did not use them. Anil got in and the first thing he did was strap himself in.

'When did you get this habit? I remember you were allergic to them in the past.'

'They're compulsory in the UK now; the fines are quite high if you are caught without them on the road, so I've got used to wearing them as I start off. What's more, I am uneasy about you not wearing one too.

'In Bangalore, I was using taxis a lot. I found my left arm searching for the non-existent seat belt whenever I got in.

'I suppose it is OK not to wear them when you are driving around in Kochi; does anyone here ever manage to get past second gear?'

'There's that,' Thankam answered. 'If anything, the traffic has got even slower in the centre of town. Except for the buses; they hurtle around lethally, killing someone with predictable regularity every month. No one seems to be able to rein them in: another example of bribery, I think.

Anil soon reached the National Highway and the toll point. When he stopped to pay the toll, stirrings could be heard from the back, but Anil and Thankam ignored them. After a few minutes, a small whimper came, 'Mmm, Ammey.' Asha was struggling up and beginning to notice where she was. 'Where is my Amma?' Panic set in. A long drawn-out wail emerged. '*Ende* Amma,' followed by a tiny sob. Asha referred to Manju as 'her' Amma only when she was really upset. Thankam brought her over to the front and comforted her, but it didn't work; at this hour of the morning mother was mandatory. When Amma was not to be seen, she put her thumb in her mouth for consolation and went off to sleep again. Thankam put a blanket over her and held her close.

A few kilometres on, Latha surfaced. 'Where is Amma?' she demanded.

'She did not come with us; she has work to do,' Thankam explained. They knew about work, but Thankam thought it prudent not to tell them she had gone to Delhi.

Asha perked up when she heard Latha at the back.

Close to Aluva, about thirty minutes out of Kochi, Anil stopped the car to get coffee from one of the small teashops lining the road; these were the only ones that still served real coffee and they were just beginning to open. The more up-market ones served "brew": instant coffee, with a strong smell of chicory, which mother and son hated

The urns in the teashops were about to boil and business was slow at this time of the day. Anil managed to get two glasses of coffee for Thankam and himself. He had to wait while the man poured it back and forth between his small pot and glass till he raised a big brown froth, but the coffee was worth waiting for. Anil carried the two glasses to the car and they drank it slowly, savouring the sweetness and its special smell. The glasses were thick and cloudy, not too clean, and one was chipped at the top, Anil noticed, as he returned them to the shop. He got in and drove on.

'This is one of the pleasures of driving here: these small teashops, which act like milestones; I had forgotten about them in the last year in England. You can get so many different types of coffee in the UK outlets and I suppose "Latte" is the closest to this, but it just doesn't compare, for some reason.'

'It's the pouring back and forth,' Thankam said, laughing.

Anil did a pit stop at Thrissur around nine-thirty for breakfast, for the girls to run around a little and for Thankam to use the toilets. The *masala doshas* were hot off the griddles and the girls were hungry.

'We are going to Ammamma's other house,' Latha explained to Asha.

'And we go back on yesterday?' Asha asked. Asha still had problems between yesterday and tomorrow.

'No, you silly, we'll go back tomorrow.'

'To my Amma's house.' Asha wanted to make this clear, but no one answered her, so she concentrated on running up and down the long dining hall in the Express restaurant, making Maruthi noises. The waiters smiled at her indulgently; the other guests ignored her most of the time. When she got in their way they pointed her back to Thankam's table; Latha would catch hold of her hand and lead her back to safety then.

Thalassery was less than three hundred kilometres away, but it generally took a whole day to get there.

After Kozhikode, Anil remarked 'Now we are into the forgotten land. The roads are neglected and narrow. Most of the bridges are bottlenecks and look at the railway crossings: so many of them and you can wait a good twenty minutes at each.'

'When we travelled during my childhood,' Thankam told him, 'Appuettan and I would bet on how many we'd get through between Kozhikode and Thalassery without stopping. At one point there are eight close together.'

Anil drove as fast as he could, which was no more than seventy kilometres an hour; an occasional stretch of wider road provided an opportunity to speed up a little, but not for long.

'This landscape is pretty; so I can stand this pace. Otherwise it'd send me round the bend. You never see this quality of green in the north,' Anil remarked.

'Even the green in England has a subtle difference; it's not so luscious and wild. I miss this when I am there, but when I see all the autumn colours in England, going from shades of green and yellow to rust and crimson, I catch my breath and think, how can anyone ever want to leave this place?'

'Yes, but the paddy fields, which used to be the main characteristic of the Kerala landscape, when I was growing up, have all but vanished,' Thankam interjected. 'People have filled up the fields and built houses. Part of the problem was the difficulty of finding and keeping labour; that's why your achan gave up on cultivating his fields.

Anil drove steadily north listening to his mother's reminiscences. He had difficulty imagining her in the role of a village-bride.

'So now we just own the house?'

'Good lord, no. Achan didn't believe in selling anything. We have whole tracts of land in Moozhikkara, now worth a lot compared to his father's times. I am beginning to feel I'd like to spend some time there each year, in Achan's house. I don't know how I am going to balance that with my work, but I must think about it.'

The children in the back slept fitfully; sometimes Asha got fed up with the journey and sat on the floor of the car to recite the nursery rhymes she had recently learned. So the car drove to the sounds of "Hey diddle-diddle, the cat and the fiddle, the cow jumped over the moon..." and "The wise man built his house upon a rock..." In Badagara, Anil stopped again at a restaurant in front of the bus stand and they had a meal of chappathis and aloo. The tea was undrinkable and coffee was not available; in this very Muslim part of Kerala not many people were coffee drinkers.

After Badagara Thankam knew she was on the home run along the coast; she sat up and started to point things out to the two girls.

'Notice the sea on the left,' she said as they drove down, approaching Mahe. 'All these little thatched houses on the left belong to the fishermen.'

Nets were strung out to dry all over the beach, which could be seen through the houses. A faint fishy smell seemed endemic to the area.

'I cannot see a jot of difference to this place from thirty years ago,' Thankam exclaimed. 'Soon we'll have to start "preserving" this.

'And you better stop in Mahe and fill up,' she added. 'It's always significantly cheaper than Thalassery.'

'I suppose that has something to do with it being a former French colony.'

'That's right. It still has some quaint residual bits from French occupation. The schools still teach French in some cases, for instance; and do you see the number of liquor shops on this one narrow road? This road pandered for all the people further north; from Thalassery and Kannoor, for instance, drinkers used to sneak in and buy their liquor here during the prohibition era.

'A roaring black-market trade flourished and a few lawyers made their pile defending the ones who were caught.'

The children at the back dozed off, listening to the comforting murmur of Thankam and Anil. When the car drew up in front of Thankam's house, they were in another world, rubbing their eyes in bewilderment. Where were they?

'Ammamma's Amma lives here, remember,' Latha announced to Asha. That itself must have been a quaint notion: grandmothers having mothers!

Appu and his son, Jayan, came running out to help them with the bags and the children. Thankam noticed Appu had become even fatter; he needs a wife to look after him *all* the time, she thought; probably lives on restaurant food.

Madhavi as usual made Thankam bristle with the first greeting. 'You have grown thin; don't you cook proper food in your house?'

'When I am fat, you say I'm fat and looking old; when I lose weight, you complain I'm thin and don't eat. How can I make you happy?' Thankam smiled and hugged her mother to take the edge off her words.

She is never happy with how I am, Thankam admitted. Why try?

Lakshmi detached herself from the gloom behind the door; she always stood behind doors, as though effacing herself. Thankam drew her out, 'My favourite sister-in-law,' she said, hugging her tight.

'You've only got one.' Appu smiled, but Thankam could see it made him happy.

'Anil mone, you have become a big man,' Appu teased Anil. 'Beginning to look like a *saive* too, fair and rosy-cheeked.'

Lakshmi disappeared in the direction of the kitchen, which was her permanent domain and Thankam followed her.

Late in the evening, when supper was over and Madhavi had retired to bed, Thankam spoke to Appu; she needed an ally.

'Appuetta, Amma is going to kick up a big fuss about Anil marrying a foreigner; it will not change the outcome; I'm anxious not to send him back to the UK upset and angry?'

'What do you know of this girl?'

'She is finishing her studies to become a solicitor and she sounds like a good person. Beyond that, what can we know from here? I saw a photo of her and Anil; that she loves him is clear in that snapshot. And he is wallowing in that affection; you can see that too.

'My only sadness is that we'll see less of him than we might have; I'd always thought he was going to come back for good. But then, things never quite work out…'

'Yes, I can see that will make you sad. But, even if they live on the other side of town, what is important is how you relate to each other, not how near they are. And England is hardly a distance these days.

'Anyway, I suggest Anil just tells her, don't make it look like he is asking permission.

'And you stay out of it. You and our Amma have always been at loggerheads with each other; whatever you say, she's going to make you feel small.

'He's got charm and she adores her first grandson; tell him to use it.'

Thankam was tired after the journey and the children were restive in the unfamiliar surroundings; so she put them on either side of her, in the bed in her old room, and went to sleep early.

The next morning, when Lakshmi prepared Madhavi's first cup of coffee, Anil took it from her.

'Let me take it to her; I need to get her on my side.'

'She's always on your side; just makes a noise sometimes.'

Madhavi glowed with pleasant surprise when Anil brought the coffee.

'My grandson brings me coffee. I'm a lucky old woman.'

'Ammammey, I am trying to bribe you,' he admitted.

'And why is that? What can a tired old body do for someone like you? However, I'm glad you are back. You are my eldest grandson; the person to set my pyre alight, so you have to be around.'

This was not going as he had hoped.

'Amma is not very happy and I want you to help me to set that right.'

'Oh, take no notice of her; she'll be all right tomorrow.'

'It's not that simple – and you mustn't get angry with me either. There's this girl in England…'

'*Ende padachone*. My God! I knew this was going to happen.'

'It's happened; please don't feel bad. How can I do anything without your blessing?' He was hugging her as he talked.

She drew his face closer to her and searched it with her rheumy eyes; something there must have registered.

'I don't believe your mother getting upset will change your mind. I'm a little afraid you won't be here when I die, but you must promise to come to do the rites. And you must ask your girl to learn a little Malayalam, otherwise how am I to talk to her?'

Anil hugged his grandmother again. 'I knew you wouldn't let me down,' he whispered to her.

Later, Anil told his uncle and mother what had happened. 'She is not such an ogre as you make her out to be,' he insisted.

Thankam and Appu glanced quickly at each other and guffawed; they knew how cussed she could be.

'You're her eldest grandson; she is very fond of you,' Appu told him. 'We have learnt to watch our step with our mother. But there is this other story going around,' Appu added. 'That you bribed her with coffee and hugs.'

'I'm off to Unni's house in the village,' Thankam announced the next morning. 'Anyone going with me?'

'I'll drop you off, but I won't stay if you don't mind. I better look after my nieces until that place becomes liveable,' Anil answered. 'You're not going to stay overnight, are you?'

'Not today. I'm going to get the place organised, get some food in, and then perhaps you and the girls can go over with me tomorrow. If you don't like it, you can come back here for the night, but I want to live in that house for a few days, as of tomorrow. First, I'll have to wake up Kalyani and that lazy, layabout husband of hers.'

Thankam took some bed-sheets and tea, coffee and a pint of milk with her, just in case.

Anil had not been to his father's old home in a long while and was surprised to see he could drive right up to the house. The walkways between the fields had been widened and firmed to make passable roads for one car; if two cars came from opposite directions, one would have to reverse all the way to the main road.

'It is only a five-minute walk to the bus stop,' Thankam reassured Anil. 'I'll get back before dark.'

Anil came inside and looked around like a foreigner. "Are you sure you'll be all right for the day, Ammey? This place looks pretty dilapidated to me.'

'Nothing that a little TLC won't set right. You go on home; I've got my mobile with me if I need you.'

Kalyani came out and asked if they needed something to drink; so Thankam gave her the tea things and asked her to get the kerosene stove in the kitchen going. She followed Kalyani in and wondered: if I am going to make a habit of coming here to stay, I'll need a kettle and a gas stove too. Then Kalyani can do some cooking for us.

She went to the back veranda to wait for the tea and considered her options. How much effort would be needed to make this place habitable again, so she could bring her children and grandchildren sometimes?

Tea came in stainless steel tumblers, almost too hot to touch, the froth worked up by pouring it back and forth into a pot many times. Anil smacked his lips at the end. 'It is thick and sweet the way I like it, with the milk, tea and sugar, all brewed in a saucepan. None of the weak tea bags and cold milk stuff as in the UK. I'm going to miss this when I go back.'

'Why don't you and Sarah learn to make tea like this? It is so easy and quick; a little messy, may be, but invigorating when you get used to it.'

'I cannot see Sarah drinking this stuff,' he said, smiling. She takes her tea without milk or sugar, with just a squeeze of lemon in it.'

Anil left and she went upstairs to her old bedroom. She opened the door to the bathroom Unni had made for her and the children on one of their holidays from Kochi; the children had made a huge fuss about the toilet arrangements in the house and gone on shit-strike.

There had been no indoor toilets or even brick-roofed latrines or night soil collectors in this little village. The men used to go out far into the large coconut grove around the house to shit, in the plot allocated for that purpose. The women had a lean-to, a coconut thatch enclosure, surrounding a man-deep pit, with two tree trunks across it for footholds. The roof was open to the elements and if you needed to use the toilets when it rained, you had to suffer in silence, or hold an umbrella in your hand as you perched. Every six months, the current pit would be covered up and a tree planted there, which would thrive exceptionally well. Then another pit would be dug near by. Thankam had flinched when she first saw it, coming to this house from her own home, where she had been used to an outside latrine, with a tiled roof.

When she came downstairs again she called Kalyani and Ambu, her husband. 'I want the compound swept properly and made safe for my grandchildren to play.'

'Ayyo! There are snakes, Ammey. Kalyani got bitten and we had to go to the Kozhikode hospital to get the anti-venom injection.'

'Right. However, if the compound is kept clean, we won't have that problem. At the moment the grass is waist high between the coconut trees; what do you expect?

'And get the whole house swept and swabbed properly.'

Thankam ferreted around in the heap of dried coconut fronds in the corner of the back veranda. 'All this should be stored in the old cowshed; nothing should be left here.'

As she prodded and poked, she saw Meenakshi's old mortar and pestle abandoned there. This was the one she used for pounding her husband's pan every day. Thankam picked it up and tried to dust it off; then carried it thoughtfully to the front veranda. She sat on the ledge, considering it, remembering the story Unni had told her a long time ago.

'How did your father permit you to marry an educated girl?' Thankam asks. They are a few weeks into their married life and there is so much they don't know about each other. 'Education is considered a crippling handicap for us girls, everyone knows that.'

'My mother could manage almost anything with my father; she had her special tactics. So all I had to do was sit back and watch the fun,' Unni explains.

'Achan, of course has a healthy distrust of educated women, but Amma's persuasive powers are considerable

where my interests are involved; she knew I'd set my mind on marrying you.

'She's pounding pan for him as usual one evening, sitting like a question mark, hunched up at his feet. "Unni wants to marry this girl and we should be making plans to meet his family," she says.

'My father is not too pleased. "I've heard Krishnankutty Nair's daughter is a bit too much into education. You and I, we managed without, didn't we?" Achan is worrying at the hair on the big black wart on his left chin and that is a sign he is disapproving.

'"Young men these days, they don't want a silly know-nothing like me. They want a wife they can talk to," she insists. Amma gave the arecanut in the mortar a good beating with the pestle making the pieces fly out in all directions. I remember one piece landed on Achan's lap; I had trouble containing my mirth. When Amma starts this fierce pounding, Achan always knows it is time to give in. Problem solved..

'When they really disagreed and he shouted at her, she wouldn't do his pan for him that day. Achan would try to do it himself, but he was uncomfortable pounding in the squatting position; his backside would rise with each thump as if he was going to fall over on his face. Finally, Amma would take pity on him and come to his aid.'

Wherever she went in the old house, she saw things needing to be done: plaster was flaking off the windowsill in the middle-room; the kitchen looked like a tip, with no clean surface space, except two rickety old tables; the toilet seat was pockmarked with lizard droppings and disuse and needed to be changed. No, Asha and Latha would not be able to cope with this level of disarray. Reluctantly, she admitted she could not camp here until the place was renovated, so she set about making a list of the things to be done. Next time, she would need to come back on her own and stay for a month.

Kalyani cooked rice and plantain curry for her with

channa dhal, so Thankam stayed on till the evening. Now she knew the house was not habitable without serious repairs, but she was strangely reluctant to leave. So she phoned Anil to say she was staying on for the night.

'Kalyani will look after me, so don't worry. Make sure you sleep with the girls, they don't know anyone else,' she instructed. Anil sounded a little uneasy but he probably fathomed this was something she had to do.

Thankam sat for a long time on the outside ledge, lost in thought, until the evening light faded, wicks of devotional lamps starting to flicker in the verandas of houses, like fireflies, through the darkening palm trees. When dusk came, Kalyani lighted the Nilavilakku and brought it out, calling '*Deepam, deepam.*' Thankam got up and faced east to worship the lamp.

This was how Unni had first fallen in love with her, when he had dropped in to see her father, and she brought out the lamp at dusk.

Thankam went to bed early that night, in the same bed she had slept with Unni all those years ago. It smelled damp and musty with neglect, but she didn't care; she had other things on her mind.

She had forgotten the total dark of the countryside; there were no streetlights here. She was often sad she never dreamt of Unni, but this night he was with her and she didn't know whether it was dream or reality.

He is sitting on the chair near the window. 'Come, Thankam,' he says. 'I have things to talk to you about.'

She is busy folding clothes to put away into the glass-fronted almirah near the window; Anil's five-year-old shorts and vests; Manju's seven-year-old frocks. She ignores him and carries on. When she goes to the almirah to put them away, he pulls her to him and she falls into his lap.

'This is where you belong; so don't run away.' He smells of the Scissors cigarettes he smokes non-stop and sandalwood soap: a heady mixture that always turns her on.

'I have to go down and see to supper for Anil and Manju,' she says carefully, but her face is burrowing into his thick chest hair, so he puts away the cigarette in his right hand and holds her close to him.

'They are grown up now; they can look after themselves. I need you to keep me together.' They have suddenly become Manju and Anil of today, in the way dreams can mock time's arrow.

'Why? Are you not together now?'

And it is not Unni's chest hair she is clutching any more; it is Mohan's and the smell of Scissors is replaced by the strong smell of Lynx shaving lotion that Mohan uses.

Mohan strokes her face and his hands move down slowly and her loins respond to his touch, warmer by the moment. Suddenly, she comes, strongly, almost violently, and wakes up, pulsing. Her left hand is holding tight to the end of her long plait and she continues throbbing for some time.

She sleeps fitfully after that and the eerie quiet of the countryside wakes her up earlier than usual. As soon as Kalyani made her a cup of coffee, Thankam set off for Thiruvangad. Appu was already up, reading the day's *Manorama* when she walked in.

'Can't stay in that house till it is renovated; it is practically falling to bits in places.'

'Well, you need more than a week to do that. Why don't you come down in December when I am here again? We'll get a contractor in and get everything done; I can supervise the work for you. I was telling Anil that you couldn't really go there to live, even for a week, with two children brought up in Kochi. You have to get the house ready and then maybe, I'll come too, and we can make a holiday out of it. And next time, bring that lazy niece of mine.'

Thankam stayed a week with her family and they drove back in time for Manju's return from Delhi.

17

Thankam prepared for a busy week ahead. Anil was off to the UK in three days and had some serious shopping to do. In addition work would have piled up at the college.

However, when she reached Kochi at five in the evening after a long and dusty drive from Thalassery, it was apparent Seetha was not in. Moli had left a note saying Seethachechi had not come, but her daughter Preethi had phoned. She didn't leave a message.

'Thank God for takeaways,' Thankam vowed. Anil went to the Western Cookhouse and brought *parattas* and chicken curry for them. As soon as Thankam phoned, Manju came to pick up her daughters; she had only got back that morning. The children attached themselves to her full of woes and questions.

'Ammey, why did you go to work, when we went to Appu ammaman's house?' they clamoured. 'Jayettan made boats for us from the silver paper inside Appu ammaman's *Scissors* cigarette boxes and we sailed them in the rainwater.'

'So, do you know how to make the boats now?' she asked, but clearly, she was distracted and barely listening to them.

'No, but we will know next time we go there. You have to come too. We visited our grandfather's big house and we went to the temple and we met lots of Ammamma's friends.'

Then they recounted a long list of sweets Lakshmi had made for them.

'So Lakshmi is still hiding behind doors and cooking all the time?' Manju remarked.

'That's right.' Thankam answered. 'And Appu Ammaman is bursting out of his clothes; he has put on so much weight. He says you have to go down there with us next time.'

'I wish I'd gone with you instead of going to Delhi,' Manju said. Thankam thought she heard a thin vein of defeat in her voice, but could not ask anything at that time. Instead she gave her a special hug and said, 'Now you are here and everything is going to be all right.'

'Yes, I know,' she murmured, but she sounded unconvinced.

Early in the morning the next day, the phone rang; it was Preethi. Her voice sounded tentative.

'Amma cannot come today; she's sick.'

'What's the matter?'

'She's in bed; she's not well.'

Yes, I gathered that, but what is wrong with her?'

'She's lying down.'

Thankam realised she was not going to get any farther with this line of questioning; the girl was going round and round in circles.

'All right. Please ring me tomorrow if she is not able to come.'

A faint 'Yes.'

Later, Thankam asked Anil to take her to Seetha's house; something kept nagging at the back of her mind. Was it the hesitation in Preethi's voice?

'Please come with me, Anil. I think I may need a man around today.'

Seetha lived in a small house near the railway lines in Vyttilla. The lanes were narrow and Anil had to dodge in and out of side roads when other cars approached.

When they got out of the car, they saw Seetha's husband, Parthan, fast asleep on the bench on the veranda; he didn't hear them as they came in. The sour smell of yesterday's drink attacked their nostrils as they tiptoed past him. An empty, orange plastic mug stood next to his head and ants were climbing in and out of it. His mouth was slightly open and a thin dribble of saliva had made snail-marks on his left cheek.

They found Seetha curled up on a mat, in the corner of the long, lightless corridor in the front of their house. The torn handloom sheet she had over her had fallen away and she seemed totally defenceless, with streaks of dried tears on her face. The old warrior in her heard her mistress, however, and she struggled up. The weave of the mat had dented a criss-cross pattern on one side of her face.

'What's the matter?' Thankam started to say, but as Seetha sat up, what was the matter became amply clear. Her face was bruised and she could not move her left arm very much; she winced as she tried to haul herself up. A tuft of hair appeared to have gone from the front of her head and one eye was half-closed and swollen; questions were clearly unnecessary.

Seetha had trouble talking through her swollen mouth; Thankam wanted to pull up the man sleeping in drunken stupor on the veranda and attack him till he screamed for mercy.

Seetha's bruises had not been cleaned. 'Why have you not gone to the hospital?' Thankam asked. 'You may have broken something.'

The tears came again, then. Thankam held her hand, careful not to move the elbows.

'They'll ask me how this happened. What do I tell them? And the whole place will get to know about it.'

'Somebody has to know and something must be done to stop this,' Thankam insisted.

'When Preethi gets married, I'm going to leave him, Ammey. If I do it now, no one will marry her from a broken home. So I have to stay.'

'I'm taking you to the hospital and I'll do the talking,' Thankam said briskly.

Anil helped Seetha into the car, while the drunken lout slept on. Preethi had gone to the house where she did part-time work and Prakash and his wife were out at work too.

In the Casualty hall at the Medical Centre, the patients sat on plastic benches with their tokens in their hands, waiting for their numbers to appear on the counter on the wall. The tannoy also announced the number, but it was hard to hear over the noise of people talking, the women at the reception explaining things to new patients, and children screaming. Some of the female patients were accompanied by men who sat stoically staring into space or reading newspapers, while their wives chased after running children, breast-fed babies or merely slumped back in their seats with illness or exhaustion. Clearly, the men considered themselves above all this disorder and need.

In the case of male patients, the women accompanying them fussed over them, fetching drinks, asking them if they hurt, if they wanted to lie down...

Thankam glanced around at the crowd and knew she was in for a long wait.

'Anil, go home, there is no need for you to wait. Come back only when I call you on my mobile. This is going to take an hour or two.'

'Are you sure?'

'Yes, you have to travel soon. Why don't you go down to MG Road and buy the shirts you need and you can get some gifts from there too, to take back for your friends. Try the "Treasure Trove"; they have good brass artefacts and sandalwood. But have an idea of the weight you are buying; otherwise you will end up paying a lot for carrying excess baggage.'

The tea vendor came by with his urn then and Thankam bought tea for Seetha and herself; Seetha perked up a little when she got the hot, sweet tea inside her.

'I don't know how you are managing with Anil mone there, without me.'

'Don't worry about that; let's get you properly healed first. You can buy food in Kochi, so it's not a big problem.

'But I have no one to tell me all the news in the lane,' Thankam teased.

Seetha needed to be away from her home for a few days, but Thankam didn't know how she was going to manage that. A day maybe, but beyond that, the husband was going to create a fuss.

'Preethi really wanted to continue her studies after she passed her school-leaving exams at the first attempt, two years ago,' Seetha suddenly said, apropos of nothing. Thankam could hear pride in her voice at her daughter's achievement. 'Prakash did not get beyond the fourth form and he started working as a casual labourer when he was only seventeen. Now he drinks like his father, beats up his wife and goes to work only now and then; it is as though he is already tired of the working life and there is no hope in him. I sometimes wonder what he is going to do when he is sixty or seventy. Now his wife works in houses and feeds his child and buys everything. Will she do anything for this kind of husband when he is an old good-for-nothing instead of a young one?

'In fact, Amma, I shouldn't tell you this: he beat her so much last month, she now sleeps in my room, not his. Like father, like son.

'Anyway, the bridegroom's people came to see Preethi last week and he liked her. Preethi knows this dream about studying is never going to happen; her uncles won't let her go back to school. Now the whole community is after me to arrange this wedding. Where was this community when my husband beat me, right through our married life? You see this front tooth, Amma?' Seetha pulled her top lip up with her finger to display it. 'This is a false tooth. He kicked me when I was expecting Prakash and my tooth came off; I was only seventeen years old then. I ran away to my father's house and I stayed there, hoping I would have a miscarriage. But, when my son was born, my father forced me to go back to this devil of mine.

'This community! Many of them have houses in the same lane. When they hear my husband shouting and starting to beat me, anyone sitting on the bench outside gets up and goes inside the house.

'Wait till Preethi is married. I'll show them.'

Finally, Seetha's number was called. Thankam took her from doctor to X-ray room, back to the doctor, paying a hundred rupees here and fifty rupees there. When all was done, the doctor pronounced no bones had been broken, but Seetha was in shock. So Thankam got in touch with Anil and he took them to Thankam's home; Seetha's husband wouldn't dare ask about her, just yet, after all that day's happenings – if he woke up at all.

Preethi phoned in the evening, asking about her mother.

'She'll come back tomorrow; she needs to rest today, don't worry,' Thankam reassured her. 'You can come over if you want to see her.'

'Did you manage to get everything you need?' Thankam asked Anil later, when they sat down to evening tea. Everyone had missed lunch and Anil had bought *vadas* and *bondas* for tea to compensate - his last big indulgence before returning abroad, he called it.

'Actually, I had no stomach for the shopping after I left Seetha. I wandered around a bit and came home. Didn't buy anything much. I can get things on my next trip home.'

'Home. Where is home going to be in the future?'

'I'm a lucky man; I have two homes when most have only one and some have none, though they don't know it.'

Manju dropped by in the evening before Anil left. He had left the nest long ago, but now a commitment had been made to another country. However much she tried to wrap it up, she knew Anil had begun to make a life elsewhere for himself and she could not be part of it from this distance.

Manju had brought food for all of them and she made a pretty picture leading her children, one on either side of her. For a little while, it appeared to Thankam the family was still intact, but in her heart she knew they had all gone.

'We never got a chance to talk properly,' Thankam began when Anil had gone inside for his bath. 'You have been sad since you came back from Delhi.'

'Dave and I spent a lot of time together in Delhi; I had a chance to see how happy I could be with him. But I thought about Asha and Latha; what if Gopi takes them away from me? So I told Dave that we must not see each other again. How can I be anything but sad?

'He's off to the UK on leave soon and I suspect he will not come back, now I've said this to him.'

Manju was crying now. 'What shall I do, Ammey? Gopi is also gone from me and now this. Don't I have any right to seek happiness for myself? I know I would never be happy if the girls were not with me. But it is so hopeless.'

Thankam went to Manju and gathered her in her arms, letting her cry her heart out. So many times, Thankam had consoled her like this in the past, when Manju had found herself in situations where the world was at odds with her.

'Don't give up so easily. We will find a way,' Thankam murmured into her hair.

As she comforted her daughter with these words, she knew it would need all her wits and inventiveness to find a solution to Manju's present woes.

Thankam drove Anil to Nedumbassery airport the next morning; the plane took off at nine, so Anil had to be there by six. Perhaps Anil sensed his mother was sad; so as he left, he turned round to her saying, 'Sarah loves India; she backpacked in the north in her gap year between school and college; now she is eager to see Kerala. I'll be back soon.' That would have to do.

When Thankam came back from the airport at ten in the morning, Seetha was in the kitchen preparing breakfast.

'Seetha, you're supposed to be in bed. Go and rest, I'll take you home this evening. Manju brought loads of food yesterday and there's plenty left; we don't need to do any cooking today.' Seetha seemed to be allergic to lying down, so she pottered around, washing out containers in the kitchen and removing stones from the rice.

In the evening, Thankam took Seetha home. She also took a parcel of rice, sugar, tea, milk and oil for the household.

Parthan was sitting outside, on the veranda. He tried to avoid speaking to Thankam by vanishing indoors when he saw her, but she followed him.

'I need to talk to you,' she insisted.

To begin with he was truculent: 'What is there to talk about?' he demanded. 'And you, what right have you to talk to anyone about anything? With the way *you* live in that house. I don't want my wife to come anywhere near you.'

'If that is what you think, perhaps you are right. I'll do my talking to the Women's Association, the Family Courts and the police.'

'This is not your business. What happens between my wife and me is not something you need to worry about. And remember, I can also talk about *you.*'

'I have made what happens to Seetha my business. If this happens again, I am going to file a charge at the Vyttilla Police Station against you even if Seetha refuses to do so.' Thankam knew perfectly well she could do nothing of the sort if Seetha didn't agree to lodge a complaint. Seetha would never agree because of the shame and the scandal. Thankam was counting on Parthan not knowing anything about the law in this respect.

She went to the car, took the food parcel out and carried it into the kitchen. As she did so Preethi came out from the outside lean-to where she was having a bath, to take charge of her mother.

'Don't let her do any housework for a few days,' Thankam said, as she left, but she knew Seetha would probably turn up for work the next day.

'She won't listen to anyone,' Preethi reminded Thankam; as though Thankam didn't know that.

Predictably, Seetha turned up the next morning, long before Thankam had got out of bed; she brought coffee, the day's paper and a huge smile as she came up the stairs.

'Look, Amma, all the bruises are going and my arm is not hurting.' This was true: the bruises had changed colour from angry red and purple to a light blue-green. When Thankam touched the one on her temple, Seetha did not wince.

'What about the elbow?' Thankam asked. 'Can you lift things with it?'

Seetha waved it around, but stopped quickly midway. 'See, it's back to normal now. I am much better off here than there; when I come here, I forget all the worries I have in that house. Here I am busy and I shut my mind to that man and his son.'

'But, I still say, you could have rested for at least another day, surely.' Thankam's disapproval was clear. 'If you come back to work too quickly and get ill again, I'm the one who will suffer, so I'm being selfish.'

Thankam turned away and busied herself getting her clothes together for the day: sari, sari-skirt, matching blouse and undergarments. However, Seetha showed no inclination to go back downstairs. Thankam turned towards her, eyebrows lifted in a question; Seetha, shook her head and left. Thankam wondered what that was about, but she didn't have to stay in the dark for long. Seetha was back in a few moments and this time, she had a determined jut to her jaw.

'That Mohan Sar-'

Here it comes, thought Thankam. She waited for the inevitable.

'I don't see him coming to our house too much these days.'

'Must be busy. In any case, they are moving out.'

'The girl has been gone a while; I am not talking about that. The food in the refrigerator does not go; it used to get eaten overnight, lots of it. So I know he does not come to see you any more.

'Preethi's father said some evil things about you. He said I can't work here. Not that I have any intention of listening to him. And where is his rice going to come from if I don't work?'

Thankam came over and sat on the bed; she didn't say anything. So that was why she got kicked around, Thankam thought. Because of me.

'Please don't be annoyed, Amma, for my saying this; so many people are making comments about you to me; I hate it. I ask them to mind their business, but when Anil was here, I was worried some busybody would say something to him.

'I want you to be happy and you've been happy this past year. But now?'

'Seetha, when people say things, sometimes they can be true. You know that, don't you?'

'Yes.'

'Mohan won't come here any more; so you can stop worrying.

'And they have been saying things to my children,' Thankam added. 'Fortunately, they did not understand. I am still a confused person. But as long as I have you, Raji and my children, it will all work out. So go down and make that *vellayappam* and stew you do so well for breakfast. I have a big appetite today.'

'I'll see whether any of that vellayappam mixture remains from the time Anil mone was here,' Seetha answered. 'You have to tell me early, like the previous day, if you want vellayappam; I need to get young coconuts to ferment the mixture and they are not easy to find.'

Since it was still Onam holidays at the college, Thankam decided she had time to go to the Kadavanthara fish market and get some seer fish, prawns, sardines and tuna. Seetha liked her sardine curry with the special *kudampuli* in it, instead of the usual tamarind she used for sambar; this was going to be a special treat for her. Kudampuli was not used for anything in North Malabar and Thankam had never got used to the taste, but it was supposed to be effective in keeping cholesterol levels down.

After the hustle and bustle of Onam, people were slow to get back to work from their villages; many would not return till after the weekend. A general air of sleepiness pervaded in the town; traffic was sparse and it was easy to get to the market. Thankam wore an old, drip-dry nylon sari and one of her ancient pairs of slippers; the alleyway to the market was filthy, particularly when it rained, and inside the market, the ground was trodden mud and slushy in places. Fish was everywhere and it was almost impossible to avoid getting some on your sari hem or slippers; she would need a complete change of clothes when she returned.

In front of the alleyway leading to the market, the vegetable and grocery shops were plying their businesses half-heartedly. Most households would have exhausted their food-budget with Onam and the shops had not yet got in a new stock of vegetables or groceries. Ummer, the man from whom she normally bought her condiments, called out to her, 'Don't you need anything from me today, *Chechi*?'

'I don't want you to palm off all your old stuff on me. I'll come when you've got new stock in.' It was all very good-natured.

She picked up a coconut from the pavement in front of the vegetable shop and shook it at her ear to test if it was good, and put it back; it sloshed too much inside; that meant it had been plucked too early and would be useless for grinding for the fish curry.

'Keep six good coconuts for me when you get new ones,' she called out.

'There is a dearth of coconuts after Onam; we've got to get new stock. All the shops are sold out. Those there are bad because the suppliers were bringing us bad coconuts when they realised the strength of the demand over Onam.'

Thankam lifted up the hem of her sari and walked carefully into the market; here too a general air of lassitude prevailed. Fish prices had come down after Onam, but very little was on sale.

Thankam saw some under-sized seer fish. Santosh, her usual supplier, came running when he saw her.

'Not much fish around, Ammey. But what we have is cheap. The seer is only eighty rupees a kilo today.' She knew it had been selling for one hundred and twenty rupees the previous week.

'It's not big enough to slice up for frying, but you could use it for curry,' he added.

'All right, I'll take one of those and slice it up for curry, will you? Can you find me some prawns as well? And half a kilo of sardines and the same amount of tuna.'

Santosh would go around to the other stalls and get everything for her. Again the prawns were small, but she took one kilo. It would do for Prawn Biriyani to cheer Manju up; the girl was doing her chicken-licken act all the time these days. The market was clean out of tuna, however.

The total cost came to two hundred rupees; Thankam parted with the money and walked out.

At the entrance to the alleyway, she ran into Janaki, Gopi's sister.

What a pleasant surprise!' Thankam called out when she saw Janaki's large backside at the door of her car, bending down to retrieve something from the floor of the vehicle. "Didn't know you were in town.'

Janaki took her time replying. She collected her things and walked over.

'Just got here this morning.' She didn't appear overjoyed to see Thankam, but then, Thankam had never seen her overjoyed.

'Does that mean Saraswathi is all right now and has come back?'

'Amma won't come back that quickly now that Manju is working. Besides, Madhavettan says she has a growth in her oesophagus. They say she is too old to be opened up and checked and she won't allow an endoscopy. She agreed to do it when Gopi was here but cried off at the last minute. So Madhavettan is just keeping her under observation, hoping the tumour won't grow and that it is not malignant.'

'Anyway, what do you gain by Amma coming here? You are both having a carefree time with no men to boss you, and Amma with me?' Janaki stared significantly at Thankam.

'Does Manju know you're here?'

'What's the point of informing her? She'll be at work or whatever. From what I am hearing she is having a ball too.'

'And what's that supposed to mean?' Thankam asked.

She bit her lip as if trying to prevent something from escaping.

'She went off to Delhi recently,' Janaki continued. 'I doubt Gopi would have allowed her to go if he had been here.'

'Actually, she asked Gopi first. Not that it is your business, anyway. I don't know what exactly you are insinuating and I can't say I like your tone.'

Janaki bristled. 'Gopi married Manju thinking she was from a respectable family, but from what we are hearing, you and Manju are leading the kind of lives my family would not want to be associated with.'

'Or you are spreading a lot of rumours. When Manju married Gopi, we did not know a few things about Gopi either. Otherwise–'

'Oh, all that was a long time ago,' Janaki interrupted. 'I asked him just before he got married and he said he had stopped consorting with any of those young men. Those were schoolboy pranks – and which red-blooded male has not indulged in a few of them? Janaki was speaking quickly trying to placate Thankam.

'He promised never again to see that crook Mani, who nearly ruined him. Mani was well known for being a rent-boy in Kovalam before he came to Kochi. He married and settled down and that was that; he tried to spoil Gopi before that, but it didn't last very long.'

Thankam knew they were talking at cross purposes and the information coming her way was gold dust, if she needed to get the better of Janaki's rumour- mongering.

'So Gopi was gay then, at college, was he? And you got him married to my only daughter, without mentioning anything to us?'

Janaki hemmed and hawed, looking acutely uncomfortable.

'And I suppose you will say you didn't know he smoked ganja as well?'

'He stopped long ago.'

'Well he hasn't. And he is still seeing Mani. I'm glad he is not here because living with Gopi can be dangerous for my daughter. What if he gets AIDS? Have you thought about how Manju would feel about all this? Selfish lot!

'So don't go round talking nonsense about my daughter and me. I'll have your guts for garters, Janaki. I'll tell absolutely everyone what Gopi has been up to, before and after marriage. So take heed.'

Janaki pulled the end of her sari and wrapped it round her as though seeking refuge in it. She hurried off into the market with a red face.

Thoughts about Manju went round and round in Thankam's head; she could not see any solutions anywhere. She dumped the fish in the boot of the car and came to the front. Sitting in the driver's seat, she put her head down on the steering wheel for a moment; she felt profoundly alone, as though the whole world was arrayed against her and her children. Then she started the car and drove home.

18

In the days after Thankam broke up with Mohan she often found herself walking from one room to another in her vast house, looking out of windows, not settling down to anything. Sometimes, when despair overcame her, she would make a mental list of all the things she needed to do and all the people who depended on her and loved her.

There was Seetha and her daughter's marriage; Seetha would not be able to cope without help of many different kinds. Manju would have to be told about Gopi's bisexuality; she must take the ELISA test. The children would also need to take tests to be on the safe side. How does one break such news to one's child? Thinking about these things made Thankam realise her own petty problems were irrelevant right now.

Mohan came round early in the morning the next day, while Thankam was having a second cup of coffee on the veranda. She smiled. 'I think you know when I'm having coffee. 'Seetha,' she called out. 'Fetch another cup for Mohan sar.'

'Who can resist the smell of Seetha's coffee?' He seemed relieved to see Thankam in a friendly mood.

'I've been looking for a place to stay and I'm sure I will find somewhere soon. It's not easy as no one is going to give me a good flat like yours for a measly thousand rupees. I am beginning to look away from the centre of town. Now

Geetha is not around I can travel in from the outskirts if need be. The ideal thing would of course be a job in Kottayam, then I can live at home. Also, I won't need to travel back and forth so much to look after our affairs there.'

'I'll let you know if I hear of any suitable flat,' Thankam said.

Mohan stayed for a few minutes talking, drank his coffee and left. When he went, Thankam found there was an unexpected lump in her throat: the meeting had cured the angst in both their minds about each other, but it confirmed the death of whatever had flourished between them briefly.

The college had meanwhile reopened. Thankam had other things on her mind, but she took the car out as usual in the morning and drove to Panampilly Nagar. Once she got into the car, she stopped thinking about Manju because she had to concentrate to avoid the potholes, the pie dogs and the motorcycles that veered in and out of the traffic.

Just past the bridge a two-wheeler skidded into her path, then recovered and proceeded without reducing speed. Must keep away from him, Thankam warned herself, so she moved to the left and slowed down to let him go. The motorcycle then became quite erratic, zigzagging and tilting over; then suddenly it toppled and the man was thrown to the right. As he hit the ground he started twitching and jerking violently; Thankam realised this was a man having an epileptic fit while riding and that the fit may have started a few moments ago when he appeared to lose control. When she looked in the mirror, a crowd had gathered round him.

Bad omen, she cautioned herself; first day back at college and what a beginning. To make matters worse, a queue of new admissions was waiting at her door: parents of students who had failed the previous batch of examinations and were looking for help for a repeat. These were the applicants who had submitted forms earlier and had now come to pick up their places. Jacob had accepted them, so all she was going to do was see them briefly before the system swallowed them up.

This was not a job she enjoyed, but as the owner and joint-manager, the applicants expected to have this brief access to her. She had no choice, so she asked the secretary to send them in one at a time. She processed each applicant quickly and sent them on to Jacob and the office at the other end of the building for counselling and other formalities.

The college had fifty places for year-twelve students and she finished the fifty by lunchtime. The tea that the secretary, Savithri, had brought midmorning was already stale and scummy by the time it reached her, so she had pushed it away. Now she was beginning to feel hungry and the ache between her shoulder blades was getting stronger by the second. She lifted her arms up and stretched, hoping to relax the tense neck muscles, thinking her work was over for the moment, so she was not pleased when a man pushed his way in, ignoring a flustered-looking Savithri, who was trying her best to keep him out.

'If you don't have an interview card, you cannot see Madam,' Savithri insisted, but the man could not be stopped.

'What-' Thankam began, annoyed, and then nodded to Savithri to let him be when she realised she was going to have to talk to him.

He came up to the desk.

'I'm from Andhra Pradesh,' he said. 'My name is Shankar Rao.' Thankam did not ask him to sit down, so he was forced to continue standing. 'My son had a place in Hyderabad at a tutorial college, but there was a family tragedy recently and I could not leave him there on his own, while I came on transfer here. He needs me.

'I know he did not apply early, but it is not his fault or mine. I was transferred here quite suddenly. This will be our first year here. I am happy to make a donation to the college or pay a capitation charge, as others may have done.'

'We don't take capitation charges and we don't ask for donations,' Thankam said, looking up at him. 'We're a small institution and like to keep it that way. What are you doing here in Kochi anyway?'

'I am the local manager of Sun Homes in Kochi and we are in the process of starting branches in Kottayam and Kozhikode, to begin with. Just recruiting staff, in fact.'

'You appear to be a special case, so I'll see whether we can find a place for your son. But what kind of staff are you taking on?' Thankam's busy little brain had seen an opportunity here. 'Do sit down.'

'Sales and marketing staff mainly, but also a manager for each town. Maybe a partner. We have a lot of applications but not too many have worked for a building firm before and even if they have, we need good references; otherwise the chances of corruption are too many.'

'I know of someone who is looking for a job and a business opportunity in Kottayam, if you are interested,' Thankam said.

'Send him on, by all means. Now, I am obliged to you, I have to consider him, haven't I?' The man smiled, obviously relieved to have got this far with the Principal.

'Something like that.' Thankam smiled. 'His name is Mohan Nair.'

'Ask him to come on Wednesday morning.'

The things I do for my yesterday's lover, Thankam mused; I must be fond of him still. And that's not bad, is it? I wonder how he thinks of me.

In another time and place, perhaps, we could have made a go of it. But in Kochi, where scandal grows from the emptiness of bored minds, who has a chance?

In the evening she phoned upstairs.

'Mohan, I have some news for you. I ran into the manager of a building company called Sun Homes today. They are opening a new branch in Kottayam and they are taking on new staff. Would you be interested? He might even offer a partnership to the right person.'

'Interested? It would solve so many problems at one go.'

Am I one of those problems? Thankam wondered, but she decided that was an unkind thought and shoved it away.

'He says to go and see him on Wednesday morning. Tell him I sent you.'

'It's kind of you to do all this,' Mohan said. 'Not many in your position would have done as much.'

'You're my friend, Mohan, and I hope that won't change. I'm sure you would do as much for me if the positions were reversed.' She noted with surprise that she really believed it.

Anil phoned late at night and stayed on the phone for a long time.

'We went to Sarah's house yesterday; her parents and brother were there. Mum, they really made me feel part of the family. Her mother is very like her, full of bubble and naughtiness.

'You know, Sarah didn't ask them for permission or anything, just said we had news for them. They of course, guessed.'

'You are a right hypocrite,' she laughed at Anil. 'Would it have made any difference if I did not give you permission, as you call it?'

'No.' Anil burst out laughing.

'So this is our usual face-saving device, isn't it?'

'Absolutely.'

'Do you know when you might be getting married?'

'Like you, her family also asked the same thing. Not before the end of the next year, I'm sure. She has to settle down in her job and I have to find another one.

'She keeps saying how lovely the ring is, shows it off to everyone.'

'There is something I need to talk to you about,' Thankam said. 'Manju might be coming to the UK for three months, on a training course. She has a choice to go in January or May and I don't know what she will decide.

'She'll need all the moral support she can get. Things are not so good at this end with her and Gopi.'

'She's being a brat again, is she?'

'Not this time. But it's her news and she will talk to you about it herself, I'm sure. Anyway, I'm taking the children over for the period, so she will be especially lonely.'

'I'm sure it will be fun having her. Don't worry about her, Ammey. She is made of sterner stuff than you think.

'Take care of yourself,' he called out as he rang off. 'Oh, and I forgot to tell you, I met Graciamma's son, that big hairy brute, John, in the shops the day Seetha went to hospital. He twirled his moustache at me and said you needed me in the house; I wasn't looking after the family properly. "A man needs to be there," he said. Stupid oaf. As though you need anyone to look after you.'

Thankam knew what that was about, so she did not comment.

'Take care, you too, and give my regards to Sarah.'

The fisherman's bicycle bell, Inji's dash for the daily gift of fish from the vendor and Mohan coming down the stairs, all happened together.

'Seetha, bring the *meenchatti*,' Thankam called out as she went to the gate to check the catch of the day. Seetha appeared quickly with one of the red, specially shaped terracotta fish-woks. It carried a slight whiff of ground coconut and boiled fish.

Thankam inspected the tuna, which she had been unable to get from the market.

'Has this been stored in ice from yesterday?' Thankam asked the obligatory question; no one trusted fish sellers; it was their job to get rid of fish, long past their sell-by hour. She peered into the basket on the back of the bike; it was lined a half foot deep with ice cubes and covered in green banana leaves to guard it from the fierce morning sun. As he lifted the leaves up, the fishy liquid drained off to the side and Inji got frantic with greed.

'Here, this is yours.' The fisherman threw two small tunas to Inji well away from the basket, so the kitten would stop getting in everyone's way, making loud demands.

'How much?' Thankam asked.

The fishermen launched into his usual spiel. 'Just caught this morning, Amma. Look at the gills.' He opened the gills to show how red they were and closed them quickly before anyone could take a proper look. 'I will give you a special price, you are my regular customer. Only fifty rupees a kilo.'

'It's only thirty-five rupees in the market,' Seetha interjected. 'Don't buy, Ammey, we have plenty of fish in the refrigerator.'

'I'll give you forty rupees,' Thankam said and the deal was clinched. The man took out his spring balance and loaded the fish into one pan and the kilo weight into the other; it was impossible for him to hold the balance rod level even if he wanted to, on his rickety balance.

'There, that's a kilo,' he said finally.

Seetha picked up another tuna from his basket and threw it into the cooking pot. All par for the course and everyone knew the rules of the game.

Mohan stood, watching this tableau and waiting for Thankam to pay off the fishermen. Then she turned to him.

'My, my-' she exclaimed. He was dressed for his job interview in Kottayam. A rust shirt over smart black linen trousers and a pure silk tie in swirls of greys and leaf greens. His black shoes were polished to perfection.

He always had been a clotheshorse, but today he looked like a model.

'If they are going to give the job for appearance, surely you will get it,' she said, laughing at him.

'You haven't forgotten how to tease me,' he answered. 'But you don't remember you gave me this shirt and tie over a year ago.'

'Did I? That was a mistake, wasn't it?' She was still laughing.

'But if you've come for my blessing, you have it. Come back with the job.' She touched the top of his head lightly.

Late in the morning, while she was signing invoices, Savithri transferred a call to her. 'Mohan Nair from Kottayam. He said he's the manager designate of the Kottayam branch of Sun Houses, madam.'

Thankam picked the phone up joyfully. 'Well done,' she declared.

'Well done, both of us,' Mohan returned. I couldn't have done it without you.'

Mohan left Kochi a week later, saying he'd come back for his things soon. He paid up his rent till the end of the month when he left.

'I think I'm going a little at a time, so I can deceive myself this is not final.'

'Why does it have to be?' Thankam asked. 'Kottayam is not far; you must come down and see Inji and me frequently.

He sat down on the veranda ledge briefly. 'This is not easy to say, but let me try.

'You've been many things to me,' he started hesitantly. 'I shall always think of you as my chechi. My favourite elder sister. I've learned many things from you.'

'Not so much of the elder, please.'

'I've acted strangely on occasion; it is not forgivable. However, I'm sure you will understand, with that large heart of yours. All my friends and colleagues started making remarks about me: What was it like to be a rich woman's lover? Did I live rent-free? Did she give me expensive gifts? They did not do justice to you or me or the way I felt about you, but they were able to destroy my self-respect. I'm sure you must have come across some of that as well.'

'Don't worry,' Thankam consoled him. 'All this will blow away soon. You have a good life in Kottayam and keep in touch with us. I am going to miss you.'

19

Thankam decided to go to the Widows Association the next Wednesday; she had been busy for some time and she had missed seeing some of her friends there. She phoned Raji. 'Are you going down to the WA today? I'm planning to go; I could come over and pick you up.'

'You are going in the wrong direction for the WA if you come to Panampilly Nagar, but it is high time you visited your old friend. Can you come over at threeish? We could have tea and go there at four to four-thirty.'

Thankam dressed carefully. She was feeling at ease with herself these days; all the frustration to do with Mohan had disappeared. Sometimes she wondered whether this part of her life was finished; would she ever love a man again? In a woman's life, the expectation of love comes to an end at some point, unless she is Joan Collins or Elizabeth Taylor, she pondered wryly; had she come to that point of no return?

She took an old necklace of black beads, tiny pearls and gold out of her jewel box, her traditional *karimanimala;* this was the necklace she wore for the *pennukanal*, the official 'seeing' day, when Unni's family came to inspect her. She had not worn it for years. A search among her bangles unearthed the pair made from the tough hairs of an elephant's tail, set in gold. To go with both, she found a pair of black-bead-and-gold earrings. She put them on.

When the red Maruthi drove into Raji's house at three-thirty, she was waiting on the veranda.

'I am dying for a cup of tea,' Thankam called out as she parked the car. 'Seetha is busy arranging her daughter's marriage this week and I have been missing her ministrations.'

'That Seetha spoils you. However, I must admit, you look as though you have no quarrels with the world. If I didn't know how lazy you are at doing any physical exercises, I'd imagine you were doing yoga.'

'Yoga, my foot! Where is the time? Manju is working full time and I do a lot of baby-sitting these days. Moli has gone off on a pilgrimage somewhere and hasn't been in for a week. I asked her what the pilgrimage was for and she said, "I want to pray for a good husband." How can I refuse to let her go after that? So, this week, it's yours truly on her own. And I must admit, I don't enjoy my tea if I have to make it myself.'

'That's the least I can do for you. I've made some *bonda* mixture as well; I only have to fry them now; so let's have a feast.' Raji went in to make up the bondas and Thankam followed her into the kitchen.

The kitchen was wiped clean and dry after lunch. A faint smell of garlic and shallots hung in the air. Both Raji's children were out at school and were now big enough to find their way back on their own, so Raji didn't need to rush out to pick them up. The whole house was quiet with that special afternoon quiet that houses acquire when housewives retire for siestas.

'Now that Shija and Ramu are a little older, I have a lot more time to myself. I'm thinking of working part-time,' announced Raji.

'What kind of work are you thinking of?'

'I was going to ask your advice. I thought of doing a course in Computer Science at the National Institute of Information Technology in Ravipuram. I might have to juggle the times a little, but they have courses starting at many different times in the day; I could find a timetable to suit me, I'm told. I've always fancied learning a little bit more about computers.

'Ramu is pestering me to buy one for the house anyway, so I might as well learn.'

Raji had the potatoes mashed and ready. So she added the chopped green chillies, onions and ginger she had prepared, and mixed them in. Then she burst some mustard seed in hot oil with a red chillie bean, some black gram dhal, and curry leaves. To this she added some chopped coriander leaves and the whole thing went into the potato mash. Thankam tasted the mixture and pronouncing it perfect, and rolled them into small balls as Raji made a gram flour batter and coated them. They fried quickly and when the golden balls were drained, Raji brought them out to the veranda with a pot of tea.

'Mmm…' Thankam expressed approval, as she bit into her first one. The inside was so hot, she couldn't shut her mouth on it; she kept it open and gulped air into her mouth to cool it.

'I was greedy.' Thankam laughed when at last she could close her mouth. 'I couldn't wait.'

Raji and Thankam took a long time over their tea and gossip.

'So what's happening? Give,' Raji insisted.

'You first,' Thankam demanded.

'No, I asked first,' Raji parried.

'Oh, all right, if you won't be satisfied without your pound of flesh. What you want to know is about my love life, I know that.'

'Love life, sex life – I'm not choosy.'

'I can answer that in one word: none. I took your advice and dismantled that relationship. Mind you, I was really angry that day you spoke to me. I cooled down fast; by the time I spoke to him two or three days later, it was better thought out, more commonsense than outrage.'

'How did he take it? Did you ask him to clear out?'

'He's not a bad sort, Raji. I talk to you only when I am upset, so you get a very lopsided view of him. Not at all fair to him. And you are my closest friend; you don't see the beam in my eye, bless you. And – I miss him dreadfully.

'He was very sweet and subsequently he talked to me about what happened to make him move away from me, emotionally. They've been giving him a hard time, all but calling him toy-boy and gigolo. It couldn't have been too pleasant.

'Anyway, he's gone and the long and short of it is, I'm on my own.' Thankam made a wry face. 'Roll on, next Mohan,' she added mischievously.

'You wouldn't dare.'

'No, I wouldn't dare, but there is no harm in thinking about it, is there?

'Actually, I had a narrow shave, what with Graciamma next door keeping her beady eyes on comings and goings before they carted her off to hospital, and the likes of Gopi's sister, Janaki, on the warpath.'

'That Janaki! She's forever stirring up trouble for someone. Silly cow.'

'Raji, the point is, I had to stop it before it got to my children; they have enough on their plates now. Anil is going to get married soon and Manju is having a tough time too.

'What surprises me is, no one told me anything about Gopi when the marriage was arranged. He has so many huge problems; I don't know whether that marriage will survive. Or whether it should.'

'Yes, Gopi was not a good choice. I had heard a few things about him, but by the time it reached me the wedding was fixed. Since this was all gossip, I didn't want to bring it to you.

'He had a reputation for smoking ganja during his college days. And then there was this thing about him and boys. Most of his friends were really surprised when he got married; they thought he'd be a permanent bachelor. But how do you know how much is truth and how much malicious gossip?'

'Do you ever? Your turn now.'

Raji pulled at her ear lobe and seemed to be considering her options.

'I fancy a little general fecklessness. How about if I take to drink now?'

Thankam knew Raji was pulling her leg.

'I sometimes think, having lived this blameless life, I'd like to sample everything: drugs, drink and dirty weekend, before I die.

'We are all inhibited by our children; it seems we have no lives of our own. A prison of love, I call it. And I can hear the two bars of my prison coming in.' She seemed happy at the prospect.

Raji's son and daughter ran into the house, dropping school bags on the veranda. Ramu had heard the word "bars."

'What bars, Ammey?'

'You two stalwarts - rods to hold me up when I stumble.' She put her arms, one on Ramu's and the other on Shija's shoulder and pretended to be a tired old woman.

'What's to eat? I'm ravenous,' Shija complained. Then they noticed Thankam. 'Hello, Thankam Auntie,' they chorused dutifully.

'There's bonda on the kitchen surface.'

'Bonda? Yummy.' They rushed off.

Raji followed them; Thankam could hear her giving instructions to her children.

'I'll be back in an hour or two. We are going to the WA. When you finish tea and have washed, do your homework before you go out to play. I'll look at it when I get home.'

At the Widows' Association, the crowd was bigger than usual. It appeared some of the women had organised a concert. Thankam had not intended to sit down and listen to amateur singing, so she was restless, wondering whether she should leave before it started. However, Raji might want to stay and Thankam did not want to make herself conspicuous. A few among the crowd appeared to have brought their teenage children with them; some were carrying musical instruments. One carried a flute case, another a *nadaswaram* of all things. A guitar leaned against the far corner and some had brought *chendas* and *tablas*. Mikes had been set up at the front.

Formalities were kept to a minimum; Parvathy announced that there would be no proper meeting as everyone was looking forward to the *music mela*. So tea would be served early and after that, the show would start.

'I didn't know about this,' Thankam whispered to Raji.

'You might be in for a surprise here,' Raji offered. 'One day when we met here, we decided we must occasionally push the boat out, enjoy ourselves, create a noise. One suggestion was a trip somewhere, the other something like this. Sunanda wanted us all to go on pilgrimage... all sorts of ideas were floated. This is the first one of those ideas actually taking shape; I think it's wonderful.'

Clearly, Raji wanted to stay, so Thankam prepared herself mentally for a long and boring evening.

The tea shop man brought a special feast for the celebration. This time, when he uncovered his offerings on the corner table, Thankam could see jilebis, ladoos and Bombay mixture. In addition the usual vadas had also been put out. He had provided spoons and plastic plates to eat out of and Fanta, Seven-up, Nimco and Thumbs-up were lined up at the back.

'We have something to celebrate,' Parvathy announced, loudly, so she could be heard over the chatter. 'Sreedevi is getting married soon. This time, the food is being provided by her.' Thankam turned around expecting a young widow, happy she was going to get a second shot at life, unlike all the others. A hand went up in the throng and Thankam craned her neck to see who it was. A middle-aged woman, plump and pretty, held her arm up, a little shyly. How wonderful, Thankam thought. To Raji, she whispered, naughtily, 'There you go. Do you think you and I will have second chances?'

While the crowd were having tea a few young boys and women came up to the front and grouped themselves as an orchestra, chenda at the back, tabla on the side, and the other instruments in the hands of musicians standing up at the edges. The vocalist who took centre stage had a mike to himself, the other singers, six young men and two women, shared.

The evening kicked off with *Vande Matharam*, Bankimchandra Chatterjee's ode to his mother country, India's second national anthem. This was the new Rahman arrangement full of verve and vigour. The chorus backed it up enthusiastically. Thankam couldn't believe how invigorating and fun it was; she had a happy smile pasted on her face right through it.

"*Ma, thuje salaam,*" the whole crowd sang at the end, joining in the rousing chorus. Thankam noticed the hairs on her arm were standing up.

As the evening proceeded, Thankam realised what she was seeing was a well-rehearsed medley of events. A young man and a girl came up to the stage at one point and mimicked a dialogue, supposedly between Atal Behari Vajpayee and Sonia Gandhi. A no-confidence motion Gandhi proposed to introduce in the lower house soon, was debated, except she still appeared to be horse-trading with the audience, to make the numbers. The dialogue was spot on, including the prolonged stops between each phrase of Vajpayee's and Sonya's shrill voice. She consulted a piece of paper every time she said anything.

The nadaswaram, a traditionally male instrument was played by a young woman; she did a spirited rendition of a classical Tamil song. A group of youngsters performed a lively dance number, to the tune of a semi-classical devotional song; the choreographer had blended the two dance forms of *Kuchipudi* and *Bharatha Natyam* beautifully. A large group of singers eventually finished off with an award winning campus song, to which they danced and waved *duppattas*.

For Thankam this was a great eye opener; she had not imagined this group capable of anything like this: either the effort or the joie de vivre.

After the performance, she went over to Sreedevi to wish her joy.

'I am surprised your family arranged a second marriage for you. This is normally not done for women.'

'They didn't arrange anything. Soman is my colleague at work; he lost his wife some years ago. We have known each other a long time and I guess we both wanted companionship. Neither his family nor mine were too pleased, but they couldn't stop us. But there are a few, if you look around, who make snide comments.'

Thankam circulated, greeting some of the other women and stopping to chat to a few others. When she went up to Parvathy to say she was leaving, a lady called Rajalakshmi was talking to her.

'You say this is a good thing, but I can't see why she needs a husband at her age.'

Thankam stood by and listened.

'Isn't this something that each person has to decide for herself?'

'Certainly not. Once you are widowed, you should lead a chaste life of prayer and looking after your family.'

Thankam made the mistake of offering an opinion.

'Can't we lead a chaste life after remarriage? And still look after our families?'

Rajalakshmi looked Thankam up and down. And who are you? the glance seemed to say.

'This is Thankam,' Parvathy hastened to introduce them. 'Please meet Rajalakshmi. She has come to Kochi after many years in Bombay. When her husband died, she decided to come back to her hometown.

'You two should know each other; Rajalakshmi also lives in Carrier Station Road.'

Parvathy's look at Thankam seemed to carry both an entreaty and a warning. Rajalakshmi addressed Thankam.

'Are you the person who lives in the big house down the lane? The one with the separate annexe?'

'Yes,' Thankam answered, not quite knowing where all this was leading.

'I have seen your house. Your neighbour Graciamma's son is a friend of my daughter's.'

She pointedly turned away from Thankam and talked to Parvathy.

'As I was saying, some widows are more intent on having a good time than looking after their grandchildren or praying for their husband's souls.' Then she flounced off.

Thankam called her back.

'We are all widows here. Are you talking about me? You know what. Why don't you get some joy into your own life, stop examining mine? You sound like a jealous wretch.'

'I'm sorry,' Parvathy said, as the woman walked away. 'She can be a bit abrasive.'

Thankam was too excited to go straight back to an empty house; so on impulse she drove to Vaduthala after dropping Raji off. Dusk was setting in as she arrived and the estate looked its best. The water birds were calling noisily to each other across the waters and the birds nearer home congregated on telephone cables to reconsider the day. Across the waters the *musaliyar* was summoning the devout Muslims to evening prayer.

She stopped for a moment on the veranda, gazing out; carpenters and masons building new wardrobes for the house across had collected their tools and were washing themselves at the outside tap. Then, as she watched, they picked up plastic bags containing their change of clothes and walked towards the security gate, where their bags would be inspected, before they were allowed to go. Inside, she could hear her daughter talking to someone on the phone.

Thankam opened her daughter's front door and walked in; as she entered she could see the call was over. It had clearly upset Manju; her face was red and she was crying. Thankam quickly dropped her handbag on the floor and went across.

'*Entha Moley?*' she asked. What is it that you are crying about?

'Dave phoned just now from London. He says he doesn't know what to say to me. When did he stop knowing what to say to me, Ammey? I have to go and see him; I miss him too much.

'He says he feels he is up against a blank wall and he doesn't know what to do next. You see, he cannot know the way we think, the way people here talk about each other, the way men can treat women and get away with it. It's all so alien and he wants to understand. Now I feel we cannot communicate with each other; I can't let that happen. He is the only man who cares for me.'

'We all care for you; you know that. When are you due to go to the UK? When you get there you can talk to him; tell him you are coming soon.'

'He knows that, but he asks why can't I go and stay with him? In my own room, as a friend, nothing more. How can I explain all our taboos to him?'

'He should understand you don't want to be compromised.'

Women colleagues stay with him all the time; he says that is normal. So he thinks I am being difficult.'

Thankam held her close and soothed her, speaking quietly to her.

'When we have children, we are not ever free after that. If you divorce a husband, there is untidiness still because of the children. One can live with that, but it does pose problems. You have to think things out properly; so, if he loves you, he should give you some time and space.'

'Yes, you're right.' Manju wiped her eyes and got up from the chair. 'I never ask about you, Ammey, it's always about me. Are you all right these days, with Anil in the UK and me about to go too?'

'I'll have to be, but the children are with me, remember. That will keep me occupied.'

Manju had to be satisfied with that.
'I'll come back soon,' she said. 'Three months will fly so quickly.'

Epilogue

Thankam prepared to welcome the elephant bearing the divine image: Shivan on his annual outing to beg food for the year for himself and his temple, which occupied pride of place in the centre of Kochi. The local residents, rich enough to live in this part of Kochi, called it *their* Shivan temple and the annual festival here was always the most lavish of all the temple festivals in Kochi. It was during the seven days of the festival that the *para* donations took place.

Asha trotted around behind Thankam as she busied herself with the preparations. 'What's para?' she asked, obviously hoping it was like Onam or Vishu when children got new clothes and sweets. "Will there be jilebis and ladoos?'

'It's the day when our *bhagawan* visits our houses and we give him food.'

'Will you give him sweets?'

'No, rice and coconut and stuff.'

'I thought *he* was supposed to give *us* food.' She had a point.

'This is when we thank him for all the food he's already given us,' Thankam explained.

'Oh.' She trotted off, pulling at her ponytail, which she had acquired just recently. It was so short, stray bits of hair dangled in front all the time. Thankam had told her it was the new fashion to have little bits like that in front.

She was back a few minutes later. 'Why is it called para?' Thankam wondered when she would lose the why habit.

'Well, actually,' Thankam began, her mind flitting back to a long-ago time when rice and rice-paddy were measured in the local capacity-measures of *nazhi*, *edangazhi* and *para*. She remembered the floury wooden measures, which were taken out in the morning daily to measure out the rice for the day.

'"Para" is the size of a big barrel in which we'll measure rice and other grains for Shivan; you'll see when the men from the temple come, because they'll bring one with them.'

Asha looked as though all this was a bit beyond her.

Latha was getting quite grown up at nine; she was into serious friendships at school and sleepovers. In fact she had a small diary, which she had shown Thankam. At the back was a page with a line down the middle. One column was headed *Friends* and the other firmly, *Not Friends*. Thankam noticed quite a few names had changed sides several times in the year. It was like crossing the floor of the *Lok Sabha*, she thought, amused. Ammu, Radha's daughter from across the road, was in the first column, Thankam registered with relief.

'Is para in the morning or evening?' Latha asked. 'I could go over to Ammu's to play carroms if it's only in the evening.'

'The procession will have left the temple in the morning on its way from house to house; today is the designated day for Carrier Station Road,' Thankam explained. 'The image and its attendants will be out on the roads all day, till they finish visiting each of the long list of houses, which are on their schedule for today. So, they'll come, most likely, in the evening.' She was guessing.

Latha ran off to play.

'You must come back when you hear the drum-beat and the elephant's bell,' Thankam called to her disappearing, mini-skirted rear. 'They'll also announce their coming with the conch.'

Seetha had helped Thankam with the arrangements for para before this and knew all the rituals, but Moli was as excited as the children. On the previous day, she had been asked to scrub and wash the engine-oil stains from the front porch with bleach and warm water. Then she wiped it dry with a floor cloth. The next morning she swept and swabbed it again; the porch had to be squeaky clean for the God's visit. The car was banished to the garage and would not come out for a day.

Early in the morning, the two older women in the house put up the decorations at the front gate; tender leaves of the coconut frond, yet to open, were forced apart and the yellow-green leaves taken off the stalk. Then Seetha split the leaves down the middle, starting from the thick end, to almost the tip. About two inches off the end were left to hold the leaf together. Now it hung free, two long strips of leaf and the hard, pointed stalk in the middle. On the stalk, Seetha impaled yellow alamanda flowers, red hibiscus and pink ixora blooms from the garden. Many of these leaf-hangings were prepared till enough were ready to cover the string, which Seetha had strung from one gatepost to another.

Moli watched with interest; this was the first time she was going to see the ceremony, because Thankam had not offered para at her house after Unni died. Being a Christian, Moli was ignorant of many Hindu customs, but in Thankam's house she was learning fast. Yesterday, she spent an hour polishing the big brass *nilavilakku* and two smaller lamps, as well as utensils such as the long-handled spoon for pouring gingelly oil into the lamps. Her hands were still slightly discoloured from all the polishing. She had also collected three young banana leaves to be placed before the three lamps in the portico; in addition burning incense and joss sticks would be placed there, she was told.

As the women went about the day's work in the morning, they listened for the sounds of the *kottu,* the slow rhythmic beat of the *chenda*, which accompanied the elephant; almost matching its ponderous progress.

The God arrived at five in the evening to the little lane, which had waited all day; six houses in the lane had put up the decorations for Shivan and Thankam's was the last. The sounds of the kottu suddenly became loud and insistent in the lane, along with the bells on the elephant and the clang of the restraining chains attached to its legs. The man with the conch gave a loud blast to alert the houses.

The elephant stopped in front of each house for the para and moved on after a few minutes, when the gifts of grain had been measured out. After each measure was made, the conch was blown. From the house opposite, the lady's little daughter, Ammu, had run in with Latha, ahead of the para, to get a ringside seat on the veranda of Thankam's house, with Asha. Thankam gave all three girls small bunches of bananas to give the elephant.

Thankam surveyed her banana leaves with a practised eye; the centre leaf was empty except for a coconut *pookkula,* an unopened bunch of coconut blooms, with the pods and flowers still tiny on each stem.

The men accompanying the elephant would light sticks of incense when they arrived. But the elephant and *pappan* both hesitated at the concrete slab over the culvert in front of Thankam's house. Eventually the pappan nudged the elephant forward with his spoke. Keshavan, for so he was called, stepped prissily over the concrete slab as though he too had reservations about the slab. The men then came in and waited for the ceremony to begin as all three girls gawped unashamedly.

'Where is god Shivan?' they asked excitedly.

'They can't see him because he's on top of the elephant,' Seetha pointed out. So Thankam lifted up Asha and Seetha picked up Ammu, to have a good look. Whatever they expected it was not a small image, the size of a briefcase.

That's not Shivan,' they insisted. 'He's *small*!' Thankam pacified them by explaining how the god sat in the temple and sent his image to do the hard work for him.

'*Ende* amma, would have liked to see para; she likes elephants,' Asha announced unexpectedly. Was she a little sad at her mother's absence? Manju had gone these last few months; Thankam wondered when she would come back. Would the three months be enough for her?

We'll have another one next year,' Thankam consoled her. 'The God comes every year at this time, in January or February. Why don't you girls send Amma an e-mail to tell her all about it?'

The man measured the grains for the God in sieves and poured them on the waiting banana leaves. At the end, the pappan said to the girls, 'You can give your bananas to Keshavan.' They were scared to go near the elephant, but Thankam led each one by the hand and they put the bananas straight into Keshavan's huge maw. Seetha brought a spare bunch of palm leaf and offered it to the animal, which tucked it behind his trunk for afters. The pappan picked up the pookkula and this too was put away behind the ivory. Keshavan's gaze at the people was passive, benign, but he had a glint in his eye, which said: in another time and place…

In the evening, when homework was satisfactorily concluded and Asha was fast asleep on the living room sofa, Latha helped Ammamma clear up supper. 'When is Amma coming home?' she asked.

'Soon,' Thankam said. She mustn't keep the children guessing, Thankam thought, but the three months would soon be over and she was also waiting for news.

'Achan has not come either.' This was more dangerous ground. 'Is Achan with Amma?'

'No, she is training in England and he is working in Dubai.' That would have to do for now.

Thankam's mother made one of her calls that night.

'The work on Unni's house is nearly complete. When are you coming to see it?'

'Soon, Ammey.' Did she hear a faint tremor of entreaty in the voice at the other end?

'Appu has gone back to Dubai. And you are further than him, I think.'

'I'm going to spend a lot of time in Thalassery, Ammey. I'll come when the schools close in April and I'll bring Manju too if she is here.

'How are the others?' Thankam asked. 'Is Lakshmi there?'

'I'll give the phone to Lakshmi, Moley. I must go for my bath.'

Lakshmi came on the line, saying, 'Amma is not too well these days; I think she's quite sad after Appuettan left, more so than usual. But she keeps asking for you also. I think you should come as soon as you can.'

'What's the matter with her?' Thankam asked sharply.

'She's lost weight and there is an abscess on her leg, which won't heal; she has to limp around. I sometimes feel she's losing the fight in her.'

'I'll come as soon as I can. But, please ring every week. And if she gets any worse, I want to know immediately.'

She's lonely, Thankam thought; her children have left in various directions. Perhaps I shall be like that soon.

Thankam considered her position. No, she decided; I have my grandchildren now. When they go, I'll still have my work, the club, Seetha, Raji… And my garden. How can I be lonely?

My children are really not that far away. Not with e-mail. It was clever of Anil to set up the computer for me before he left; I can write to them daily if I wish.

She went to her room, booted up the computer and typed in Anil's and Manju's e-mail addresses. She wrote:

It's evening here and I have just lighted the nilavilakku and brought it to the veranda. How many years and in how many houses I have done this!

I thought I'd write to you both before the day is quite finished.

The College is doing well and I am enjoying the work. The spoken English lessons are popular with the students and the library is a godsend for some of them.

I have made many new friends at the Widows' Association and you should see me zipping around in my new Maruthi.

I hope all is well with both of you. The girls are well and growing fast; they keep me young at heart.

Come back soon, and if you can't, I must think of coming over with the little ones.

Printed by BoD in Norderstedt, Ge